ADVANCE PRAISE FOR

CONFESSIONS OF A TEENAGE JESUS JERK

"I'll never slam the door on a *Watchtower* hopeful again without thinking of Tony DuShane's hilarious, original coming-of-age novel. Addictive, informative, heartbreaking, and utterly satisfying." —Janet Fitch, author of *White Oleander* and *Paint It Black*

"An absorbing and poignant exploration of the dilemmas facing a youth growing up within a conservative religious community—where even the mildest sexual thoughts could land you among the post-Armageddon forever-damned." —C.D. Payne, author of *Youth In Revolt*

"*Confessions of a Teenage Jesus Jerk* is astonishing and hilarious, evoking shades of John Kennedy Toole and C.D. Payne. Tony DuShane's got a sharp new voice that's sure to be noticed; I have no doubt he'll garner fans fast." —Katie Crouch, author of *Girls in Trucks* and *Men and Dogs*

"A truly original take on familiar, omnipresent subject matter is a rare and precious thing. And subject matter doesn't get more familiar or omnipresent than the coming-of-age and sexual awakening of an American suburban teenage dude. But I guarantee you've never read coming-of-age like this before. Smart, funny, touching, and more fun than a Jehovah's Witnesses ethnography could be reasonably expected to be—a real winner." —Frank Portman, author of *King Dork* and *Andromeda Klein*

"Darkly funny and authentically kinky, Tony DuShane's first novel is a surprisingly sweet coming-of-age story told through the eyes of a horny, Jehovah-battered, *Watchtower*-wielding, door-to-door proselytizer. I may never answer my doorbell again." —Mark Haskell Smith, author of *Moist*; *Delicious*; and *Salty.*

"Watch out Armageddon. Here comes DuShane! A mushroom cloud of excruciating laughs, and wicked twists. Deserves to be placed in drawers in every motel in the country." —Alan Black, author of *Kick the Balls*

"Tony DuShane's highly original novel lives at the fecund corner of religion and sex. *Confessions of a Teenage Jesus Jerk* captures the ache of an adolescent heart drunk on a combustible cocktail of Jesus, hormones, and visions of escape. You'll pull for this most sympathetic hero and hope he finds a god of his own." —Seth Greenland, author of *Shining City* and *The Bones*

"DuShane writes like a dirty angel. Raw and inspired. He is not afraid of the dark. Spread the word." —Rachel Resnick, author of *Love Junkie: A Memoir*

CONFESSIONS OF A
TEENAGE
JESUS JERK

Tony DuShane

Soft Skull Press · New York

Library of Congress Cataloging-in-Publication Data

DuShane, Tony.
  Confessions of a teenage Jesus jerk / Tony DuShane.
     p. cm.
  ISBN 978-1-59376-263-6
  1. Christian teenagers—Fiction. 2. Jehovah's Witnesses—Fiction. 3. Christian teenagers—Sexual behavior—Fiction. 4. Adolescence—Fiction. I. Title.
  PS3604.U758C66 2010
  813'.6—dc22
                              2009040420

Cover design by Goodloe Byron
Interior design by Neuwirth & Associates, Inc.
Printed in the United States of America

Soft Skull Press
An Imprint of Counterpoint LLC
2117 Fourth Street
Suite D
Berkeley, CA 94710

www.softskull.com
www.counterpointpress.com

Distributed by Publishers Group West

10 9 8 7 6 5 4 3 2 1

CONFESSIONS OF A

TEENAGE

JESUS JERK

One lone pubic hair sprung out from my baby-smooth pelvis area. I didn't even see it start to grow. It just made its appearance and told me more were coming.

I raised my hand to my cheek and felt for hair and there was no stubble. One pubic hair below. Adulthood cometh.

I had a crush on every girl. There was Olivia from history class who stood a foot taller than me. I liked Allison who said hi to me one time in pre-algebra. I was so nervous I turned around and walked away. I thought she was going to make fun of me for being a Jehovah's Witness. I couldn't understand why a pretty girl would want to talk to me.

Allison and her friend giggled and that was my last chance with them.

But I loved Jasmine from our congregation even though she was in high school and I was still in junior high with her younger sister, Camille.

Jennifer Hansen told me that Camille had a crush on me. I asked Jennifer about Camille's older sister, Jasmine, the girl I really loved, and she said, "Jasmine's a bitch."

The next day at school I sprung into action as my lone pubic hair goaded me to.

What do you do if you know for sure a girl likes you? You ask her to go steady.

It's the most important thing I learned in eighth grade from the worldly kids. Anyone who was worldly wasn't a Jehovah's Witness. Jasmine and Camille were Jehovah's Witnesses.

Camille liked me. She wasn't Jasmine and she wasn't bad.

Jasmine was out of my league and Camille was right in front of me.

I needed to kiss someone. Everyone else was kissing each other at school. I saw it all over the hallways. Every girl I could've had a chance to kiss was worldly and I would always walk away when they'd try to talk to me. I was a nervous wreck when it came to girls. A few more pubic hairs may have brought my confidence up. Or a mustache.

Ben, the Spanish kid in homeroom, had a mustache. He kissed a lot of girls.

No mustache, one pubic hair, and Camille liked me. Her breasts were starting to show themselves. She had full lips over her crooked teeth.

She wasn't her sister, Jasmine, but she was decent enough and I'd known her since we were kids.

Having a girlfriend could show my classmates that being a Jehovah's Witness didn't mean I was a fag like they'd sometimes call me.

In typing class we learned how to type without looking down at the typewriter. The keys had the letters blacked out so we couldn't cheat. We copied what was written on the chalkboard. Thirty type-writers clacking in unison. It could've been the newsroom at the *San Francisco Chronicle* except we all wrote about the history of the American flag.

I couldn't salute the flag at school, but I could write about it.

Every morning during flag salute I stood and held my hand on my belt buckle so it looked like I was pledging allegiance if you saw me from the back.

I was tired of answering, "Why don't you salute the flag?"

Every year, on the first day of school, we had to give our home-room teachers a note explaining why we didn't, as Jehovah's Witnesses, salute the flag. My eighth-grade homeroom teacher read the no-flag salute note that I gave him, grunted, and tossed it in the wastebasket, never to reference it again.

In the morning he would ask one of the students to lead the flag salute. Before that name was called out my hands would clam up. About once a month he forgot about my note saying that I was a Jehovah's Witness and he called on me to lead the pledge.

"I can't," I said. He looked at me, confused, then remembered I was one of those Jehovahs and asked someone else. The other kids looked at me weird until the bell rang for first period.

Persecution.

And two minutes of heart pumping every morning during the flag salute.

Every day I prayed not to be taunted as the non-flag-saluter.

At the Kingdom Hall we heard Jehovah's Witness kids had gone to jail for not saluting the flag in the 1930s and '40s. During those two minutes, the possibility of doing time in a maximum security prison bounced in my skull.

Camille liked me, not Jasmine. I was settling, but it'd clear up a lot of embarrassing things in my life.

So, after typing my essay on the importance and history of the American flag from the chalkboard, I put another piece of paper in the typewriter and wrote:

> Dear Camille,
> "Will you go steady with me?
> From,
> Gabe"

My hand shook from nerves as I slipped the note in her locker.

Once the note disappeared into the air vent of that dark space of her locker, the deal was done.

I saw her the next day. She smiled at me. The biggest smile I had ever seen from her, showing all of her crooked teeth. Usually she smiled with her lips shut, hiding her teeth, but she showed them to me and I waited for her to answer my question.

She said, "Hi," and touched my arm.

No girl ever touched my arm like that. It was electric.

I guess I needed that first pubic hair to get an arm touch. My pubic hair and that touch on my arm worked its way to my mouth.

"Come here," I said.

She followed me out the hallway doors and we turned the corner. There was a secluded area where no one could see us, with a couple of stairs that led to the janitor's office. The door was closed and we sat on the steps.

We stared into each other's eyes. I thought I was going to faint but I did it. I reached over and I put my hand on her hand and let it stay there.

She smiled. I couldn't hold her unblinking gaze and she looked away. I was nervous. IT was getting excited down there.

Hand-holding was related to dating and being engaged. In the eyes of the congregation we were too young to do either.

I got scared and put her hand back on her lap. We sat there for a few minutes in silence.

"Let's go," I said.

We ate lunch with Jennifer, who was also a Jehovah's Witness. We talked about Mr. Adams. Mr. Adams was a Vietnam veteran and everyone said his butt was shot off during the war. I think it was true because when he wore his pants they hung straight down his legs. No butt. I wondered how he pooped.

We all laughed and the lunch bell rang.

Camille was my girlfriend.

See! Being a Jehovah's Witness doesn't mean you're a fag.

I got home from school and Mom was awake. She had my note asking Camille to go steady.

Betrayed.

How did, what the, how in the— ?

Mom told me about dating and courtship and how I wasn't old enough to date. I needed to be at least eighteen, and if I started dating Camille before then, it could lead to fornication and I could be kicked out of the congregation, disfellowshipped.

She told me that Serena, Camille's mom, was really upset about the note and how I was pursuing her daughter.

I would've rather been in homeroom during flag salute and thinking about how there could be a time when I would go into a maximum security prison for my faith than talk to Mom about fornication. It was like she saw right through my pants to my lone pubic hair.

Everyone knew.

Jasmine knew.

My pubic hair had led me in the wrong direction.

I learned a valuable lesson that day. Camille and Jasmine weren't to be trusted in the area of romance. I'd have to continue to love Jasmine from a distance even though they both thought I was in love with Camille.

If I tried to set the record straight it'd be trouble with our parents.

It reminded me of when I was in fifth grade and Jasmine was in sixth and Jasmine told on me for swearing, for saying "duck" but with an *f*. It upset Serena. Mom and Dad lectured me about profanity.

I wished Jasmine and Camille had grown out of that. I'd thought they'd finally learned to keep things from their mother.

Going-steady type things.

No, I was an open book straight to my parents via the Camille and Jasmine connection. Jasmine would have to wait.

And Camille ate lunch with me every day. We never brought up the note or why she told on me. She'd just smiled her crooked teeth in my direction. I noticed how jagged her teeth were. She still dressed like a little girl, with her Raggedy Ann shirt. And she developed a new laugh. When I'd tell jokes she wouldn't just laugh, she'd violently laugh, over-laugh, scary demonic laugh.

Har, Har, HANH, Har, Har, HA!

It wasn't that funny.

Peter and Jin ate lunch with us as well.

Jin ate his Ho Hos and he really liked Cheetos and Doritos. He was the junk food king. Before he spoke English, real English, when he first came to America when he was seven, he could say McDonald's and Coke. Before he could understand who Captain Kangaroo was, he could ask his mom for a Three Musketeers candy bar.

It was starting to show. The square Korean face he came to America with had become rounder. He was slower during P.E. when we'd run around the track. And he couldn't even do one pull-up.

Peter and I met Jin when his mom and dad brought him to the Kingdom Hall when we were seven years old. Our parents tried to get us to call him by his American name, Jimmy. But we heard his mom say Jin too many times when she'd try to get him to greet us or to sit quietly during the *Watchtower* study.

It was too weird to call him Jimmy, so we stuck with Jin.

Peter liked Jennifer Hansen.

Jennifer told him she liked his dirty-blond hair and his freckles. She liked that he wore baseball jerseys that went halfway down his forearms. And his tiny kissable lips. That's what she said, "kissable." But they hadn't kissed yet. Every lunch hour was a meeting of all the Jehovah's Witnesses in junior high.

Some kids asked me if I was dating Camille. She must've been telling people we were. I said we dated for a little while but it didn't work out.

Her answer to my typewritten note was given to me in a Bible lecture from my parents.

Dating? No.

I guess she was trying to show her girlfriends that all Jehovah's Witnesses weren't lesbians.

Every day I waited for more pubic hair to come.

Jennifer wrote Peter a note and stuck it in his locker. We found it after school before we walked home. He immediately ripped it open. I smelled perfume come from the envelope and he read it. He smiled.

"What's it say?" I asked.

"I can't tell you."

"C'mon."

"It's between me and her."

He put the note in his backpack. It was easy for him. Jennifer didn't blab to her mom every time Peter wrote her a note or secretly held her hand behind the backstop during recess.

"Do you love her?" I asked.

"What do you think?" he said like it was a stupid question.

Camille drove me crazy. She started wearing makeup. Too much makeup, overdosing on eyeliner and lipstick. It was gross. And her laugh I hated more and more. I didn't want her near me.

She betrayed me and still wanted to be my girlfriend.

Kevin was a guy I talked to in typing class sometimes. He liked Foreigner and U2. I knew who U2 was so he thought I was cool.

I walked over to his bench at lunch. He wore his Class of '85 jersey. Junior high graduation was two months away. He sat with the popular kids, Gary, Ken, and Josh. Josh had thrown a spitball at me and called me a Jehovah Bible faggot in history class a few months earlier.

"Can I eat with you guys?" I asked.

Kevin looked at me and laughed. It wasn't the same Kevin from typing class.

"Go preach Jehovah to someone else, dork," Josh said.

I wished I was big and strong and could punch Josh in the eye and make him cry. They all laughed. Kevin laughed. I walked over to Jennifer, Peter, and Camille, vowing it was the last time I'd eat with Camille.

In P.E., after lunch, there was a Japanese kid named Kendall. His front teeth were too large for his lips to fully cover them and he wore the same pair of glasses that my dad did. If they were sunglasses, he'd look like a studious cop. I asked if I could eat lunch with him the next day.

"Tomorrow is a chess tournament in room 103. You can come to that," he said.

The next day I played chess. I got some moves wrong and was beaten within three minutes. I stayed and watched the other nerds play chess.

Between Camille and the nerds, I picked the nerds. When Peter and Jennifer were together they were in their own little universe. They'd stare at each other and whisper secrets of love.

I was jealous of Jennifer and wished she hadn't taken Peter from me.

I saw Camille in the hallway and said hi. She asked if we were broken up. "We were never together," I said.

She walked away. It never dawned on me that she didn't move her arms when she walked, that they always hung to her sides.

Dad called me into the bedroom. He had a Bible in his hands and that Kingdom Hall elder look in his eyes.

"I heard about Camille," he said.

Yeah, old news.

"Did you touch her?" he asked.

My heart raced. Did Camille tell that we'd held hands? How bad was that?

I didn't answer, but my red face filled in the blanks. If I was hooked up to a lie detector it would read off the page. Screaming, HE touched HER—THEY held hands ALONE—CALL the ELDERS.

"I'm going to ask you again, and keep in mind thsat if you tell me the truth, Jehovah and the elders will consider it a confession, and it'll be better for you." Then he bent over close and looked me right in the eyes while I tried to avoid his stare and looked at the ceiling.

"Did. You. Touch. Her."

I burst into tears. He just watched me as I sobbed. I finally let it out.

"Yes, I touched her," then waited for the wheels of justice to turn.

He looked at me. Disappointed. Heavy in the face.

"I could lose my position as an elder because of this," he said.

I didn't realize how far the hurt would go because of my sin. I didn't think it would affect anything other than my pleasure or Camille's.

"Camille's mom needs to know."

I nodded my head slowly. It was the beginning of the end.

"Where did you touch her?"

It was painful to tell Dad.

"By the stairs near the janitor's office at school," I said in between sobs.

"Was it her breast, her vagina?"

I looked at him confused.

"You need to be honest with me, Gabe."

"I touched her hand. We, we held hands."

"And . . ."

"That's all we did."

It didn't even occur to me that Camille had a vagina. I hadn't thought that far ahead.

"If I called Camille right now, she'd tell me the same thing," he said.

Where's the lie detector, I'll pass with flying colors.

"Yes, call her," I said. "You thought I went to third base with her?"

"I needed to know." Then he read me a few paragraphs from the *Youth Book* published by the Watchtower Society about holding hands and how it could lead to fornication and sins like fondling breasts and touching vaginas.

"You're not going to call the elders?" I asked.

"I don't need to," he said.

I made a mental note of that for future reference.

The next day at lunch, I sat with Kendall and his friend. Kendall had a calculator his dad had bought him for $300. We looked at the amazing technology, and then Camille, Jennifer, and Peter sat down next to us for lunch. Camille sat close to me.

I wondered when Armageddon would come so I wouldn't have to sit next to Camille at lunch or ever worry about worldly people making fun of me.

Aunt Laura sent me a postcard of the mountains in Utah. I turned it over and saw she'd written how much she missed me and that she hoped I was doing okay in school. My cousin signed the bottom after my aunt, "from Karen." The last time I'd seen her was when she lived closer and she and Aunt Laura came over to our apartment for dinner, when we were eleven. Since we didn't celebrate any holidays, Dad tried to do something special on non-special occasions so there wouldn't be any chance that we were participating in a pagan ritual with our worldly relatives.

Karen was six months older than I was. She always made fun of me for being a Jehovah's Witness. She would lay it on thick about all the stuff I couldn't do.

"I went to the greatest birthday party for my friend Jackie," she'd said the last time I'd seen her. "Oh, I forgot. You don't go to birthday parties. Why is that?"

"Because it says in the Bible."

"Where?"

"I don't know."

She was a monologist. Her words spewed so fast I could almost see the letters of alphabet soup falling from her mouth to the ground.

"Are you still Jehovah walking?" she asked.

Before I could answer she was already on her next thought.

"It's hot. This fucking sucks. Hey, do you like Duran Duran?"

"Yeah, I—"

"They're European. Mom bought their record. I play it on the stereo she gave me for Christmas. Oh, yeah, you don't celebrate Christmas. That must suck."

It sucked but I couldn't let her get the best of me, so when she stopped to take a breath I said, "Yeah, but I'm doing what God wants me to and you're not, so you better watch out at Armageddon."

"How do you know what God wants you to do?"

"Because I read it in the Bible."

"Where does it say you can't celebrate Christmas?"

"I don't know, but I'll ask Dad."

"Then how do you know anything you're doing is what God wants you to do?"

I wished I could walk on water right in front of her to show her I knew what I was talking about.

"My mom says Uncle Alan gives too much money to the Watchtower people, so he stays poor. Mom says Auntie Linn is a Jehovah because she has voids in her life."

"My mom doesn't have voids."

I thought she was talking about a disease. She was already onto the next thought.

"What's green and red and goes one hundred miles an hour? A frog in a blender. I went to the school dance last week with Erin. All they played was crappy music. I hate Foreigner and Styx. I still like Queen. Dad says Queen are gays. He likes Van Halen. Van Halen is okay. He made me listen to Cheap Trick. Yuck! I'm bored. Can Jehovahs kiss girls? I bet you haven't kissed anyone yet. Mom said we can travel to Utah in a few years."

Dad interrupted her monologue and had us come to the kitchen with the rest of the family for a prayer before we ate. Before I could reply to Karen.

I can kiss any girl I want, I said in my mind while Dad thanked Jehovah for the food we were about to eat. *I have to have a bodyguard to keep the throngs of Gabe fans away so I can get on with my normal life.*

Dad asked God to bless those who weren't as fortunate to eat like we did.

"In Jesus' name, amen," Dad concluded.

The prayer was Dad's stealth way to bring some Jehovah to the gathering and to show his sister how happy we were so that she could become a Jehovah's Witness and our family could be together in the new system.

Karen miraculously stopped talking to chew her food and drink her juice.

After dinner and after her several wins at backgammon we played stop-time. It was something we'd done every time we saw each other, since we were little. We touched our fingers together while sitting on my bed with our eyes closed. We floated above the apartment building. Dad came in and interrupted us.

"What was that?" he asked later.

He hadn't seen Karen and me play stop-time before. I explained what it was and he told me that Karen's grandma on her dad's side was an American Indian and it could be a communication with the spirits, like a séance. He told me never to do it again just in case it was a sin. It didn't feel like I was doing anything wrong.

That was the last time I'd seen Laura and Karen.

Easter vacation came and Brother Miller let all the young Witnesses come over to the pool at his apartment complex after we preached in the morning. I had my swim trunks in my book bag, which was also filled with a Bible and *Watchtowers* and *Awake!*s.

The sun was out. Ally was one and a half years older than I was and she wore a one-piece bathing suit. She'd developed a lot faster than the rest of us. I kept stealing glances at her long blond hair, her round nose, and her breasts.

"Her tits," Peter whispered to me as we lay out on the hot cement.

I laughed, "Shut up—she'll hear you."

Ally jumped off of the diving board and did a cannonball. I stole a glance at her round butt.

Peter and I said words like "tits" and "balls" and "dick" when we were alone. Sometimes, when we sat together at the Kingdom Hall during *Watchtower* study we would write swear words and show them to each other, then cross them out before anyone saw.

I wrote "fuck" under an illustration of Lazarus being resurrected. I showed it to Peter and he tried hard not to laugh, but snot came out of his nose. I quickly crossed the word out.

There was another time that Peter wrote "asshole bitch" next to a scripture in the *Watchtower*. I laughed really loud and my punishment was that I couldn't sit with Peter for three months.

Jasmine and her sister, Camille, showed up a little later at the pool. They both wore one-piece bathing suits. Jasmine's was aqua blue and Camille's was beige. Camille's hips were bigger than Jasmine's. Jasmine had long legs. Dark legs. She didn't need to tan because her father's background was Italian. Camille's dad was German.

They put their towels next to ours and lay out in the sun with us.

The smell of suntan lotion on a girl is so different from the smell on a guy. It's like honey butter.

Camille was right next to me and Jasmine was on the other side of her.

"Go for it, man—she still likes you," Peter said.

I tried to ignore him because I didn't want Camille to get the wrong idea. She'd had her chance. Those crooked teeth would never meet my lips.

Jasmine, oh Jasmine. The beautiful and too-mature-for-me Jasmine. She'd talk to me sometimes, but I was scared of her and never let the conversation carry itself out to completion.

It wasn't quite that I loved her; my obsession was that I wanted her to love me, so I could make the choice later.

I couldn't talk about my feelings for Jasmine to anyone for fear I'd lose her forever. I couldn't even tell Peter, my best friend. The whole Camille situation really messed things up for me. It was so confusing I couldn't figure out how to explain it to Peter.

I went to the bathroom to check for more pubic hair. Still only one.

Peter went over and picked up Jasmine to throw her in the water. I wished I had thought of that. But I didn't want Jasmine to be mad at me. Jasmine twisted and squirmed and Peter had her arms in his and was winning the battle. I noticed a little smile on Jasmine's face and it made me jealous, so I jumped up to help him dunk her in the water.

Her soft arms in my grasp sent tingles through my spine. Once we got her in the water she came out and her dark brown hair was covering her face and she was coughing.

Peter ran toward Ally and she took off running. Her breasts bounced as she ran around the pool and Peter was in pursuit.

"You guys are lame," Jasmine said.

Camille smiled her crooked teeth at me and it was time to jump in the deep end and tread water. Peter and Ally fell into the water together and we all started splashing each other. Camille jumped in to join the fight. Jasmine stayed on her towel, propping herself up on her elbows, looking at the sky. She was a photo of a sophisticated Italian woman, reading a book in front of a café in Rome. We were a bunch of loud kids disrupting the flow of the universe and craving pubescent attention.

I came home and Mom was awake and wearing her robe.

"How are you feeling?" I asked.

There was a heavy sigh before she said she was okay.

She made tea. She'd stopped drinking coffee three years before because the doctor told her it was bad to drink if she had chronic fatigue syndrome.

She sat on the sofa and turned the channel to *Phil Donahue* on our wired remote that went from the coffee table to the TV set. I put on dry shorts and a shirt and sat with her.

"Are you wearing wet underwear?" Mom asked because I hadn't changed out of them after swimming.

"Yeah."

She looked at me and said, "Bubbles."

It was the first joke I'd heard her tell in a long time. I laughed as I went behind the partition in the living room where my bed and dresser were to change into my dry underwear.

"Bubbles" was a spoon that Peter's stepdad, Terry, had brought with him to the Kingdom Hall when we were kids. If Peter fussed or got out of control when he was younger, Terry would say "Bubbles" in his ear and bring him to the back of the Kingdom Hall and beat him with a wooden spoon that had little bubbles drawn on one side and the word "Bubbles" written on the other. I didn't know why Mom remembered Bubbles when we were watching *Donahue*. Maybe it was a show about child abuse or Dr. Spock.

If Peter wore a short-sleeve shirt to the Kingdom Hall when he was a kid you could sometimes see bright red marks on his arms where Bubbles had made contact.

Terry was a jerk.

I changed out of my wet underwear and came back in dry underwear and Mom had fallen asleep on the couch. I gently took the remote from her hand and changed the channel to watch cartoons.

• • •

One time I had lunch at Peter's house when I was about eight years old and Peter smelled like poo.

Jin was there and still didn't speak too much English yet. But he plugged his nose and said a bunch of Korean stuff.

I laughed and said, "Who farted?"

Peter sat and didn't laugh or move.

"Peter farted," I said to Jin.

"Peter far-sed," Jin said. "Peter poo."

"Cut it out," Peter's mom told us while serving grilled cheese sandwiches.

Peter sat catatonic, like he had frozen in a position of trying to hold his anus tight. We sat and ate.

I asked Mom later why Peter smelled like poo sometimes.

"Because some boys who don't live with their real fathers smell like that. You should feel sorry for him, not make fun of him."

Peter's real father was worldly and in a state correctional facility. When Peter was about two years old his father had held a gun to his mom's head when he was drunk and Peter saw the whole thing. He was too little to remember so his bowels remembered for him.

I felt bad and promised to myself never to say anything when Peter pooped his pants. His mother divorced his dad and married Terry, a Jehovah's Witness who had come into the organization after he returned from Vietnam.

Peter only smelled like poo a few times after that. The memory of his father assaulting his mother gradually left the memory of his anus.

On Easter Sunday, Dad was assigned to lead the service group into the preaching work. Every time Dad went out in service, I had to go out in service. Mom stayed home and slept.

Since no one else showed up Dad decided to conduct the service group with just him and me. He made me read scriptures based on the *Watchtower* article we were going to hand out about Jesus and how we should be reflecting on his sacrifice for our sins and not participate in pagan holidays like Easter and Christmas, which are really disrespectful to him.

He took the territory card out of his pocket and we drove to Hemlock and Hillcrest and started preaching house to house.

A group of kids were hunting for Easter eggs on their front yard down the block.

Dad rang the first doorbell to get things started.

"Hunh?" said the man who answered the door. He had no shirt on and only pajama bottoms. His hair was sticking out all over the place.

"Good morning, sir. Can I show you the latest issues of the *Wat*—"

The man slammed the door. I think he said "asshole" as he turned away. I knocked at the next house.

"What?" someone said from behind the door.

"Uh, we're Jehovah's Witnesses," I said.

"It's fucking Easter for Christ sake."

Dad and I persevered to the next house, where some noise was coming from the inside.

"Someone's up and home," Dad said as he rang the doorbell, ready to give a witness.

A woman came to the door with glitter on her face. Behind her was a man dressed in a bunny suit, and kids surrounded him eating candy.

"What's wrong with Easter?" the woman asked.

"It's pagan," Dad said and tried to explain why before she interrupted him.

The woman looked at me and said, "I feel sorry for him," and shut the door.

I felt a little sorry for myself as well.

Later that afternoon I rode my bicycle around Millbrae. I stopped at a deli to buy Pop Rocks and Coke. I never drank Coke and ate Pop Rocks at the same time since Kendall told me it would explode in my stomach.

Sitting with my bicycle on a bench in downtown Millbrae made me feel like an adult.

Downtown Millbrae was a handful of mom-and-pop stores up

and down Broadway. Photo supplies, hardware gear, pizza places, Chinese food, and Walgreens and Safeway were the grandfathers of downtown. There were dental offices, and streets connecting Broadway led to the Millbrae Library and parking lots.

On the flat part of Millbrae there were rows of apartment buildings, and the houses looked like junkyards. As the hill gradually elevated, the small houses arranged themselves around manicured lawns and fresh paint. The trees gave them shade.

Then the incline went steeper up the mountain where the houses were large and had swimming pools and sweeping views of the San Francisco Bay Area. The San Francisco International Airport extended south to Millbrae, and from the top of the hill you could watch planes gracefully land and take off without listening to the roar of their engines.

In the flat area of Millbrae you couldn't see the dance of the runways, but your ears would get used to the sonic thunder.

I turned my bicycle up Hillcrest and rode south on Broadway. Around the corner I saw Jasmine walking.

"Jasmine," I yelled.

"What are you doing?" she asked.

"Just riding around. Where are you going?"

"Home," she said.

I went over the scenarios in my brain and came to the conclusion that giving her a ride home on my bicycle wouldn't get me in trouble if she told her mom.

"I'll give you a ride," I said.

"How?"

"You sit on the seat and I'll stand forward and pedal. Peter and I do it all the time."

She agreed and immediately put her hands on my sides to steady herself.

Giving Jasmine a ride was one of the best ideas I'd ever had. As I rode I lost balance for a second and we almost fell to the ground.

"Stop it," she said while laughing.

"I'm not doing it on purpose."

Then I did it on purpose and she laughed more. She brought her dark hand up to her mouth as she laughed. I waited for her to put her hands on my sides again and we continued riding.

I wished all the worldly kids at school could've seen me riding a pretty high school girl home on my bicycle. I stopped in front of her house, where she lived with Camille and their mom.

"Wanna come in for some juice?" she asked.

I got a vision of Camille's crooked teeth and declined.

All the way back to my apartment I still felt the touch of Jasmine's hand grasping me as I pedaled her home.

I wished I was riding a motorcycle and she was on the back. Our hair blowing in the wind. Cigarette hanging from my mouth. Going nowhere, just riding.

Peter punched his locker.

"Are you okay?" I asked.

"Bitch," he said and punched it again.

He showed me the letter that was slipped into his locker.

> *Dear Peter,*
> *You're a great guy. I'm really sorry but I think we should break up. I'm too young to date and my dad is mad. He's going to call your dad later.*
> *From,*
> *Jennifer*

"What happened?" I asked.

"I don't know."

Peter's stepdad, Terry, waited for him to get home from school. We both walked in the door since we were going to get Peter's skateboard and go out again.

"Peter, sit down. Gabe, please leave," Terry said. His white T-shirt didn't go all the way to his pants, so I could see his hairy gut exposed.

Peter was grounded again. He was locked in his parents' bedroom with nothing but a tape recorder and Bible drama tapes produced by the Watchtower Society. Volunteer Jehovah's Witnesses acted out the parts of people like King David or Moses or the Apostles and Jesus so we could be entertained and educated at the same time.

He got the "you're too young to be dating" lecture, but he also got in trouble because someone had seen him and Jennifer holding hands.

I was secretly glad she had broken up with him because we got to eat lunch without Jennifer or Camille.

Jennifer's dad put the fear of God into her. Literally. At school she stopped Peter in the hallway. Peter smiled. He thought they were going to get back together.

"Peter, I like you, but fornicators won't make it into the new system, so I'm glad Jehovah stopped us before we sinned and lost his favor."

Peter's smile dropped.

"Okay, thanks," he said.

"I'm going to try to be a better Jehovah's Witness and not lead a double life," she continued.

"Okay?"

"You should, too. Then, in the new system, when we're adults, we can talk about getting married."

"Okay?"

"Thanks for understanding," she said, touching his arm like Camille had touched mine earlier in the year.

"May Jehovah bless you both," she said to us.

We walked to our lockers, too dumbfounded to speak about what had just happened with Jennifer.

The next week we graduated from junior high. I couldn't wait to get to high school and see Jasmine every day. I pictured her introducing me to all her sophomore friends, embracing me every morning, her being as excited as I was that I would finally be a freshman.

The first week of high school Peter showed me something called a skate key. It was a tool to change your skateboard wheels and loosen your trucks in case you wanted to make sharper turns.

When Jared and Tom found out Peter had a skateboard, they started eating lunch with us. Tom had a Hacky Sack and we'd kick that around after we ate.

I didn't feel like a gay Jehovah's Witness for the first time in a while. I asked my parents for a skateboard so I could be more included in the group. They promised me one if I learned the names and order of all the books in the Bible.

I studied for two days and came to them with the memorization and passed the test. I had a hard time remembering the order of Galatians, Ephesians, Philippians, Colossians. Dad said it's easier to remember if I think General Electric Power Company, G, E, P, C.

I bought a Powell-Peralta and soon Peter and I were skateboarding back and forth to school.

We practiced skateboarding with Jared and Tom. On days when Peter was absent, I could eat with Jared and Tom and not feel weird.

That semester I also got all A's and B's on my report card. I brought it home to show Mom and Dad. They were happy but Mom reassured me that since Armageddon would be here before I got out of high school, there was no need to engage more than necessary in worldly activities.

The brothers at the Kingdom Hall talked about the world of mankind like the *Titanic*.

"If you were on a ship that was sinking, would you polish the brass? No, you get on a lifeboat."

Getting on a lifeboat meant being a Jehovah's Witness and going out in service and to all the meetings.

Getting good grades was like polishing the brass on the *Titanic* as it sank.

I stopped doing most of my homework. In English class I excelled and aced the tests, especially the essay tests, without studying. I had an instinct for words, so the teacher decided I should be in an advanced class called College Prep Composition. It was actually an easier class than the lower one.

I didn't tell my parents I had advanced, because it was fun and I was polishing the brass on the *Titanic*, but only a little bit.

"Class, settle down. We have a lot to cover before the day is over," Mr. Phillips, our science teacher, said.

Everyone calmed down and I took out my textbook and continued to soak in that wonderful spring day.

"Today we're going to have sex education," the teacher continued.

Persecution imminent.

Mr. Phillips gave me a stealth look and I picked up my notebook and went to the library. The class watched me leave. I felt like a spotlight had switched on and I should've started singing Vegas show tunes. Sex ed was embarrassing enough without having to leave every time it was taught in class. The Watchtower Society published a brochure called "School and Jehovah's Witnesses" that we had to give to our teachers:

> Many schools are also providing explicit education in sexual matters, including contraception, masturbation, homosexuality, and abortion.
>
> Sex education is generally provided without moral guidance. In fact, it is not infrequent that educators themselves will criticize the moral standards of the Bible. Therefore Witness parents are very concerned about what is taught in sex education classes.

One book used in some schools, entitled *Dreng og pige, mand og kvinde* (*Boy and Girl, Man and Woman*), says, "Each individual must have the right to satisfy his sexual needs independent of age, sex, and—as far as it does not invade the rights of others—the method used." So, as to sex relations with animals, this book states: "In this country [Denmark], . . . it is lawful to satisfy sexual desires in this way." Yet God's Law to Israel said: "Anyone lying down with a beast is positively to be put to death."—EXODUS 22:19.

As emphasized earlier, Jehovah's Witnesses try to follow the Bible's moral principles and to inculcate these into their children. Therefore they do not want their children to receive sex education from those who do not respect these principles. Thus if Witness parents feel their children are being indoctrinated with ideas, and/or visual matter, that blatantly undermine principles being taught at home, they may request that their young ones be released from sex education classes.

—"School and Jehovah's Witnesses,"
Watchtower Bible and Tract Society 1983

On Saturday morning I was assigned to preach with Brother Albertson. Brother Albertson had a big nose and his eyes were kind of glassy because he used to do a lot of drugs. He stopped doing drugs, and even though Jesus turned water into wine he couldn't even touch alcohol anymore. He was really enthusiastic when it came to preaching.

I knocked on the first door. An older woman answered.

"Hello, ma'am. I'm asking your neighbors today, have you ever wondered what happens when we die?"

"You're a precious young man, but no thank you," she said and shut the door.

Brother Albertson rang the next doorbell.

"I'll get it," a girl yelled to her mother from inside the house.

She opened the door and it was Lorie from science class. I saw her tank top exposing her newly formed breasts. Brother Albertson had his Bible ready. She looked at me and my face turned red so fast my ears looked like they'd been bitten by a poisonous spider indigenous to the deep Congo.

Brother Albertson started his presentation. "Can I read you a scripture I think you'll find comforting?"

She gave a meek smile and shrugged her shoulders.

"It's Revelation chapter 21 verse 4, 'And He will wipe out every tear from their eyes and death will be no more.' Doesn't that sound wonderful?"

"I guess," she replied. I felt the blood rush to my face and prayed she just thought I had a sunburn.

"This issue of the *Watchtower* talks more about a time when those living will never die. Would you like to read it?"

"Okay." She held the *Watchtower* between two fingers and let the magazine go limp.

My heart beat so fast I could feel the throbbing in my teeth.

"What's your name?" Brother Albertson asked.

She said Lorie.

Brother Albertson thanked her for her time and she looked at me and shut the door. On the sidewalk Brother Albertson wrote her address and name in his book. Next month he'd come back with the latest issue of the *Watchtower* to offer it to Lorie.

"She looks about your age. It's good she sees you doing God's work. You're setting a good example for her," Brother Albertson told me.

The blood slowly left my face and went back to my liver and my hands and my knees. My chest hurt.

Monday before class, Lorie asked me why I was Jehovah walking. I told her because I'm a Jehovah's Witness.

I didn't want her to ask me more about it, even though it was the first time she'd ever spoken to me. I'd sat two rows behind her in science class since September. I stared at her curly blond hair and her wonderfully revealing tank tops.

I wanted to drop the Jehovah subject and go to my desk even though that was the first time I knew for sure that her eyes were hazel. Without looking psycho I could gaze upon her full lips as they moved while she spoke to me—because she was talking to me, the misfit Jehovah's Witness, the guy she'd avoided eye contact with for most of the semester.

"Why are you a Jehovah?" she asked

I said I forgot my pencil in my locker and left class and ran to the bathroom to splash cold water on my face. Then I looked in the mirror and said a prayer to Jehovah for strength.

I sweated my fever out and my sheets were wet. When I woke up the partition between where I slept and the living room seemed to be rippling, like a small wave in a lake.

It shook me awake and I realized it was probably a fever hallucination.

There was a moment when I thought the demons were messing with me. I called out for Jehovah. I knew how easy it was to invite them into your house. The wrong record. The demonic film. A secondhand pair of jeans worn by a woman who practiced séances or played with tarot cards and the demon door was open in your house.

Sister Sheehan told me about a time when the demons took all the blankets off her bed and held her down for a minute. The elders traced it to a Fleetwood Mac album where Stevie Nicks was dressed like a witch.

"Are you okay?" Mom had heard me yell to Jehovah from the kitchen.

I moaned and she came to my bed. She put her hand on my forehead; then she rubbed my arm that was exposed outside of the blanket.

I was completely comforted. I let out a weak cough and closed my eyes, basking in Mom's affection.

"You're soaking wet. Do you feel okay enough to take a shower?"

"How old were you when you left Norway?" I asked.

"Two." Mom seemed put off by my instant lucidity.

"Do you remember it?"

"No, honey."

"Do you ever want to go back to Norway?"

"Yes, probably after Armageddon, when the new system is here. We can all go over there."

I thought about the new system.

I thought of a time when the whole earth would be filled with Jehovah's Witnesses. When I wouldn't have to worry about flag salutes, when my bed wouldn't be part of the front room, when I could be married and have sex in a house with my wife. Anywhere in the world I wanted. Paradise would be mine. A place where I wouldn't have strep throat or ever die.

"How did Grandma Liz die?" I asked, referring to her mother.

Mom looked at me like she was wondering *where that came from.*

"She died from an accident."

"What accident?"

Mom pulled her hand away from my arm. She pulled her whole body away from me.

"An accident," she repeated and went into the kitchen to retrieve her tea.

I wasn't satisfied.

"How?" I yelled from the bed, and then my throat hurt from trying to talk too loud.

She was silent. I waited. I put my hand around my throat to feel my swollen glands.

Dishes clanked in the kitchen. She didn't respond. I dropped the subject.

She came back. She was crying.

I didn't feel sympathy for her. She was hiding something from me. I was determined.

"What accident?" I pushed.

She raised her voice: "She died. She killed herself."

In the back of my mind I knew there was something fishy about Grandma's death. Maybe I had asked when I was a kid and I knew the "accident" answer was a bogus one. I couldn't remember.

I was unrelenting.

"How did she kill herself?"

Mom was crying and pacing in and out of sight beyond the

partition, to the front room, then back past the partition in front of my bed. She stopped and looked at me.

"She killed herself by slitting her wrist," she yelled.

That's all I wanted. I wanted the truth. Grandma died. I now knew exactly how. I didn't need to know why. Not yet, anyway. Mom sat down on the bed and fought her emotions.

"We'll see her in the new system when she's resurrected," Mom said.

"She'll be resurrected?" I asked.

"Yes, Jehovah will then ask her to decide if she wants to be a Jehovah's Witness or not. If she does, you'll be able to meet her."

I didn't particularly care to meet her. The thought hadn't even come to me. I was too busy with my new house and having great sex with my wife in the paradise of the new system.

After Mom went back to bed, Dad came home from work. He grunted when I said hi to him.

"Have you been watching TV all day?" he asked.

"No, I just turned it on."

"Have you read the latest *Watchtower*?"

I knew if I lied he'd have a question for me about the current *Watchtower* that I couldn't answer and I'd have to read it more thoroughly for a later quizzing.

Dad always kept the latest *Watchtower* in his back pocket. Every chance he got, he'd pull it out. He'd take it out at work, at Grandpa Barry's car repair shop, and read it on his breaks, to find a few moments of spiritual solitude in a worldly environment.

The pressure he'd been under from Grandpa Barry to "leave the Jehovahs" had ceased years ago, but whenever Grandma Sara visited the shop to bring Grandpa his lunch or something, she'd ignore Dad completely. Like he wasn't even there. Like he was a mechanic and she was a customer—not like she'd birthed him and raised him and her blood coursed through his veins.

Grandma loved Jeff, Dad's stepbrother, who lived above the shop and also worked there. When she saw Jeff she'd light up, double kiss him on the cheeks, and find out about his latest band and travels. Even though he was her stepson, he was her pride and joy.

He hadn't joined "the cult" and messed up her grandchild with all that "cult" stuff.

Dad's persecution. He wore it on his sleeve. Every day was an endurance for him. In the Bible, Jesus said some believers would have to leave their biological family in order to join their spiritual family. Dad was enduring and he'd come home to find me in bed, watching television, getting influenced by Satan's world, not reading the *Watchtower* to protect my mind from the satanic influences in the worldly associations I had at school every day.

"No," I answered.

He turned the TV off and I read about Noah's day in the *Watchtower* and how being a Jehovah's Witness is like being in the ark he built, though I would've rather seen the end of that *Starsky & Hutch* rerun.

I went over to Peter's apartment and we played Pong on his Atari 2600. He leaned close to me and said, "Did you know women can make their pussy lips move while you have sex with them?"

"Really?"

"Yeah, Todd told me he had sex with a worldly girl, and she made her pussy lips move and it was the best feeling in the world."

I didn't know pussies had lips and stored that in my memory for future reference.

Todd was a Jehovah's Witness. He was eighteen. I wouldn't dare tell anyone about Todd's secret because not only could he kill me with one punch, but I wanted Todd to know I was cool, if he ever found out I knew and I was okay with it. But I wasn't completely okay with it. I was kind of scared that if I didn't tell, I could be in trouble with Jehovah. I just pretended that it was probably another Todd he was talking about.

"Have you ever touched it?" Peter asked.

"What?"

"Your penis?"

I laughed. I didn't want to talk to him about it. Then again, I wasn't getting too much education on the topic anywhere else, so I thought, why not? But I stopped just in case he was trying to trap me into saying I touched myself so he could make fun of me in front of other people.

"I don't know. Let's just play," I said.

We kept playing Pong. It made its beeping noise every time we hit the electronic ball to each other. The silence in the air screamed, "Masturbation! Self-abuse!"

"I played with it a couple of times," Peter finally confessed.

"What was it like?" I tried to pretend I had never touched myself.

"You know what it's like. C'mon, tell me if you've played with yourself," he said.

Quotes from the *Watchtower* flashed before my eyes:

Masturbation is indeed a "hurtful desire." It is also "uncleanness," for it is an immoral practice, and this explains why the masturbator generally is ashamed of himself and hides his repugnant act from the sight of others.

Abnormal, mentally deranged people are notorious masturbators . . . many mentally disturbed priests and nuns are chronic masturbators.

—*Watchtower* 1973, September 15

Masturbation can lead to homosexuality.

—*The Youth Book*, page 44

"I may have tried to touch it," I said.

"Ha, I knew it," Peter replied in a way that made it seem like every family member I had and everyone in the congregation was going to jump out of the closet and yell, *"Surprise!,"* and Peter was going to be rewarded in paradise for getting me to confess to my deranged act, and I was going to be disfellowshipped, excommunicated for my uncleanness, and never be able to speak to Peter or Jin or Jasmine or Ally again.

"I knew it because I do it too. I've been doing it all the time. It feels great," Peter said. I stopped looking for the condemnation entourage.

"Have you cum yet?" Peter asked.

"What's cum?"

"That's the best part, man. I can't believe you haven't cum."

We stopped playing Atari and Peter turned toward me.

"You rub it up and down, right?"

"I think so, no, well, I touched the tip of it," I said.

"Next time rub it up and down, and think of the pussy lips that Todd told me about."

"What did Todd tell you?" Peter's mother, Mandy, came into the room.

My body went ice cold.

"Oh, he said there's a game called *Choosy Blips* for Atari that we should play."

She looked at me.

"I hear it's really good. My friend at school has it," I backed Peter up. She left the room. I wasn't sure she was convinced.

"Tell me after you do it," said Peter, and we started playing Pong again.

Freshman year was over and with summer came extra time for going out to preach.

Mom and Dad would only let me have Witness friends and all my Witness friends preached more during the summer months, so there wasn't much choice.

It wasn't too bad to go out in service in the morning. Maybe I'd get a little embarrassed because Lorie from science class or Jessica from P.E. would see me at their doors wearing a suit and tie and holding a Bible. But I felt like I was doing right by God. Even on tough preaching mornings, there was a unique joy of accomplishment.

And some of the Witnesses in my congregation were even funny. There was Brother Temple, who always joked about how bald he was or how he'd never get a wife unless *fat and bald* became the new *thin and handsome*.

Whenever I partnered up with Sister Sorisho, she talked about music. She liked reggae and ska and would tell me about bands I should listen to, like the Specials and Pato Banton. Her husband wasn't a Jehovah's Witness; he was a graphic designer. They met each other at a Richard Hell and the Voidoids concert in 1976. He would come to the congregation meetings once in a while with his wife, and the elders would always ask him if he wanted a Bible study. He'd politely shake his head no and walk away.

He and his wife really loved each other. She was cool with him not being a Jehovah's Witness, something that was completely foreign to my understanding. To everyone's understanding. Wouldn't she be sad when Jehovah killed him during Armageddon?

Sometimes I went out in service with Ally or Arlene or Peter. Arlene was two years older than I was. She hung out with older people in the congregation but when they weren't around she'd stoop down to our level. Even Jasmine and I preached together during the summer. One time when I preached with Jasmine I wore my yellow tie and a brown suit. I thought the contrast was cool.

At the morning service group, Brother Miller was the director. On weekdays Sister Sorisho offered her apartment for us to meet in.

Jasmine wasn't there when I arrived. The service meeting had already started, and there was an empty seat next to Sister Feeney. Brother Temple joked once to me that Sister Feeney looked like Mrs. Roper on *Three's Company*. As I sat down I tried not to giggle at her curly red hair and bad makeup.

"We all have a choice to make. Are we on God's side or are we with the ruler of this ungodly world?" Brother Miller opened his Bible. "Follow along with me as I read 2 Timothy chapter 3 verse 4. 'In the last days, men will be lovers of pleasure rather than lovers of God.' These are the people we have to be with at work and at school every day. We need to make sure their worldly ways don't influence us to choose the side of Satan. And, if their hearts are good, they'll listen to our message."

Brother Miller always liked to make dramatic pauses. He would pause after expressing a thought and look around the room and squint his eyes, like he was trying to look deep within our souls to make sure we fully understood what he was saying.

Sister Feeney nodded her head in agreement; then she sneezed. When Sister Feeney sneezed, it was more like an elephant roar. She wouldn't cover her nose because her sneezes came on like a smack to her face. I got some residual spray on my slacks.

I looked around the room just in case I'd missed Jasmine when I first came in and sat down. There were about twenty people there, all of them ready to go out preaching. All of them dressed like it was Sunday worship.

Jasmine wasn't there. Distracted, I missed hearing which part of the scripture everyone was supposed to turn to for the next part of the lecture, which was about what we should discuss with potential disciples later that morning. Sister Feeney leaned her Bible toward me so I could follow along with the verses.

The front door knob shook. The hinges creaked. Then Jasmine entered. Her long dark hair and blue flowered dress flowed as she made her way into the field service meeting. It all happened in slow motion. She wore dark nylons and black shoes with about two-inch heels, still chaste enough by Jehovah's Witness standards. If her heels were any higher, an elder would probably send her home to change before she would be able to go out preaching.

Jasmine squeezed in behind Sister Sandoval's chair. There were no more seats available, so she stood. I looked at her but didn't make it too obvious. Her olive skin pierced my heart. A couple more pubic hairs had sprung from my body, and they all pointed at Jasmine. She was on my mind more and more.

Sister Sandoval wore flat shoes that fully covered her toes. I liked to stare at sisters' toes. I felt weird doing it, so I would always wait until everyone bowed their heads in prayer at the service meetings before I could catch glimpses of the little piggies.

No one ever thought my relationship with Jasmine was anything but platonic. No one would ever guess that I had dark, lustful thoughts whenever I saw her brown eyes. It would be frowned upon for us to go out in service together if there were a sexual interest. As far as everyone was concerned, we were just spiritual comrades.

Mom used to babysit Jasmine and Camille. I really liked that because I didn't have any brothers or sisters to play with. When I was eight years old, before Mom got chronic fatigue syndrome, she took all of us to the park near the recreation center in Millbrae. There were monkey bars, and Jasmine could skip three bars at a time because her arms were longer than mine. I noticed her then. She was unique. I ached for her.

"Come on, you try it," she said.

"I want to see you do it again," I replied.

Jasmine jumped up onto the bars and concentrated as she skipped hand over hand across the apparatus. Her concentration turned into a smile when she saw how intensely I looked at her.

"I bet you can't do it." Jasmine jumped down. I smiled at her and said, "Let me push you on the swing."

As I pushed her I touched her lower back with my hands. A charge went off through my nervous system. The electricity in my sciatic nerve could've started an earthquake.

Brother Miller finished discussing the *Watchtower*s and *Awake!*s that everyone would offer to the public, and it was time for him to say a prayer to bless the service day. Everyone closed their eyes to concentrate on the divine communication except me. I kept my head bowed down, but my eyes were on Jasmine's dark shoes and skinny ankles, which were barely visible behind Sister Sandoval's chair.

Jasmine and I were assigned to Sister Sandoval's car group. There were five people in the group, Brother Miller, Sister Sandoval, me, Jasmine, and Sister Feeney.

Sister Sandoval had lost her husband to a brain tumor when he was twenty-two years old. Going out in service was the only thing that kept her from completely breaking down. She didn't smile anymore and was very serious about preaching. She had five Bible studies. Dark hair sprinkled her upper lip, from her Nicaraguan heritage.

As we left the apartment and walked to Sister Sandoval's car, I finally got the chance to talk to Jasmine.

"Hi," I said.

"Hi, Gabe."

The monkey bars of love were in the air.

"That's a nice dress," I said.

"Thanks. I don't think a yellow tie goes with a brown suit."

Sister Sandoval unlocked the driver's side door. Her car was a Datsun 510. Two-door. It was small and had fold-down seats for passengers to squeeze into the back.

Brother Miller asked if I had the latest *Watchtower* to offer.

"Yes, right here."

"It's good to see you're prepared," he replied.

Just then Sister Sandoval unlocked the passenger door, and Jasmine got in the back seat. Brother Miller was right behind her. I had to sit pushed up against Brother Miller as we drove off to the territory where we would preach. I wanted to be pushed up against Jasmine, not a short, curly-haired elder with too much aftershave.

We reached the assigned territory on Chadbourne Avenue. Everyone piled out of the car and worked the block by going house over house over house. Sister Sandoval preached with Sister Feeney, and Brother Miller preached alone.

Jasmine and I approached the first door, 812 Chadbourne.

"You want to go first?" Jasmine asked.

Being the gentleman, and to show her that I could take the lead, be a good spiritual head, a good father-type figure, you know, a good boyfriend if she needed, I went first.

I'd perfected the mediocre knock over my years in service. I knocked softly enough for no one to hear me inside the house, but loudly enough not to raise suspicion that I really wanted to avoid talking to people about the Bible on some mornings, especially when I preached in an area where I knew a few of my school friends lived.

When I was in fourth grade, Leslie and Anne-Marie from my elementary school answered the door once when I was in service with Dad. It was my turn at the door. I stood catatonic as the girls giggled at me in my suit and tie and Dad talked to them about the importance of the sacrifice of Jesus Christ.

The next Monday Anne-Marie came up to me while I was eating lunch with Stan and Charles, who didn't know I was a Jehovah's Witness.

"Why do you go streetwalking?" she said.

My heart pounded as I was about to be discovered as the weird Jehovah's Witness. I tried to ignore her, but Stan and Charles were stoked that she was even talking to us.

"What are you talking about?" Charles asked. It was the first time he had ever talked to Anne-Marie, and he wasn't going to lose the opportunity to keep the conversation going.

She tossed her blond hair back. "Gabe was reading the Bible at my door with his dad. He's a Jehovah. Why are you a Jehovah?"

I swallowed a bit of my ham and cheese sandwich and hoped the question would just go away. It hung there in the air as Charles, Stan, and Anne-Marie waited for an answer.

"I don't know, I just am," I felt my sandwich creep back up my esophagus.

Anne-Marie walked away and Stan and Charles hit me with all the same questions I got whenever I was found out. Can you dance? Why don't you celebrate Christmas? Can you drink Coke?

There was no answer at the door so Jasmine and I started down the stairs to the street and onto the next house. As Jasmine walked in front of me, a wind from God lifted her dress up. I saw a small beauty mark above the back of her left knee under her nylons. Erotic.

"I bought *The Joshua Tree*," I said. I knew she was a U2 fan.

"Is it good?"

"Really good. I can tape it for you."

"Sure."

We walked.

"I want my dad to buy me a black vest like Bono wears on the cover."

"He's the guitarist, right?" she asked.

"No, he's the singer. He's my favorite member of U2."

"*Thriller* is great," Jasmine said. I forgot she was a Michael Jackson fan. I'd heard she was positive that she would marry Michael one day since he was a Jehovah's Witness.

"It's as good as *Off the Wall*?"

"No, way better. 'Billie Jean' is my favorite song. They played the video on California Music Channel the other day. You should get a white suit like he wears in the video."

I could be her Michael Jackson.

I wanted to hold her hand, but that would be out of the question. I wanted to caress her, to run my fingers through her silky soft hair, but that would set into motion events I didn't care to enter. The questions from the congregation elders regarding my intentions toward Jasmine. The questions from my parents. The investigation by the congregation to make sure Jasmine and I didn't engage in any other misconduct, or sexual activity. The lectures that I was too young to think about marriage and didn't even have a job to support a wife would soon follow.

As we walked slowly along the sidewalk I brushed up against her and pretended it was an accident. I could smell the strawberry shampoo that she used in her hair. I wanted to eat that hair.

"Gabe, how about you work with me for a few doors. I'd like to hear your presentation," Brother Miller said, interrupting my lust.

"Sister Feeney is going on a Bible study, so Jasmine, could you preach with Sister Sandoval?" he added.

Jasmine walked over to Sister Sandoval, who stood on the street corner reading her Bible, getting ready to approach the next house.

I ached to hug Jasmine goodbye. This was not how I'd envisioned my perfect morning preaching with Jasmine turning out.

At the next door I gave my mediocre knock and waited with Brother Miller. Brother Miller smiled and gave the door a harder knocking; each knock was a thud to my eardrums. I was almost sure Yvette from English class lived here. I was tired of explaining my religion to cute schoolgirls and jocks from class. I was sick of being accosted with questions in the school hallways. "What were you doing last Saturday?" "Was there a funeral? Because you were all dressed up." "Are you a Jehovah?" "Does that mean you're a virgin?" "Can you drink coffee?" "Are you allowed to dance?"

A college-age woman in sweats answered the door. She looked like she had been jogging. Her sweatshirt was unzipped down to her tight stomach, exposing her chest, heaving from being out of breath.

"Hello?" she asked.

"Hi, my name is Gabe and this is Brother Miller and we're here to talk about God and how he—" She slammed the door.

Brother Miller and I walked back to the street.

"If you talked a little slower and had more confidence in what you're saying, the householder might take the *Watchtower*," Brother Miller suggested, scratching his curly hair while dandruff made a snowfall onto his blue suit jacket.

"Do you know who the shortest man in the Bible is?" Brother Miller asked in a lame attempt to bond with me.

"Nehemiah. Knee High Miah," he answered his own question and laughed.

I laughed to keep Brother Miller happy. To silence him. Jasmine had beautiful knees. So delicate. I thought about putting my hand on one of her knees.

"Did you know the Bible talks about tennis?" Brother Miller continued. "Moses served in the courts of Pharaoh."

After a few more doors and tries at slowing down my presentation, Brother Miller and I met Sister Sandoval and Jasmine back at the car. Jasmine got in the back seat and I went in right after her. The back seat was so tiny I could brush up against Jasmine's leg without anyone noticing.

"Actually, Gabe, I'd like to take you on a Bible study with my student Bill. He lives right over there, so we can walk," Brother Miller said.

I looked at Jasmine. I wanted to cry. I huffed and got out of the car.

A Bible study usually lasts about an hour and is just like it sounds:

You study the Bible. When people study the Bible with Jehovah's Witnesses, it's usually in their homes. Even though my whole body ached for leaving Jasmine, at least I wouldn't have to worry about kids from school seeing me preach outside for the next hour.

"Can you pick us up in one hour at 32 Willow Ave?" Brother Miller asked Sister Sandoval.

Ahh, they'd be coming back.

As Brother Miller and I walked to his Bible study, he focused like a boxer who was about to get into the ring and spar.

"Taking walks is good when you're out in service," he said. "It helps keep your mind sharp so you'll be ready to defend the word of God if you need to." Brother Miller inhaled deeply and gripped his Bible. The neighborhood we walked through was filled with manicured lawns and luscious gardens. The smell of spring was in the air.

I kept my head down just in case one of my school friends drove by.

Bill, Brother Miller's Bible study student, invited us into his apartment. It was a dark basement apartment, in the back of a house. Bill had barely any furniture, so I sat in a folding chair. The studio apartment smelled like eggs and bacon. Bill's mustache looked like there was dirt on his upper lip. His left eye wandered. It was hard to tell if he was looking at me or at someone behind me.

"Let's begin," Brother Miller said. "Do you remember in last week's study we talked about the world? What is the world?"

Bill flipped through his study book. "The world means people who aren't Jehovah's Witnesses."

"Very good. And who is the ruler of the world?"

"Satan."

"Can you give me a scripture from the Bible to back that up?"

"First John 5:19, 'the whole world is lying in the power of the wicked one.'" Bill looked up from his notes.

"Right, and if we aren't for God, then who are we for?"

"That means we're against God and for Satan."

"Very good, Bill. Gabe, please read John 12:31 for us."

I read as Bill listened. He had no elastic in his white socks, so they crept all the way down his ankles to his nylon Keds with Velcro straps.

"Thanks, Gabe. So Bill, are you for God or Satan?"

"I'm for God," Bill said with a whimper.

"I'm sorry, we didn't hear you?"

"I'm for God, I'm for God. I hate Satan!" Bill said.

"That's great!" Brother Miller smiled, then realized Bill was crying.

"Bill, what's wrong?"

"I. I hate Satan, but I'm for Satan."

"How?" Brother Miller squinted his eyes to see into Bill's soul.

"Well, I guess I've been for God the last few days. I haven't smoked a cigarette in four days now," Bill said.

"Have you been praying to God about not smoking?"

"Yes, I did. One day I prayed, but I broke down and smoked half a pack later. That's because I sinned against God anyway during that day, so I figured I may as well have some cigarettes."

Brother Miller sat in a second-hand patio chair, blocking my path to the front door. In an emergency, I figured I could use my chair to climb up to the window in Bill's bedroom. I'd just have to kick out the screen.

"Bill, that doesn't mean you're for Satan. You're trying to make changes and God sees that. He knows you're on his side."

I wondered if Jasmine was having fun with Sister Sandoval. I wondered if Jasmine still thought of me as a little kid, if she was under the impression I still wanted to go steady with her crooked-toothed sister.

"But, there's more." Bill hit his fist against his knee, then let out a grunt, waking me from my fantasy. "I. I'm for God."

"I know, Bill. What is it?" Brother Miller asked.

"Well, uh, I—" Bill looked at me.

"Go ahead, it's okay; we're brothers here," Brother Miller assured.

"I masturbated that day."

My face went flush. I felt cold tingles down my spine, like a skeleton hand was massaging my back.

They talked about masturbation at the Kingdom Hall sometimes during the three weekly meetings. It always made me blush. I would tilt my head slightly down in the hopes that no one would see my embarrassment and assume I was a transgressor of masturbation. I flashed to that day I played Atari with Peter.

Bill was confessing it *all* to Brother Miller. I would never tell anyone other than Peter that I touched my penis, especially Brother Miller. I'd rather die at Armageddon if I had to.

I tilted my head slightly lower and tried to think of something else so my face would feel less hot. I hoped Bill didn't have too much more confessing to do, since I wanted to be with Jasmine.

Brother Miller pulled out his Bible and read Colossians chapter 3 verse 5, "Deaden your body members that are upon the Earth as respects fornication, uncleanness, sexual appetite . . ." and Matthew chapter 5 verse 30, "If your right hand is making you stumble, cut if off and throw it away from you. For it is more beneficial to you for one of your members to be lost than for your whole body to land in Gehenna."

I tried to keep my mind blank and my head less crimson.

"You know," Bill started, "thanks for helping me today, but I have one more thing to confess."

If only I had a gun.

"I, well," Bill said trying to hold back the tears, "when I masturbated I bought a pornographic magazine, and I still have it."

"Bill, these desires may seem natural but we must fight them because they are a part of our sinful flesh. And Satan wants us to succumb to our hurtful desires. Gabe, how do you deal with sexual desire?"

I brush up against Jasmine and feel her soft body. I intoxicate myself with her scent, with a smile in my direction.

Then I ache with desire unfulfilled and touch my penis later.

"I pray to God for help," I replied.

"And does he help you?" Bill asked.

"Yes, trust in Jehovah," I said.

Brother Miller comforted Bill and let him know that God still loved him and even though he took a step back from His favor, God would forgive him.

Brother Miller said, "When I reached puberty, I had a problem with masturbation. Do you know what I did?"

I pictured him squinting and concentrating as he stroked his penis. It made me never want to masturbate again.

"I kept a calendar with me. On days when I masturbated, I put a black dot in the corner of the date. I kept it on me as a reminder. I finally stopped. I looked at a month on the calendar without any black dots and prayed to Jehovah with thanks for helping me to beat that filthy habit."

As we left, Bill shook my hand. The only thing I could think about was how soon it would be until I could wash it.

After waiting for a few minutes outside of masturbation Bill's apartment, we decided to walk down the hill to Lyon's restaurant, where Sister Feeney conducted her Bible study.

Jasmine, Sister Feeney, and Sister Feeney's student, Helga, whom I'd met a few times before, sat in a large booth. They were praying.

"Dear God in heaven," Sister Feeney prayed, "please bless our efforts to learn more about you and please give us your Holy Spirit so Helga can accept you and become approved by you. And thank you for the food we're about to eat. In Jesus' name, amen."

Helga didn't bow her head all the way and she kept her eyes open. She said a low-volume "amen" at the end of the prayer.

After they finished praying, Brother Miller and I slid into the booth. The booth was meant for eight people. I was able to sit next to Jasmine, but there was no excuse to scoot right up next to her.

Helga's husband had told her that she better quit studying with that Jehovah cult. Helga defied her husband because she felt there was something right about Jehovah's Witnesses and that they might be the true religion. So Helga had asked Sister Feeney if they could meet at Lyon's restaurant to study the Bible and she could tell her husband she was having lunch with a friend and not be a liar.

"I tried to read the Bible on my own, but I don't know where to start," Helga said after the prayer and showed Sister Feeney the scripture that scared her at Jeremiah 5:8: "Horses seized with sexual heat, having strong testicles they have become. They neigh each one to the wife of his companion."

She was Sister Feeney's Bible student, yet Brother Miller couldn't help but interject, "The Bible can't be understood in one week; it takes time and research. It's good that you read the Bible. Try to read it every day. It's inspired by God."

Sister Feeney took control with her prepared presentation: "I brought you a book that we can study together." Sister Feeney showed Helga a little blue book entitled *The Truth That Leads to Eternal Life* and gave an overview of the chapters and what Helga would learn:

*Satan is very real and he's misleading the entire Earth;

*False religion will be destroyed and only those who are Jehovah's Witnesses will be saved through Armageddon and make it into the new system;

*All those who have died will be resurrected; and

*We'll be able to live forever with them on a paradise Earth.

"Do you understand how easy it is to realize that we are the truth?" interjected Brother Miller. "We are the only religion who would rather go to jail than go to war. We are the only religion who tells the truth that there is no such thing as hell. Hell is not hot; it's just another word for the common grave." Brother Miller's testimonial was his last since Sister Feeney gave him an evil stare. He wanted to express humility, so after that he kept to nodding his head vigorously every time she made a point he agreed with. He wanted Helga to believe the truth to the core of her soul. To the marrow of her bones.

After finishing the Bible study, Sister Feeney took a few sugar packets from the table and put them in her purse.

Our waiter's name tag said Charlie and his polyester black pants only went down to the tops of his ankles. He refilled Helga's and Jasmine's coffees, and Sister Feeney was moved by the Holy Spirit to preach to him.

"Charlie, do you know the earth will one day be a paradise?" Sister Feeney asked.

goodbye to everyone. The car drove down the street and Jasmine's dark hair glistened through the rear window.

I walked up the stairs and embraced my morning with Jasmine. Her touch. Her smell. Her aura.

When I got to my apartment, Mom was sleeping.

I lay on my bed and closed my eyes, watching my mental home movie of Jasmine.

Dad drove me over to the car repair shop to stay with Uncle Jeff so he could take Mom out for dinner.

Jeff lived in a small converted apartment above Grandpa Barry's shop where he and Dad worked. I called Barry Grandpa Barry, but he was really Jeff's father. By the time I found out we weren't blood related it felt weird to suddenly stop calling him Grandpa.

Jeff played bass and sometimes went on tour with bands or played in a jazz band at an expensive hotel in San Francisco that would only let people over twenty-one in to see his show.

Jeff was technically worldly but Dad witnessed to him and Jeff listened.

Dad felt confident leaving me with Jeff since Dad was sure Jeff would become a Jehovah's Witness one day.

He was playing his bass as I walked up the stairs. When he saw me he stopped.

"Hey, kiddo," he said.

"Hey, Jeff."

"I bought an Intellivision, this new video game player, if you want to check it out."

He showed me how to work the controls. I played Asteroids while he continued on the bass.

Jeff's hair was growing past his shoulders. Dad said that Jeff had stopped doing drugs and committing immorality and was thinking about going to the Kingdom Hall.

The phone rang.

"Hello? . . . Oh, hi . . . I'm sorry, I . . . it's hard to explain . . . No, it was nothing to do with you, Stella. It's . . . no." Then he put his hand over the mouthpiece but I still heard, "No, the sex was great.

I'm just . . ." He uncupped his hand and said, "Yes, the Jehovah thing . . . Stella? . . . Stella?"

He slammed the phone down.

I stared at him and he looked at me. He pointed to the television and I took that as my cue to continue playing the video game.

Only the sound of Asteroids being shot out of space hung in the air. Jeff got a beer out of the fridge and sat on the couch, hypnotized by my skills at Asteroids.

I couldn't take it anymore.

"Uncle Jeff, I have girl problems, too."

"With who, kiddo?"

"Her name is Jasmine." I felt like a weight was lifted off my shoulders.

"Jasmine Passeri?"

"Yeah." I forgot he would know who she was, since he had come to the Kingdom Hall and met her and Camille a few times in the past.

"She's cute," he said. I didn't think someone as old as Jeff would find Jasmine good looking.

"What's the trouble?"

I told him the situation—I spilled my guts out. He laughed about Camille and how I'd screwed things up more by trying to be her boyfriend.

"It's not as messed up as you think," he said.

"How do I fix it?" I asked.

"It'll work itself out. Just wait a few years. You'll have all the girls clamoring to hang out with you."

The thought of a bunch of girls wanting to hang out with me sounded so foreign, he could have been saying it in Finnish.

Sophomore year had just started. I walked across the school courtyard to history class. The wind gusted from the east. It almost knocked me over. It was so strong my penis felt it through my sweat pants. My penis thought the wind was my hand or a woman and got fully erect. Throbbingly erect.

It was something that was happening more and more.

My penis pointed toward my history class.

It made me embarrassed and self-conscious when I got erections for no reason and my penis pointed straight out. I tried to position a book around it and walk toward a wall. I stood outside of the class and prayed for it to go down before the bell. Before I was tardy. The bell rang and my penis took that as a sign to continue its full erection. I ran to my seat in the front row and sat down as fast as I could.

I heard Eileen and Kelly laughing in the back of the class. I leaned forward in my chair to camouflage my unrelenting sexual organ.

I never understood how the rest of them, my pubescent comrades, could hide their erections so well.

Peter and I ate dinner at Jin's house.

Jin's mom and dad spoke broken English but his mom understood enough to get by. She was pleasant enough and said things like "Water?" "Two helping food?" "Hand washing?"

Hyun Gi, Jin's dad, spoke very little English. Jin would try to act normal with us there, but we'd hear a spattering of Korean and Jin would tense up and get up to leave. All of a sudden when we were around, there were chores that needed to be done. Jin had to take out the garbage, clean the bathroom—and one time he even had to go wash the car. We helped him with that chore.

The family car was a station wagon. Hyun Gi had wanted it painted yellow, so he made Jin help him and they painted the car in the driveway with house paint and paintbrushes. There were brush strokes on the car and some of it was already chipping off, showing the white underneath.

When Hyun Gi spoke, he sounded like a commander in the army. Jin would reply softly in Korean, trying to hide his embarrassment. I didn't understand a word and it amazed me that they were actually saying things that made sense. I was also a bit intimidated because I didn't know how much they were talking about us.

"Hand washing?" Jin's mom asked us, and we all nodded our heads. We knew the drill and Jin reminded us before sitting down so his mom wouldn't make us get up.

We had to stand up to pray before eating. Hyun Gi would pray in Korean, and we'd get the cue to say amen as the family started to sit back down.

Hyun Gi said something in Korean and laughed and laughed. Jin snickered and his mom gave us fake smiles and nodded her head. Hyun Gi made another remark and pointed at us.

That meant he told a joke that he thought was so funny he wanted Jin to translate it. But his jokes were pathetic and didn't translate well. The first time it happened, Jin translated the joke: "How does a tuna fish pee in a toilet? The other way." It must've been huge in Korea, but Peter and I still waited for the punch line. Then Hyun Gi said the joke louder and slapped his hand on the table and laughed louder. His mom had the same smile and nodded her head at us. The special-ed girl in our history class who had a crush on Peter always smiled at him with the same vacant look.

Over the years Jin got smart so that when Hyun Gi would tell a joke, Jin would get creative with the translation. "I farted and it was a Hershey squirt," he said. He spoke really quickly with a mumble so Hyun Gi wouldn't catch any English. He could understand proper, slowly spoken English and not "I-farted-and-it-was-a-Hershey-squirt."

Peter and I laughed and milk actually blew through Peter's nose. Hyun Gi was happy to be bonding, finally, with Jin's American friends. Jin had a sick sense of humor when we ate with his family.

Apart from the awkward chores, the game of mistranslating made dinners quite interesting at Jin's house.

After Hyun Gi tried his material with us, the rest of us had to help clean the dishes. Hyun Gi went into the other room and got the *Watchtowers* out so he could lead the family Bible study. Fortunately, their family Bible studies were in Korean, so Peter and I got out of it and went skateboarding while Jin looked like he was being sent to a work camp.

"Thank you, thank you," his mom said as we finished with the dishes.

"Later, dude. Enjoy your bitchin' Bible study," Peter said, and we got the hell out of there.

Mom's Miles Kimball catalogue came in the mail. The company sold an assortment of medical-type products; skin cream for acne, corn removers, discounted tampons, women's protective panties, and Comfort Cross Wrap Bras. Middle-aged women posed in bras and granny panties on pages five through seven. I could almost make out the darkness of the nipples of a woman with long gray hair in her support bra on page six.

When I got home from school, Mom was asleep.

The woman's blue eyes on page six reminded me a little bit of Ally. Her square Nordic shoulders and large breasts. I imagined what her breasts looked like under that bra. What would it be like if she were standing in front of me, only in her bra and panties in my bedroom that was pathetically partitioned off from the living room in our small apartment?

I thought about Ally in her bathing suit and her boobs bouncing as she ran away from Peter at the swimming pool. I thought of the curve of her butt when she did the cannonball off of the diving board. I looked back at the gray-haired woman in the catalogue.

"Do you like my new bra?" she would say.

Slowly my head would nod and I would ask her what breasts look like.

"Let me show you."

She would unhook it from the back and pull it off. There would be two breasts with nipples in front of me. The $21.99 bra on the floor.

I looked at the picture of the woman and put my hand down my pants. I had been touching myself a lot. It was the most wonderful feeling in the world. At that moment I forgot about my family. I forgot about God and Jesus and the Kingdom Hall and the elders and preaching every Saturday and the kids in school making fun of me for wearing a suit and coming to their doors with my Dad as he told their parents about the Bible and the promise of a coming paradise Earth after God murders worldly people at Armageddon. I felt the top of my penis and I blanked out what scripture it was where Jesus told his disciples that they should look at the birds in the fields because God clothes and feeds them and if he cares for the birds and the lilies, God would always take care of us.

After a few strokes I pulled my hand out of my pants and looked at the woman in the bra. Then I felt bad. I knew God was watching me and didn't want me to touch myself. At the Kingdom Hall I learned that even looking at a woman so as to have a passion for her was a serious sin. I thought about Brother Miller's masturbation calendar and his Bible student's beady eyes and sweaty mustache. I thought about my recommendation to him to trust in Jehovah when he felt like masturbating.

I put the catalogue down on my bed and went to the front room and turned the TV on. Blood still rushed down there. Charges went off in my brain. I flipped the channel to the news. It didn't take my mind off of what I had started with the woman in the support bra because the female anchorwoman moved her mouth and looked into my eyes. I flipped to a boxing match on the Spanish language station. Dad never let me watch boxing; it was too violent. I changed the channel to cartoons and there was an old Bugs Bunny cartoon on.

Elmer Fudd went to get his rifle to hunt Bugs Bunny. I took a deep breath and concentrated on the TV set. Bugs Bunny changed into a policeman's uniform and came up behind Elmer to ask what he was doing. "Hunting wabbit," he said.

The intense throbbing in my pants started to go away. As Bugs Bunny teased Elmer Fudd and he got more and more frustrated I laughed and forgot about the woman in the support bra. Elmer walked to a clearing with a few trees and Bugs came up behind him, this time dressed as a woman rabbit, with lipstick and fake breasts in a red top. Bugs wasn't wearing a skirt or underwear or pants. It was the first time I realized Bugs Bunny was naked. Bugs Bunny had put on fake eyelashes and blinked them at Elmer Fudd. My horniness came back. I quickly changed the channel. I couldn't stop picturing Bugs Bunny dressed as a woman and I started thinking about Ally's big breasts and the woman in the bra catalogue.

I put my hand on IT, but over my pants, and there was some relief. There was a fire in there and the only way to put it out was with a caress of motion. IT had a mind of its own and was communicating with me.

Mom came out of her bedroom.

"What are you doing?" she asked.

"Nothing!"

I put my hands behind my head like I had been relaxing them there the whole time.

"Come help me make dinner," she said.

I stood up, but my penis stuck straight out. It pointed from underneath my pants. She walked to the kitchen and I quickly sat down.

"Let's go," she said coming back into the living room.

"I don't feel so well," I said.

I dropped to the floor and crawled to the bathroom. She sighed and went back to the kitchen. I stood up and ran into the bathroom and waited. I looked at myself in the mirror in shame.

"Are you okay, dear?" she asked through the bathroom door.

"Yeah, I mean, I just need to use the toilet."

Then the blood rushed from my organs and legs to my head. I'd left the Miles Kimball catalogue on my bed, opened to the picture of the woman in the bra. My heart pulsed as I opened the bathroom door to see if Mom had retrieved my sexual contraband. I crept out of the bathroom and walked to my bed. Mom put chicken breasts in the oven. I put the catalogue under the mattress.

IT needed. Later that night, all I could think about was the bra woman under my mattress. The woman in the bra. My penis. Mom and Dad were asleep so I tiptoed to the bathroom with the catalogue under my shirt. I pulled my pants down and sat on top of the toilet. I looked down at my throbbing penis and pulled out the catalogue from under my shirt. It opened easily to the bra page. I fondled it and pulled away. Once wasn't enough. I felt up and down again and stopped. IT begged. I stroked up and down a few more times and a surge went off in my brain where I couldn't stop stroking. All of a sudden white liquid shot out onto my brown T-shirt that I wore to bed. And shot out again. I put my hand over the gush to stop what I had done. White liquid streaked across the Miles Kimball catalogue and onto the face of the gray-haired woman.

A calmness settled on me. Then guilt and evidence I needed to clean up. I wrinkled up the catalogue and threw it in the toilet and flushed. It wouldn't go down. I flushed again and water rose to the rim, then started to splash on the floor.

"Are you all right, Gabe?" Dad woke up and called from the other side of the door.

"Yeah, just a minute."

I grabbed all the towels and put them around the toilet as it overflowed. The catalogue clogged up the bottom, so I splashed my hand into the toilet water and yanked it out.

"Did you overflow the toilet? The plunger is out here. Let me in so I can help."

He usually wasn't that helpful. Dad started twisting the door knob. "Is it locked?"

I did a super-bionic scan of the bathroom for all the white liquid evidence.

There was a skylight in our bathroom with just enough of an opening that I could toss my dying sperm on the gray-haired woman's face out to the roof of our apartment building.

Dad gave me the plunger and I turned away from him so he couldn't see that my penis was taking way too long to go soft in my underwear. He never knew the twisted sexuality I had performed on myself.

Uncle Jeff came to the Kingdom Hall a couple of times a month. Dad always looked up to Jeff. If there was one person in his family that he wanted to make sure didn't die at Armageddon, it was his stepbrother.

Dad loved to tell stories about how when he was in high school, his older stepbrother protected him and made sure to upgrade Dad's status from nerd to cool cat. A greaser who would monkey wrench with cars and gradually grow to be one of the popular kids. All because Uncle Jeff treated Dad better than he had ever been treated before.

The least Dad could do was get Jeff right with God. Outside of the Kingdom Hall, Jeff kept his Jehovah's Witness friendships secret. He wasn't sure about all the Armageddon stuff, but he felt bad about Grandma not talking to Dad, and Jeff saw the excitement in Dad's eyes when he attended a congregation meeting.

Brother Connelly, Jake, gave Jeff a job doing construction work. Jeff didn't want to work at Grandpa's shop even though he still lived upstairs when he was in town, and he'd stopped playing in the jazz band because the temptation of drugs and women was too strong for him. Being surrounded by drugs and women, Jeff knew his limitations . . . if it was in front of him, he'd snort it or fuck it. That's what he said.

Jeff needed a transition. He was coming to meetings at the Kingdom Hall but couldn't comment or go out in service or give talks because he hadn't quit smoking yet.

(He still drank whiskey, but Jesus turned water into wine.)

Brother Connelly had more work than he could handle and agreed to let Peter and me work with Jeff for $5 an hour. That was a lot of money for us at sixteen.

We moved concrete and painted fences and caulked. Every time we used the caulk we made jokes. Could you show me your caulk? That's a lot of caulk. I've never seen a caulk so white and long.

Jeff smoked his Camel non-filters.

He left Peter and me to finish a job because Jake needed his help with a drywall job for another client. We were left painting a fence in an old woman's backyard on Hillcrest. She kept looking out the window at us. Every time we saw the curtain move, we did a freeze frame—held ourselves really still. She closed the curtains and we went back to painting the fence a bright white, cracking ourselves up.

Curtain open, freeze. Curtain closed, back to work.

She didn't smile at us or know we were playing a game.

"She probably thinks she's stopping time whenever she opens the curtain. Or she's—" The curtain opened again and we froze.

The curtain closed and snot blew out of my nose from holding in my laughter.

"What will we do if she comes out here?" I asked.

"Dude, stay still if she—" the curtain opened.

The curtain closed, then opened again fast. My lips were quivering but the rest of my body stayed catatonic for the game.

Curtain closed. We moved slower just in case she did that again.

"What if she comes out here thinking that she stopped time and undresses us?" I asked.

"We should take our pants off and keep working like nothing's wrong."

It was a good idea, so we took our pants off to our tightie whities and continued to paint the fence.

The curtain moved and stayed open for a really long time.

"What . . . do . . . we . . . do?" I asked and began to consider a future as a ventriloquist. Three minutes felt like an hour.

Finally we gave up and started painting again. The curtain closed and stayed closed for the next half hour.

"What the fuck are you little nimrods doing?" From around the side of the house came a deep growl, which turned out to be the voice of a big fat guy in a tight tank top.

We were holding paintbrushes in our underwear, looking really suspicious.

"Working," we whimpered.

"You're scaring my grandmother. Why are your pants off?"

"It was hot?" Peter said.

That sparked my adrenaline. I didn't know if this guy was going to hurt us or call the police or what.

"Get out of here," he yelled.

"The paint, we—" Peter said.

"And our pants," I said.

"Get out of here before I shove this brush up your ass," he said and meant it.

"What the fuck?" Uncle Jeff came to the back of the house and saw a big fat guy threatening to shove an implement up our asses while our pants were off. Without hesitation Jeff had the guy's face pressed into the grass and his knee on his neck. The man, face still pressed into the dirt, mumbled for air and tried to explain.

Jeff looked at our guilty faces and at the fat guy he was assaulting and realized there was more to the situation than he'd thought.

"Put your pants on," Jeff said to us as he slowly let go. The fat guy bounced up, ready to fight. Jeff fixed him with a stare, eye to eye, and the fat guy looked away and let his body slump, knowing Jeff would be the alpha male in a fight.

He explained how frightened his grandmother was in the house and said that we were messing with her, and Jeff kept a stern face, like Dad sometimes got, and told the fat man that Peter and I would apologize to his grandmother.

"She's really freaked out. Would you guys mind just leaving?"

"No problem," Jeff said and shook the man's hand.

We lost the job for Jake Connelly. Later he asked if we thought it was fair that he docked us a day's pay. We agreed.

That was the last time Peter and I took our pants off at work.

We loaded the paint cans and brushes into Jeff's truck. It smelled like cigarettes and he lit another but kept the windows down so Peter and I wouldn't gag.

We drove down Hillcrest to the stoplight on El Camino. Silent tension hung in the nicotine-thick air of the truck.

Jeff looked at us and laughed.

"You both are out of your fucking minds, you know that?"

Peter and I nodded our heads.

"What time do you need to be home, Peter?" Jeff asked.

"Whenever."

Jeff made a U-turn and pulled into 7-Eleven. He bought three two-liter plastic bottles of wine cooler and some chips. He drove us to a parking lot near the airport by the runway, where we could watch the jumbo jets take off for Vegas or Oklahoma or Nagasaki or Paris or Norway.

Jeff, Peter, and I passed one of the wine cooler bottles.

"What do you want to do with your life?" Jeff asked us.

Pioneer. Get married. Have sex. Become an elder. Make it through Armageddon into the new system.

"I want a girlfriend," Peter said.

Jeff took a drag from another Camel non-filter.

"I'm sure Terry would just love that," he said.

I pictured Peter's stepdad locking him in a room with only Bible drama tapes for a month.

"He wouldn't have to know."

Jeff took off his Snap-on Tools baseball cap and tossed it onto the dashboard.

"No, I guess he wouldn't. What would you do after you got your girlfriend?"

"Kiss her."

"No, I mean, you got your girl—what are you interested in?"

Peter and I looked at each other.

"Marriage," I said.

Jeff took a big swig from the plastic wine cooler bottle.

"Stop talking like the *Watchtower*. If you could have anything you wanted. If there really were genies in bottles, what would you wish for?"

"A million dollars," I said.

"That's a start," Jeff said. "What would you do with the million dollars?"

"I'd buy a car," I said.

"A million dollars goes a lot further than that."

"I'd go live in Hawaii and surf," Peter said.

Jeff hogged the wine cooler bottle that was nearing its end.

"Now you're talking."

"Have you been to Hawaii?" I asked Jeff.

"No, but I've been to Mexico. The water is turquoise, and it's cheap to live there. Gabe, you may want to move to Mexico with that million dollars. You'd be the richest man in Baja."

"What was it like," I asked . . . a little buzz from the sweet wine cooler crept up on me. "What was it like when you played bass with Santana?"

"It was fun at first. It all starts to become a blur when you're on tour. It actually gets really lonely and boring on the road. Different city every night. That's why it's too easy to take drugs and get in trouble. You have sound check at usually five o'clock with a bored sound engineer and club owner trying his best to screw you out of money and then there's nothing to do for hours until you're scheduled to perform. I'd get bored hanging out with the guys and Carlos."

Yeah, right. I couldn't picture someone as famous as Santana being boring.

"So we'd just do nothing. Someone would offer a line of cocaine and you gotta numb your head if you're going to play the same songs, the same notes, night after night to a blur of people who look exactly the same in every city."

"Did you have lots of sex?" Peter asked.

"I ain't drunk enough to tell you boys about that." Jeff decided to put his hat back on and unscrew another plastic two-liter bottle. This time it was orange-flavored.

"You got to remember, worldly girls, they can sometimes give you diseases. I had to get tested twice for syphilis. They stick a tube right up your pee hole in your dick. It's the worst feeling in the world."

Peter and I took gulps from the wine cooler. The alcohol settled in. It felt like floating. It felt like being on one of those planes, going somewhere exotic with Jasmine, holding her hand to comfort her as the plane ascended, making Camille and Ally and everyone jealous of our travel adventures.

We sat and watched a 737 take off. The roar of the engine shook all the cars in the lot.

"You ever hear of pussy farts?" Jeff asked.

Peter and I laughed and shook our heads.

"It's when a girl gets air in her vagina—it happens sometimes when you're having sex. When you're done, her pussy farts."

Peter, Jeff, and I laughed. I ached so bad to hear a pussy fart for myself. I ached so bad in general.

"What do girls like when you kiss them?" I asked.

Finally, an adult. A formerly sexually active adult. Uncle Jeff, ready to give us the skinny. The technique. The edge, so when Peter and I got our next girlfriends, we'd be the best kissers they'd ever had.

"Roll your tongue around hers and," Jeff paused to burp, suck from his Camel, and let the smoke run out of his nose as he continued talking, "touch her softly. Touch her neck. You'll want to be rough in your mind and you can do that later, but first be tender. Rub her elbows lightly. If you're sitting down and she's wearing a skirt, touch the back of her thighs like you're handling cotton. Then pull away. It's like hypnosis. They'll be begging for more. Go back and give her more. They want it as much as you do; they just want it a little differently. And they want you to be a little edgy. A little bad. They'll tell you they want a nice guy but they really want someone who has got a bit of animal in him, a little passion. If you can stand up to her or her parents, then she'll feel safe with you. And feeling safe to a girl is like when you get a boner. They want safety. They want you to take control. They also want to talk. Let them talk. If you really want to get a girl, talk all night. Cuddle and talk.

"You'll have her until you want to dump her and move on.

"And, don't let her talk sometimes; pull back, especially if she's pretty. If everyone's been telling her she's beautiful all her life, give her an insult once in a while. Nothing harsh. Tell her she has shit in her teeth or eye boogers. Remind her she's human and eats and shits like the rest of us."

Where was my notebook or tape recorder? I was buzzed. Planes took off every minute. I hoped Peter remembered more than I did.

Thigh. Back of the thigh.

Talk. Don't talk. Touch her elbows. Elbows. Remember to rub her elbows. Back of thigh.

Peter and I played catch with a Nerf football in the alley downstairs behind the Chinese restaurant.

He threw the ball over my head and it went into a puddle.

The ball was heavier and spiraled water through the air when we threw it to each other.

Our clothes got wet and muddy.

Peter and I pulled together our notes of the knowledge Jeff had hit us with, about what girls wanted, like rubbing their elbows and thighs.

"Jared said when he kisses girls they like it when you roll your tongue along their teeth," Peter said.

I couldn't wait to try that.

Peter took the ball and soaked it in the puddle, getting it completely wet.

"Let's go," he said.

I knew what he was talking about. It was time for some teenage terrorism. It was our vice. Our buzz.

We hopped the fence to the apartment building next door and another fence after that.

Then we walked up a driveway to El Camino. The sun was starting to go down.

Right before hitting El Camino there was a fenced-off area containing industrial-sized garbage cans. We sat there. My blood pressure jumped and my legs shook.

Traffic went by on El Camino. We couldn't see it because the fence was too high, but we heard it. Then it stopped. We were about a quarter block from a major stoplight, and it would soon start again.

"You first," he said.

"No," I said. My arms felt like rubber.

"Do it." Sometimes Peter got a crazy look in his eyes, and I didn't want to be the guy who wouldn't. I didn't want to be a pussy.

We waited.

The light turned green and the traffic started up. I threw the wet Nerf football as high as I could, and it landed with a thud on the asphalt on El Camino.

Traffic continued. Then we waited.

"Go get it," I said, fearing that a police officer had seen the ball flying into traffic and was waiting for the perps to collect their property.

Peter ran into the street and came back with the football.

"We have to get it wet again," Peter said. We found a spigot in one of the carports for the apartment building behind us.

Back at the garbage cans we squatted and listened. Traffic started up and Peter threw the wet Nerf football high through the air.

Boom. Boom. Thud. Screeeeeech.

We ran like Olympic stars, hurdling fences like Crockett and Tubbs pursuing bad guys, back to our apartment building. We couldn't stop laughing and could only imagine the damage, since even looking could get us caught.

It wasn't really fun. It scared me to death.

But I liked that feeling.

And it was another experience with Peter that I knew would carry us into adulthood when we both had our families and barbecued together and had lots of sex with our wives.

Crazy wild sex.

The-floodgates-are-opened sex.

Twenty-four-hour-boner sex.

Walk-around-the-house-naked-and-stop-only-to-hydrate sex.

Marriage. Girls into women. We were coming dangerously close to losing our teen years. We needed stuff to talk about when we became adults. We needed some crazy antics. We braved danger, punishment, and sometimes arrest. It was a checklist. We needed it for reminiscing at future barbecues. We just needed it.

It was Mom and Dad's seventeen-year wedding anniversary. I was out of the apartment trying to cause car accidents and injuries on El Camino and creating great stories to talk about at barbecues when Peter and I were older and had wives.

Seventeen years ago they'd vowed to stay with each other forever. They were worldly when they got married and I was in Mom's belly becoming a human being.

When they came home from dinner, Mom seemed excited. They'd gone to the Sixteen Mile House and had expensive steaks. She showed me the box of chocolates that Dad gave to her. I couldn't remember the last time Mom smiled. We shared some of the chocolates as Dad held her hand and gave her kisses on the cheek. A lot more affection than I was used to in the house.

Dad had given Mom a movie too—*Five Easy Pieces*, starring Jack Nicholson. It looked boring, though Mom mentioned they'd seen it at the drive-in on their first date, in Dad's '57 Chevy.

"When was that?" I asked.

"August 20. And we got married two months later!"

I ate more chocolate, and then I felt like throwing it up. If their date was August 20 and I was born in May and they had to get married two months after their date. That means? That means that was probably the day they had sex and she got pregnant with me.

I went to the kitchen and had a glass of water to keep from hyperventilating at the thought of Dad and Mom having sex. Having sex and I was actually there. I was sperm. I was in Dad's balls; then I was in Mom's belly.

Dry heave. Breathe.

Visions of white liquid flashed before my eyes. Sticky white liquid on the seat of Dad's car. The other sperms. They could've been my brothers. I beat them all to Mom's egg. I had a sense of pride, then tried to push the thoughts of Dad's balls and Mom's vagina and sperm out of my brain even though they kept popping into my head like flash cards.

Seventeen years ago Mom had to drop out of high school because her stomach protruded and she was always sick and throwing up.

Seventeen years ago they got married while I lay waiting to squeeze out of her, ready for a social security number and for breathing on my own.

The whole family, I'd been told, came to the wedding except for Mom's mother, Liz, since she was dead.

Next to our Bible study books in the front room was a photo of Grandpa Tor and Grandma Liz from when they were young and still lived in Stavanger, Norway. Grandma had the same round cheeks as Mom. Her gaze was directed beyond the camera taking their photo. Grandpa Tor had his arm around Grandma and in his hand was a burning cigar.

Grandma wrote Grandpa Tor a letter, two years before I was born, when Mom was fourteen. She wrote it before she killed herself with a sharp razor blade in a bath of warm water. Grandma Elizabeth was at her lover's house, and it was time to expose her secret affair to her husband and family without having to tell them face-to-face.

It was a very Norwegian way to communicate something that hurt too much.

These days, Mom's chronic fatigue syndrome had her sleeping sixteen-plus hours a day. There was nothing anyone could do about it. She had to ride it out. She just needed to sleep.

It could be stress-related, the doctor had said. It could be that she'd never gotten over her mother's suicide. Years earlier he'd suggested that she go into therapy to get the help that she needed.

"All the help she needs is right here," Dad had said at the hospital and held up the Bible.

Therapy was a big no-no for Jehovah's Witnesses. A therapist wouldn't understand the truth about God, so why go to one for support or help? Therapists had a secular education and could steer people away from Jehovah with their double-talking ways.

Seventeen years. Two hundred and four months. Over six

thousand two hundred and five days Mom and Dad had been married. After their encounter in the front seat of his Chevy. After their sin of premarital sex. Before they really knew how wrong it was before Jehovah God to have sex without marriage.

Dad hated seeing Mom ill. All would be perfect after Armageddon in paradise in the new system. So at least there was hope. They knew they were fortunate enough to have found the true religion and to have the opportunity to live together forever. With each other. With their son and his future wife. With their grandchildren. And in the resurrection, Mom could confront Grandma about her love affair and suicide and resolve more than she could've in this worldly system of things with a therapist who didn't have the hope of living forever because he or she wasn't a baptized Jehovah's Witness.

There were sixteen Jehovah's Witnesses who went to Mills High during my junior year. There were Peter and Jin, of course, along with crooked-toothed Camille, love-of-my-life Jasmine, and Ally with the big boobies. Then there were Jennifer Hansen and her older sister Kim, and John Carson and his brother David. There were two brothers from the Spanish congregation who usually got soccer games together at lunch, so I barely saw them. Three sisters and one brother were from the Japanese-speaking congregation. They were very closed off from everyone, including us, and would draw pictures and talk Japanese to each other like they still lived in Japan and had been mysteriously plunked down on a school in the Western Hemisphere by a UFO.

Jennifer stopped Peter and me in the hallway. Their relationship had been strained since their junior-high-school love affair. Jennifer still liked Peter and she was certain that the promise that they would be together after Armageddon, when they were older, was still valid. Peter, growing pubic hair himself, was captivated by all the women he could choose from, so Jennifer was far from his radar.

"I have great news," she told us. Even her manner of speaking was pure. Clean. I felt a tinge of envy over her clean conscience. It made me feel like I was riding the fence. Teetering on dangerous ground with my thoughts of lust and continued masturbation. I tried just to put that out of my mind most of the time.

"Principal Silva agreed to let us set up a booth so we can answer questions about the Bible and distribute literature," she said, like she'd just been voted homecoming queen.

"Wow, I didn't even know you were asking him for permission," Peter said.

"Well, it was Kim's idea. He said we can only do it at lunchtime, as long as it doesn't interfere with our class work, and we can set up right by the library."

"Cool," I said, not really thinking it was that cool.

"John and David are helping us. The principal said we can't go and distribute literature, but if someone comes up to the table and asks questions we can offer them what we want."

We stayed silent. John had a crush on Jennifer. He didn't speak to Peter too often, and every time Jennifer, Peter, and John were in the same vicinity John would get really quiet and a look of defeat would come across his face.

"So, do you want to help us work the table?" she asked.

Good wholesome association. Get to know each other better in the cleanest of circumstances. Jennifer had plans for Peter.

"Probably not; you never know. Sometimes I have to catch up on homework during my lunch break," Peter said.

"You can do your homework at the table," Jennifer countered. "Can I put you down for a shift, Gabe?"

"I, uh, lunch is an important time for me to not think about anything and relax, because, uh, after school I do so much studying and preparing for service and preaching, lunchtime is my only recreational time." I could've been a political speech writer.

She gave us both evil eyes of judgment.

"It's for Jehovah, you know," she said and stomped away.

I looked at Peter and he looked at me.

"No way," I said.

"Yeah, wow, dude."

Jennifer tried to recruit Camille, Jasmine, Ally without success. The brothers from the Spanish Hall pretended they knew less English than they really did and the brothers and sisters from the Japanese Hall really didn't know enough Ingrish.

The booth was set up. By the door to the library. Peter, Jin, Jared, Tom, and I played Hacky Sack on the other side of the courtyard. Camille, Jasmine, and Ally went to Burger King in Ally's car. They started leaving campus more and more. I told Peter we should go to Burger King with them.

Mills High had an open campus during lunch so all the kids could leave and go to delis or fast-food joints to eat. Carrying a Burger King bag with you at school meant you had a car or knew someone with a car. Instant upgrade in status. Even nerds with Burger King bags at lunch might get picked earlier for softball games at P.E. and invited to parties that they wouldn't have been invited to previously. Not like my parents would let me go to worldly parties anyway.

Ally had a Bible study with her worldly school friend Margie. The first time we went to Burger King we all piled into Margie's four-door Renault. Jasmine and Ally sat in the front seat and Peter, Jin, Camille, and I sat in the back. I ended up sitting on Jin's lap, which was soft from his continuing weight gain and quite comfortable actually.

The second time we went I told Jin to sit in the front and Peter crammed next to him. I waited until Jasmine, Camille, and Ally situated themselves in the back seat. Jasmine sat behind Margie, who was driving, so I went over to the back door and said to Jasmine, "I'd sit on your lap, but it might be easier if you sat on mine."

Without fuss. Without a sign of anything from anyone. Normal. Status quo. Jasmine got up and I edged in underneath her and she sat on my lap.

She wore shorts and I wore shorts. Her bare legs touched my bare legs. She held on to the front bench seat as we went around corners. Margie had a way of driving erratically. We hit a bump and I grabbed Jasmine so she wouldn't fly too high. She didn't look at me weird when I put my arm around her waist to keep her steady. I let my hand stay on her waist. She let my hand stay on her waist.

I looked out the window and pretended like my hormones weren't raging.

Like I wasn't sporting a soft-on.

Like her bare legs against mine happened all the time. Her

birthmark on the back of her thigh was slightly raised from the skin. I felt it in all its glory.

Every bump we hit was a lap dance. Every turn was a gyration.

The next time we went to Burger King, I ended up sitting on Ally's lap. She was a little bigger than me. Jasmine sat up front, but the ride was still fun. On the way home, Ally sat on my lap, and my soft-on came back. I put my hand around her waist to steady her and wished I could reach six inches up, to the forbidden zone, to feel those enormous breasts. I prayed she wouldn't feel my penis inching closer and closer to her as she shifted her weight over every bump and slid on every turn.

Peter and Jin decided it was a lot more fun just to play Hacky Sack during lunch and didn't want to go to Burger King with the sisters anymore. Without Peter and Jin, there was no convincing reason for me to go.

Back to the Hacky Sack with Jared and Tom it was.

"Your Jehovah friends are selling books and *Watchtowers* over there," Tom said as he joined us for Hacky Sack at lunch. "Why aren't you guys helping them?"

"We're lame, but not that lame," Jin said, swallowing the rest of his corn dog.

"They asked me if I wanted a Bible study. Is that what you guys do when you do your streetwalking?" Tom continued.

"Kind of," Peter said. We wanted off the topic. We wanted high school normalcy. The literature and information booth that Jennifer and her sister set up was like a screaming billboard that there were Jehovah's Witnesses in the high school. Meaning more questions, more questions.

After most meetings at Millbrae Kingdom Hall, everyone in the congregation stayed and associated, making plans for service, catching up with each other. A few of the elders would go into a room in the back and shut the door. Dad went in there sometimes. There were nights when they would only stay in there for about ten minutes. Then the door would open and out would come the elders. Sometimes they were in a good mood.

There were times when the elders, including Dad, would enter the room and the door would close and Mom had forgotten to ask Dad for the keys to the car so everyone in the congregation would filter out and Mom and I would be alone in the Kingdom Hall. Waiting for that door to open.

We couldn't knock on the door; that was unheard of. Even if they were in there for hours. We didn't know if they were having a judicial committee because someone from the congregation had sinned and had either been caught or was confessing to them. They'd listen to the testimony and decide if the person was repentant and had mended their ways. If so, they could stay in the congregation. Maybe they couldn't comment at the *Watchtower* study or give talks at the meetings, but they could still associate with others in the congregation.

If they were unrepentant, they'd be disfellowshipped. Excommunicated. Expelled.

Which meant no one could talk to them or acknowledge their presence. They were dead spiritually as far as everyone was concerned and would be killed at Armageddon.

They could try to come back, but they needed to mend their unrighteous ways, and they would have to change their attitude and attend every meeting, Tuesday, Thursday, Sunday, sitting in the back of the Kingdom Hall and not talking to anyone or singing any of the three Kingdom Melody songs interspersed throughout the meeting.

It usually took a year of continuously being ignored before they could be reinstated. When they were reinstated, people sometimes said that being disfellowshipped was the best thing that ever happened to them. It made them truly appreciate what they lost by being out of Jehovah's organization and realize how precariously close they'd come to dying, since Armageddon could have come while they were in that spiritually dead state.

So what went on in the back room was highly confidential.

We got phone calls at the house all the time. If Dad answered the phone in the kitchen, he'd tell whoever was on the other end to hold on and have me hang up the phone when he picked up in the bedroom. He'd unravel the extension cord and take the phone from the bedroom into the bathroom, the only room in the apartment with real privacy. For masturbating and for Dad's Jehovah's Witness elder business.

And we always had an idea when someone was about to be disfellowshipped because Dad would be gone a lot and a few weeks later we'd hear the announcement, "Brother Smith has been disfellowshipped" or "Sister Smith has been publicly reproved."

If the person disfellowshipped wanted to be reinstated someday, they had to show their humility and attend the meeting when the disfellowshipping was announced.

Everyone would try and not glance at the person after the announcement.

When Sister Hawthorne was disfellowshipped, I accidentally looked over and saw her. Sister Hawthorne held her head very still and tears dripped from her chin to her lap. She wasn't wiping them away. She was taking her punishment with dignity.

But a lot of times if there was an elders' meeting after the regular meeting, it was a short one. The elders would come out in a good mood, laughing at whatever joke was just told.

Peter said an elders' meeting was code for smoking pot. Whenever they came out laughing, we'd crack up and Peter would whisper, "Elders' meeting."

"Hello?" I answered the phone.

It was Brother Knox. He asked for Dad. He didn't say hi or ask how I was doing. I knew it was elders' business. He didn't say who he was, but I could tell from his voice.

"Dad, phone," I yelled.

He got up and unraveled the phone from the cord in the bedroom and went into the bathroom.

"You can hang up now," he yelled.

I hung up the phone and picked it up really fast. I put my hand over the receiver. I prayed Mom's chronic fatigue syndrome would keep her in bed. I just had to know what one of those frequent bathroom phone calls was about.

"It's Brother Knox."

"Jason, how are you?"

"Not so good; that's why I called."

"What can I help you with?"

"Well, this is really hard to say. I mean, I don't know if we sinned, but . . ."

"Brother Knox, Jehovah gives mercy to those who confess their sins. You're a good brother in the Kingdom Hall. You'll make a great elder one day. Know that I'm your friend and Jehovah is your friend. Feel free to talk."

"We committed sodomy," Brother Knox said.

I made a mental note to find out exactly what sodomy was.

"With who?" Dad asked.

Blow job? Butt fuck? It had to be one of those.

"My wife," Brother Knox said with a chuckle. "I'm sorry. I didn't mean to laugh," he continued. "I just could never fathom having sex with anyone else."

"This might be hard, but you need to give me all the details," Dad said. I pictured him sitting on the toilet, phone tucked on his shoulder to his ear, with a notepad, ready to start the process of taking charge of the fate of Brother Knox.

"We started to have sex, it was, we were in missionary position, we were kissing, and in the heat of the moment, I stuck my penis in and started, started going in and out, until my wife stopped me. I didn't know my penis was in her butt."

Aha, sodomy = butt fucking.

"How many times did you go in and out?" Dad asked. That shocked me. It was so explicit. I started to get a little hard-on.

"I think about five."

"Did your wife enjoy it?"

"Hold on a second," he said and left the phone. My heart pounded. I hoped Dad wouldn't come out of the bathroom to get a drink of water or something while Brother Knox talked to his wife about all the gritty details.

"Hello, Brother Dagsland?" Jason's wife got on the phone.

"Hi, Sister Knox. Go ahead and tell me your side."

"We were in the heat of the moment, he stuck it in about five or six times, I almost didn't realize it was in the wrong . . . area. . . . I was concentrating on his eyes and our kissing."

"Did you enjoy it?"

"I enjoyed our kissing. The minute I figured out he was in my . . . my butt . . . I told him and we stopped. We didn't, uh, finish the sex, because we both felt bad."

"Thank you, Sister Knox. Could you put your husband back on the phone?"

Jason came back to the phone.

"I just need to make sure—did you ejaculate into your wife's butt?"

"No, like she said, we didn't finish sex after that."

"Brother Knox, you understand that practicing sodomy is against Jehovah. It's a sin because it's a homosexual practice and we don't want to have anything to do with homosexuality."

"We sure don't."

"I doubt we'll have to form a judicial committee meeting about this, but we may go ahead and schedule a shepherding call. Another elder and I will come over to your place and discuss the seriousness of the sin and talk about how if it was a regular practice, you could be expelled from the congregation."

"Don't worry, we're not practicing—"

"I know, you're a good brother. It's just a necessary procedure, and there won't be any further action."

Brother Knox wept on the other end.

"Brother Dagsland, Alan, thank you [sniffle] so much [sniffle]. We just wanted to [sniffle] make sure we're still right with [sniffle] God."

"Everything will be fine. I'll call another elder and we'll set up a time for next week to come by."

I heard Dad hang up the phone, so I hung it up on my end and poured myself a glass of milk. The phone rang again and I grabbed it just to make Brother Knox embarrassed that he'd have to go through me again to get to Dad. Dad answered at the same time and I was stuck.

"Brother Dagsland, it's Brother McMurphy."

"Hi, Steve. I'm glad you called. We have a situation with the Knox family. Do you have time next week to go on a shepherding call with me?"

"Of course." Brother McMurphy was a young elder, eager to do whatever he could to advance and go deeper into the fold of eldership.

Dad told Brother McMurphy, Steve, about the sodomy case. Steve gave a lot of serious-sounding "hmms" and "okays" while Dad filled him in.

"The reason I was calling was to talk about ways that I could start having more responsibility in the congregation. I'm so happy I can help with this case," Steve said.

They finished the call and I hung up the phone really fast and sat at the table drinking the rest of my milk.

Dad came out with his elders' briefcase, which was about three times the size of a normal briefcase and had a combination lock on it. He walked through the kitchen without saying a word, grabbed a pair of tongs, went on the balcony, and lit some documents on fire. When they burned all the way, he came in and wet the ashes before putting them in the garbage can.

I wondered what case those papers were notes for. Or if it was a letter from the Watchtower Society that all elders were instructed to burn after reading, kind of like *Mission: Impossible*.

My alarm went off at 5:30 AM. Dad was already in the bathroom getting ready to go to the District Convention, which happens every summer at the Cow Palace. Ten thousand Jehovah's Witnesses from all over California come out for four days of Bible lectures and association.

The program didn't start until 9:30. Dad and I had to get there early because he was one of the elders overseeing the calculation of contributions received during the assembly. Hundreds of contribution boxes were set up at key locations to make it easy for anyone to help cover the expenses of the assembly.

The sisters weren't allowed to do as much as the brothers, so most of them worked in the morning making food that would be sold during the afternoon lunch break. Because I was under eighteen, the only job for me was to help make sandwiches along with the sisters.

You never knew who you'd be working with at the hoagie assembly line. I stood next to a cute girl with a slight overbite. Her hair was cut new-wave style. It was blond and covered half of her face. She could've been the lead singer of Missing Persons. I wondered how she got away with having such a worldly haircut.

The sisters and younger brothers and I wore plastic gloves and hairnets. Missing Persons on my right was on cheese duty and I was on ham duty. I retrieved the bread after she put a slab of cheese on it. I smacked on a slice of ham and handed it to my left, to the two elderly sisters next to me, so they could add the lettuce leaf.

The elderly sisters took their job very seriously and kept holding up the assembly line with their precise placement of the leaf.

Sandwich-making duty started at 6:00 AM and finished by 9 so we could be in our seats for the Bible lectures, and the sandwiches would be ready for the lunch break at noon. We were hundreds of tired Jehovah's Witnesses working in the warehouse room. At 7, people finally started to get talkative, and there was enough chatter in the building so I could ask Missing Persons her name.

Helene, with an *e*.

She had recently come to San Francisco from Denmark, so she was a foreigner, which may have explained why she got away with having a worldly haircut.

She handed me her bread with cheese and I felt her warm soft hand. I touched it for a second longer than a touch. It was a moment. She looked up from her pile of cheese slices into my eyes.

Her blue eyes took me to a future of flying to family gatherings in Denmark and our fair-skinned kids running around Scandinavian Airlines while Helene and I drank Aquavit and cuddled under our blanket, debating whether we should join the Mile-High Club.

Her hand would fit perfectly into mine as I walked her around the assembly, showing her off to the other brothers.

She would have a few housecleaning accounts like Jehovah's Witness sisters always seemed to have, to supplement our income. We'd have candlelight dinners and sex.

"What brought you here so early?" I asked.

"My boyfriend is an attendant and needed to be here by 6:00 AM. I came with his family since I'm staying with them for a few weeks, so I figured I could help out with the sandwiches. What about you?"

What about me? Oh me, well, I'm not an attendant and just fantasized our life together and you essentially killed it.

"My dad is the elder who handles contributions."

She nodded her head and continued handing me bread with cheese slices and I avoided touching her hand every time.

Helene's boyfriend came to pick her up from her sandwich duty. He was so, so ugly. His chin intruded into his face and she gazed upon him like he was Bono or something.

I took my gloves off and walked out of the warehouse into the main corridor. I'd done my duty for Jehovah. I'd helped make hundreds of sandwiches to feed to some of the ten thousand Jehovah's Witnesses who were coming that day to assemble, associate, and listen to Bible talks.

After years of consuming and smelling the food from the lunches, you don't question it. I wonder who got rich off of setting up the hoagie contract with the Watchtower Society for the USA. Eight yearly assemblies for Jehovah's Witnesses from Northern California at the Cow Palace alone. Even a half-cent profit on every transaction would translate to millions every summer.

- apple and cheese Danishes
- sausage-egg-muffin sandwiches for breakfast
- pudding cups
- Shasta cola and lemon-lime

While being lectured on the harms of smoking, we were being pumped with bad cholesterol and put on the path to future obesity.

I always thought sisters got fat from having babies, but to watch them open up that third apple Danish for breakfast, well . . .

Since I'd been baptized a year earlier, Dad said it was okay for me not to sit with Mom and him and that I could sit with Peter and Jin that year during the district assembly session. We'd saved our seats early in section 22, so I sat down.

Peter looked through the binoculars at all the pretty sisters as they made their way up ramps put in place to accommodate the handicapped brothers and sisters. They showed off their new curly perms and flowered dresses, and the daring ones were showing their fishnet stockings.

Peter was on the hunt and kept nudging me awake and handing me the binoculars.

"Oh, her."

"Check out this one."

"Damn," he wrote in really tiny letters in the notepad he wasn't taking notes in to express his admiration of a seventeen-year-old sister from Tracy or a twenty-year-old from Livermore or a sixteen-year-old from Richmond Congregation.

He nudged Jin, but Jin gave him a dirty look because he was trying to follow along with a talk that discussed how we know we're living in the last days and Armageddon would come at any moment.

Later, when the chairman on the platform announced lunch, we got in line to retrieve our sandwiches and pudding cups and such. We ate standing in the Ring. The Ring was a large hallway that circled outside the stadium seating but was still inside the Cow Palace building structure. It was the center of activity during the lunchtime break, and we didn't want to miss out on meeting brothers and sisters from other congregations. We wanted to be popular. We wanted to meet girls.

After we ate our hoagies and our pudding cups we bought some liver-wrenching coffee and walked around the Ring. Eating that food for four days of the assembly always made me constipated. The district assembly food was designed to constipate you, to keep you in your seat during Bible lectures and talks by missionaries and local people who didn't give in to the temptations of Satan through materialism or sex or peer pressure.

Families held hands with their children so they wouldn't lose track of them. It was a Jehovah's Witness amusement park. It was a concert of Jehovah's Witnesses.

The Ring opened up to the front corridor, where the main doors to the Cow Palace were located. Thousands of Witnesses were getting introduced or reacquainted. Spiritual brothers and sisters. The security attendants kept track of anyone who was out of place. Inside the main arena, above the seats, there was a dark room. In that dark room were more attendants with special red-dotted badges and binoculars. Stealth crowd control. Anyone who had a beard or long hair or looked out of place was noticed and checked up on. Walkie-talkies kept the red-dotted attendants in close communication with each other.

Darren and Arlene walked up to me, holding hands. They had gotten engaged a few months before. He promenaded her through the Ring, hand in hand. It was okay to show that type of affection once you got engaged. Arlene was about to turn eighteen. They were waiting until then to seal the deal and have sex on their honeymoon.

I avoided eye contact with Brother Clark, who was slightly retarded. He was eighteen and had an attendant badge, two qualifications that normally made you an automatic Jehovah's Witness babe magnet, but not in his case. If I was seen talking to him, it would bring my babe attraction points down by association—although being only sixteen meant my points were already pretty low. He walked with an odd limp, kicking his left leg out before placing his foot on the ground. His right leg was fine, making his limp even weirder.

No, he wouldn't be holding hands with any sister unless she was in a wheelchair and had a neck brace. And a goiter.

Camille tapped me on the shoulder. I was happy to see Jasmine with her.

And as long as I stayed on track and became an attendant at eighteen and either worked at Dad's shop or got a job as a janitor, I could tell Jasmine of my lifelong love for her, and we could get on with our own courtship.

Camille was my block, the buffer that separated me from Jasmine. She always made sure, even when we were just standing together, that she was between us. If I was talking to Jasmine at the Kingdom Hall, she'd come clear across the Kingdom Hall, without moving her arms when she walked, to be included in the conversation and stand close to me. I'd always take a side step and navigate myself in Jasmine's space.

It had been years since I'd asked her to go steady with that type-written note. Years since Mom had approached me with that note, which Camille had freely given to her mom to give to my mom so she could lecture me on the harms of fornication. Back then, I'd taken that action on Camille's part to mean "no."

I now had more pubic hair. I'd started to develop a better

understanding of sisters. And any information I received from Jeff or any other brother or *Three's Company*, I absorbed like a sponge.

I didn't want to get a sister's phone number while Jasmine was in the vicinity. I saw her three times a week and she still sent chills down my spine.

Pathetically, Camille still acted like we were together and had never broken up. We didn't go on dates. I never held her hand or kissed her. But her body language was territorial. I'd asked her to go steady when we were in the eighth grade, that's true, but if that was sealed like the seven scrolls, I'd still be engaged to Pamela, to whom I'd proposed marriage when I was six years old. I couldn't tell you what Pamela even looked like anymore.

Brother Abrahamson approached us. He was from Burlingame Congregation and they met in the same Kingdom Hall as our congregation. He owned a vacuum cleaner shop. He was tall with black hair, trimmed neatly. He'd gotten baptized at the same assembly I had the year before. Brother Miller had preached to him one day while he was out in service and Brother Abrahamson had progressed quickly from Bible student to baptized brother to regular auxiliary pioneer, which meant he had to get in sixty hours a month in preaching.

"Hi, Gabe. Hey, ladies," he said.

This isn't a pick-up joint. . . . Wait. It is.

"Hi," Camille and Jasmine said in unison. Camille stood a little closer to me and I bent down and retied my shoelace, then took a side step away as I stood up.

"We should go out in service together," Brother Abrahamson said to me.

"Sure," I said.

"Let me get your phone number. I don't think I have it."

I scribbled my number on a piece of paper I tore out of my small scrapbook.

"Jasmine, you should come with us. Why don't you give me your number as well?" he said.

He was picking her up and using me as a springboard? I didn't even see it coming. I was impressed and ticked off.

Camille took a half step closer to me.

Jasmine grinned as she gave him her number.

Brother McMurphy walked up and handed Brother Abrahamson an attendant badge.

"Better late than never," Brother McMurphy said.

"I got to go—I'm attending section 24," Brother Abrahamson said. He left and Jasmine's face lit up.

"I don't like that guy," I said to Camille or Jasmine or whoever would listen to me.

"He's only been baptized a year, but he seems nice," Camille said.

"He's kind of cute," Jasmine said. I didn't like the way she said that.

I was sure Jasmine would tell her mom about getting Brother Abrahamson's phone number. A twenty-two-year-old attendant with a badge. I couldn't fully express my feelings to her because I knew she'd tell her mom. Why did Camille and Jasmine trust their mom so much? Didn't they realize their mom cramped my style? She was my cock block. I'd heard the phrase cock block on *The Alex Bennett Show*.

I was getting phone numbers, but that didn't mean I'd forgotten about Jasmine. Maybe it was harmless. Maybe Jasmine was waiting for me to come of age. Anyway, I had some phone numbers and addresses to collect, myself.

Just then I heard, "Dags," and turned around to see Peter and Jin approaching. They didn't stop walking around the Ring, and I fell into step with them.

"Bye," Camille said.

Her "bye" felt like gum on my shoe I needed to scrape off.

Jasmine, my darkest secret. Peter and Jin had no idea of the jealousy brewing in me because of Dan Abrahamson.

We ran into Gary, Vince, and Gibby from Fremont Congregation. I hadn't seen any of them since the year before. So we turned around and walked with them in the opposite direction. The six of us, like a band. Talking. Laughing. Joking. Giving each other nudges, pointing to 3 o'clock and 6 o'clock and high noon, to all the well-bred Jehovah's Witness girls surrounding us in the Cow Palace.

Curly hair.

Straight hair.

Flowered dresses.

Nylons.

Breasts.

Hips.

Smiles.

Blue eyes.

Brown eyes.

White.

Black.

Indian.

Spanish.

Vietnamese.

Glasses.

No glasses.

Perfumed.

Deodorized.

With addresses and phone numbers.

With protective fathers.

With elder fathers.

With non-believing fathers.

Potential.

Future wives.

Future fiancées.

With delicate hands that would fit perfectly into my hand.

Painted nails.

Cute "hi" waves.

They looked at us, and we looked at them. And talked. I added to my address book, careful never to take an address or phone number if one of our crew wanted it instead.

The Code.

Vince and I couldn't both ask Desiree from Tracy Congregation for her number. One of us went for it first, or whispered, "The one on the left is hot," and the other one knew that unless the speaker changed his mind, the one on the left was off limits.

Grandpa Barry had bought me a camera; it was my "in"—my

tool to woo the opposite sex innocently, without screaming, "I want to jump your Jehovah's Witness bones!" Instead, I would ask them, "Can I take your picture?" And what girl who had spent two hours curling her hair just right and matching her flowered dress with the right stockings and shoes and then changing them five times before leaving for the assembly would not want her picture taken?

Sometimes I'd take it and they'd run away right after I flashed the camera, never to be heard from again. I had a pile of pictures of girls with no idea who they were. But some of them would stay after I took their photo. I could get their addresses with the line, "Where should I send you a copy of the picture?" which sometimes resulted in a long-distance correspondence with a sister or two after the assembly.

I'd make mix tapes for them after I asked in letters what kind of music they liked.

Mindy Smith from Livermore South Congregation: "Rock 'n' roll and stuff."

Rachel Pirker from Sonoma Congregation: "Bauhaus."

Rose Moulag from Vacaville Congregation: "New wave and punk."

Hilary Nelson from Las Vegas (visiting her local cousin): "Rockabilly, you know, like the Stray Cats."

Desiree Robinson from Redwood City Congregation: "Ska, and I love Fishbone."

When the mail arrived at home my parents gave me the sisters' letters without too much worry. They liked my long-distance relationships, especially with Cyndi Rattray from Nova Scotia. They really liked her. How could I touch her breasts or vagina from four thousand miles away?

It was important to distinguish ourselves from the rest of the sea of Jehovah's Witnesses, most of whom sported the same clean-cut look and suit jackets and ties from JCPenney or Mervyn's. My friends and I had found out about *vintage clothes*. Jin had driven Peter and me to the gay district of San Francisco to buy our suits and shoes for the assemblies. American Rag was on Polk and Sutter, and it was there that I found my look. Three-button suit, cuff links, and wingtips.

I studied the band photo on the back of the cover of the Specials' first record. And I had a copy of the Untouchables' latest record. All the ska band members wore wingtips or creepers. Dad said, "No creepers, they look worldly," like they were a venereal disease, but wingtips were something Grandpa wore, and Dad got a kick out of me being into something from his father's generation.

Dad had a lot of rules that weren't quite rules from the Bible but his interpretation. For example, I couldn't go to concerts unless it was to see a soul band. A Flock of Seagulls, no way. Smokey Robinson, no problem.

I found out about ska and played "What's Gone Wrong" by the Untouchables for Dad. He really liked it. And, added bonus, the band was black, which meant it was okay to go to that concert. He wanted to supervise Jin, Peter, and me at the show and told their parents he'd keep an eye on us.

The opening band was Fishbone. Also black, but when asking Dad if I could go to the concert, I conveniently didn't play songs like "Lyin' Ass Bitch" or any songs with a fast driving beat.

When we drove into the parking lot of the Circle Star Theater in Redwood City—it was a theater with a rotating stage in the middle of the floor—there were *Quadrophenia*-looking guys on their motor scooters and punk rockers drinking 40-ounce beers in the beds of pickup trucks. I prayed Dad wouldn't turn around.

Lorie from school was there wearing a tank top revealing breasts that were enlarging by the minute. She talked to me and gave me a hug. We were outside of school and I was at the concert, which must've meant I was okay to hug.

And Denise was there. Her parents dropped her off and picked her up early, before the Untouchables came on stage. She had blue eyes and long, natural curly hair, a kind of sexy Persian look to her. She hugged Peter and Jin and me.

Jared and Tom and Chris with the crown haircut that he bleached at the tips met up with us.

I asked Dad when the concert started if we could go up to the front of the stage, since no one sat in their seats but rushed straight for the front right when Fishbone started.

"As long as I can see you," he said.

It was my first slamdance. I got one over on Dad. He was at a punk rock show. He never talked about it later. I think he didn't want me to know that I'd steered him like a lamb to that counter-culture den of borderline un-Christian entertainment.

Or maybe he saw how happy Jin, Peter, and I were and didn't want to spoil that.

Or maybe he saw a little of himself in us?

At the assembly I was sporting my wingtips and three-button-suit jacket. That set me apart. Well, it set our whole crew apart. We looked like a mod softball team walking through the ring of clones.

Our haircuts were all the same. Short on the sides and back but long on the top. Not too long to be branded as worldly, but long enough not to look too clean-cut if we shook it out of its unbreakable mold of hairspray and gel.

As Peter gave April his phone number an attendant came up to us and asked us to return to our seats.

"Give me one second," Peter said, and the attendant said, "Now."

He waited and watched as we walked up to section 22. We were jealous of the power of the attendant. I vowed never to be so strict when I turned eighteen and it was me walking the corridor and Ring with my KEEP MOVING and PLEASE RETURN TO YOUR SEATS signs.

The Ring of desire. It was a mating ritual. I would respect the purpose of the Ring when I was eighteen and married. I would respect my younger brothers and make sure they had the time they needed to close the deals of address exchanges with members of the opposite sex.

The afternoon session started, and as elders lectured on the sin of fornication and encouraged young people to pioneer or to go volunteer and live a life of poverty for Jehovah at the Watchtower Bible and Tract Society (also referred to as Bethel), we sat and took notes and passed around a pair of binoculars. Some people brought binoculars so they could see the speaker better from the faraway seats or so they could watch the Bible dramas, which were about the parallels between our lives and Abraham's or how Lot's wife turned into salt when she looked back and craved the old world of Sodom and Gomorrah and how we don't want to follow her example and crave anything in this current world that's on its way to destruction.

We'd all clap our hands when the speaker would say things like, "And don't you want to give a reply to Satan, who is taunting Jehovah?" and "Would you like to send your love to the brothers in Nigeria?" and "Isn't it great that we have found the truth and have escaped this wicked world?"

Clapping hands.

Affirmatives.

Recognition.

Some of us weren't paying too much attention and would just clap when everyone else clapped. Some of us were using our binoculars to scout Stephanie in section 13, a sister who'd just given Peter her phone number, or Sharon in section 17, who liked my wingtips.

At the end of the assembly day, the chairman took the platform and announced Brother Schrader would give the closing prayer. Brother Schrader was inspired to thank Jehovah for every talk given during the program, naming every title and thanking Him for his wondrous ways. Then he became inspired to ask God to look over the foreign lands where there was much persecution and to help our brothers behind the Iron Curtain where they were under particular duress. Please help them. His inspiration became more of a sermon. I glanced at the feet and toes of the sister in the row in front of us. Black toenail polish.

Brothers with attendant badges couldn't close their eyes during the prayer. They needed to keep watch over their assigned sections. Anything could happen, from an elderly person passing out to some implanted apostate jumping up on the stage and yelling, "You're all being lied to!" That had never happened in my life as a Jehovah's Witness, but you'd always hear stories from other conventions where something like that had happened.

After the assembly day was over, each congregation had a section to clean. Ours was section 222–224 in the box seats. We swept and mopped it clean every night because a sign of cleanliness is close to Godliness.

Every year for eight weekends the Cow Palace welcomed Jehovah's Witnesses from different regions of California. Different congregations were assigned to one weekend for a program that repeated itself eight times. We'd always make sure we left it sparkling clean and the owner would comment on how clean a people we were, and the chairman announced that. We'd all applaud because there was a potential for the owner of the Cow Palace to become a Jehovah's Witness by our fine example, and we showed how separate we were from the world. We may have saved his everlasting life just by doing our part in picking up gum wrappers or discarded lettuce leaves from hoagies.

The sister with the black toenail polish turned around and put her Bible and song book in her purse. She helped her younger sister put her coat on. She had motherly qualities and perky breasts under the blue vintage vest she wore over her white men's dress shirt. She may have also shopped at American Rag. She had style and long black hair. Her nose was French, but the right kind of French, Canadian French. They had smaller versions of the French nose. Perfected via interbreeding with . . . whomever the French bred with in Canada. She smiled at me, breaking my hypnotic stare.

Black toenails was from Antioch congregation. Not the biblical Antioch that the Apostle Paul preached to, but Antioch, California. It's on the way to Sacramento from San Francisco. Too far unless I had a car, but within letter-writing distance and secret rendezvous distance, if we both planned a trip to San Francisco with our friends, to attend a concert, like seeing the Cure at the Cow Palace, or something similar.

Her name was Caitlin, and I took her picture and got her address and phone number. She had sloppy handwriting and she wrote really fast. I noticed she kept looking toward her dad while we were talking. It was clear I needed to pursue the conversation later. I asked her if she sat in the same area every day, since there were two more days left for that assembly.

"Yeah, pretty close."

"I'll look for you," I said.

Her dad looked at me and I said "hi" to diffuse his stern look of disapproval. He turned around.

"He's disfellowshipped," Caitlin said.

The word sent an electric shock through my back. It was like saying my father's a transvestite who had an operation to replace his dick with a vagina.

If you're a Jehovah's Witness, it's about the same.

"Will you still look for me tomorrow?" Caitlin asked.

"Of course," I replied.

But it would be hard when my parents would later ask, who's Caitlin, if they found out her father was disfellowshipped. It would be trouble for me.

Or.

It would be great because maybe her father would be totally cool and drive us to secluded places to make out while he was shopping or doing things that disfellowshipped people do.

She turned and I touched her arm.

"Yes, Caitlin, I'll definitely see you tomorrow."

She smiled.

I was giddy with schoolboy lust. Caitlin had style and there was something about her that made me want to toss all other phone numbers I had in my pocket into the trash. A Jehovah's Witness getting an address and phone number at an assembly is like getting a blow job on a first date for most people.

I went to our assigned cleaning section. Jasmine and Ally had mops in their hands and smiled at me as I approached.

"Nice timing. We're almost done," Ally said, leaving me with Jasmine while she returned her mop to the brother in charge.

"Dan Abrahamson asked me for my phone number," Jasmine said.

"Remember, I was there," I replied.

I pulled out my conquest, wanting her to see it. She read the writing and her mouth dropped.

"Caitlin Friedman?"

"What, you know her?" I said.

"Her dad's disfellowshipped, he goes to Antioch Congregation, and they share the Kingdom Hall with Vacaville Congregation, where Carla goes," Jasmine said. Carla was a friend of her cousin's.

"I already know that," I said.

"Do you know why he got disfellowshipped?"

"We didn't get that far in the relationship."

It was *my* phone number. Dan Abrahamson had gotten hers and now she was scoffing at mine.

"Because he voted in the last presidential election," she said.

Voting is apostasy because it means you're not looking to the Watchtower Society or God's Kingdom as the solution to all of our problems. Caitlin's dad was a registered Democrat. I had no idea what that meant at the time.

According to the *Watchtower,* being disciplined by your parents means they love you.

According to the *Watchtower*, being disciplined by God means he loves you.

The elders administer discipline from God by means of the Watchtower Society, or the Faithful and Discreet Slave who feeds God's chosen people (Jehovah's Witnesses). The feeding is spiritual.

A glossary of terms used to categorize and describe the various types of sin:

Sin

The elders may get involved, but don't necessarily have to, in addressing the sins committed by people in the congregation. If you lie, you can obtain God's forgiveness for yourself. If you gossip or slander and ask the person you sinned against for forgiveness and he forgives you, all is taken care of and the elders don't need to be brought in to clear up the matter.

However, there are sins for which the elders must form a judicial committee to discipline the person and make sure the congregation is clean.

Uncleanness

The lightest of the sins, uncleanness usually involves some kind of immorality. It could mean you were making out with a woman and in the heat of the moment touched her breast and stopped right there.

Loose Conduct

The broadest category of sins, loose conduct can refer to sexual behavior or other things. As it applies to sexual behavior, it means you touched someone's sexual organ or sucked on a woman's breast. Loose conduct can also mean that you murdered someone or that you got a DUI. Or that you molested a child. But if the molester doesn't confess to the sin and only the victim comes forward, then the molester isn't punished because you need two witnesses in order for justice to be served. The molester is clean as far as the congregation is concerned and the victim is strongly urged not to tell the police, since the Bible tells us not to take our brothers to court.

Fornication

Fornication comes from the Greek word *pornea* and signifies sexual sins. Penetration of a woman with a penis or finger (if the perpetrators are not married) or another object is fornication.

Bestiality (pronounced "best" as in, "That's the best thing I've heard!") is fornication. I was one of the 0.001% of American sixteen-year olds who knew the proper pronunciation of the word bestiality.

Sodomy, like what Brother and Sister Knox did, is also fornication.

Adultery. That sin is pretty straightforward.

Apostasy

Among Jehovah's Witnesses, apostasy used to involve teaching anything against the Watchtower Society's interpretation of the Bible. The definition was changed in 1980 to mean even believing anything against the Watchtower Society's teachings.

Apostasy can also be defined as joining an organization run by a church or a political group.

It's automatically assumed you're an apostate if you decide to leave the Jehovah's Witnesses.

Sins and their definitions periodically change. Jehovah's Witnesses go back and forth on certain issues and have confused many people over the years with varying interpretations.

If you are found guilty and unrepentant (even if you say you're repentant) and if you sinned a few times before telling the elders (or if your sins were reported by someone else) you can be disfellowshipped. But without a confession, two people must have witnessed the sin.

The elders had no problem holding eight-hour, repetitive, monotonous judicial committees to break someone. It was their chance to play spiritual *Miami Vice*.

A glossary of terms used to categorize and describe the various types of discipline administered by the elders for the above categories of sin:

Private Reproof

The judicial committee believes you are repentant of your sin and takes away a couple of privileges in proportion to the gravity of your actions.

Privileges that Can Be Taken Away

For a Brother	For a Sister
Commenting at the *Watchtower* study and other meetings	Commenting at the *Watchtower* study and other meetings
Pioneering*	Pioneering
Helping with microphones or being an attendant at the meeting or assembly	
Being a ministerial servant**	
Being an elder	

*A pioneer vows to preach forty-five to ninety hours a month
**A ministerial servant is almost an elder but does not participate in judicial committees or elders' meetings

Public Reproof

You can be publicly reproved when your sin is public knowledge or, in the case of DUI, can be made public record, and your name was in the *Millbrae Sun* police blotter. Public reproof is announced to the congregation from the platform and usually includes a talk about what you did. All your privileges are taken but you're still allowed to talk and associate with Jehovah's Witnesses. Some Witnesses may decide not to associate with you for a while.

Disfellowshipped

Excommunication. No one who is a Jehovah's Witness can speak to you unless they want to be disfellowshipped, too.

If you've been a Jehovah's Witness all of your life and you've followed the counsel of the Watchtower Society never to have friends who aren't Jehovah's Witnesses, then you've just lost every friend you've ever had. Even your family can't speak to you.

Someone who is disfellowshipped in their thirties after only having been a Jehovah's Witness for a year or two is a completely different story from someone in their thirties who is a janitor or window cleaner and works with other Jehovah's Witnesses and has been in the organization since they were born and has no worldly friends.

To be reinstated into the congregation, it takes one year of going to three meetings a week, not talking to any of your friends who ignore you anyway, and writing a letter to the congregation stating how you've changed your ways. A huge commitment with absolutely no moral support.

In the early 1970s you could say hi to a disfellowshipped person, but that changed.

If someone disassociates voluntarily, other Jehovah's Witnesses treat that person as disfellowshipped.

The above rules change constantly and are hidden from the public. Do you remember the Michael Jackson video "Thriller"? There was a disclaimer at the beginning of it stating that Michael objected to the occult and that he didn't want to promote a belief in life after death. That was put there so Michael Jackson wouldn't be disfellowshipped, but only publicly reproved in his congregation in the Los Angeles area for participating in that video.

That was apostasy averted.

After the Sunday *Watchtower* study at the Kingdom Hall, Jin, Peter, and I were supposed to go swimming at Brother Lucero's house.

The rainstorm came out of nowhere.

"What should we do instead?" Jin asked.

Jeff, who'd been coming to the meetings at the Kingdom Hall, spit his nicotine gum into a wrapper and put it into his book bag.

"You guys are welcome to play video games at my place," he said.

I pictured him buying us two-liter wine coolers and giving us more insight into the ways of women.

"Is that okay, Dad?" I asked.

"Make sure it's okay with Peter and Jin's parents," he said.

Jeff dropped us off and gave me the key. He saw the question mark on my face.

"I got stuff to do, guys. Help yourselves to whatever you want."

We walked through the darkness of the shop until I felt for the light switch at the bottom of the stairs that led up to Jeff's.

I checked the fridge for wine coolers while Peter set up the video game console.

No wine coolers.

Jin saw some powdered doughnuts in the cupboard and looked at me.

"Have 'em," I said.

Jin smiled, making his face look even pudgier.

Next to the stove was an R-rated video. *Fast Times at Ridgemont High*. R-rated movies were forbidden. Un-Christian.

I had always wanted to see *Fast Times at Ridgemont High*. I knew the character Jeff Spicoli, played by Sean Penn, from people at school who imitated him. When Tom and Jared talked about the movie one day I even pretended I'd seen it already because I didn't feel like explaining why R-rated movies weren't Christian.

"Guys," I showed Peter and Jin the contraband. "Let's watch this."

"Dad would kill me if I watched that," Jin said while white powder sprayed out of his mouthful of doughnut.

His dad still didn't speak English, but he was scary as hell when he yelled at Jin in Korean. He was definitely from North Korea. A commie Jehovah's Witness.

"Your dad will never know," Peter said after he'd already grabbed the tape and hit the rewind button in the VCR so we could start from the beginning.

In one scene of the movie, Judge Reinhold goes to the bathroom after he sees Phoebe Cates in a bathing suit. He starts pumping away. Masturbating. Peter, Jin, and I got real quiet and didn't look at each other. My face was flushed.

Then Phoebe Cates takes off her top in Reinhold's fantasy as he continues to masturbate. Her breasts exposed.

She was. Wow.

Peter, forever the bold one, got up and rewound that scene again.

I couldn't get up without anything obviously protruding from my pants.

Phoebe Cates pulled off her bathing-suit top again.

The wonders of technology. The video tape player. FFWD and RWD. What would they think of next?

Later in the movie, Jennifer Jason Leigh has sex with a ticket scalper.

And she shows her vagina for the camera. A full bush of hair.

Her boobs are smaller than Phoebe's. But that triangle between her legs. I don't think I had ever seen one before. One that moved on video.

After we watched the movie, Peter and I started playing video baseball on Jeff's Intellivision. A little while later we realized Jin had been in the bathroom quite a long time. It was really quiet.

We turned the video game down.

"He's jerking off," Peter said.

We laughed.

"What's taking you so long, Jin?"

"Done in a minute," he said, his voice a little higher than normal. His round face glistened as he came out of the bathroom.

Peter and I decided to leave him alone. Jin got embarrassed about that stuff and I was about to win video baseball in the third inning, anyway. The video game only went for three innings. Jin found a bag of chips and sour cream dip in the fridge.

At six o'clock the phone rang. Dad told me that Jin's mom called and wanted him to come home.

"I can come pick you guys up," Dad said.

"Nah, Jin and Peter are taking the bus. Can I stay overnight?"

There was a pause at the other end of the line.

"Okay, but you need to be home by 8:00 AM to make service tomorrow morning."

Whenever I asked Dad for a little extra freedom, he always got me to give a little extra to God.

It was a deal.

My friends left. I was alone. *Fast Times at Ridgemont High* went right back into the VCR. I rewound and replayed Jennifer Jason Leigh as she sat naked on the couch. Her bush. Her belly button. Her small feet. I rewound over and over until I was done. I used a paper towel to wipe up my sperm as they lay on the floor. Spilled to the earth, the little guys. I wondered how long they lived and swam until they died. I wondered if maybe I committed murder every time I masturbated. I prayed to Jehovah to forgive me and put the video away, vowing never to let Jennifer Jason Leigh's body entice me to wrongdoing again.

Jeff came home. I was glad because it felt weird being alone in his apartment for so long.

"Dad said I could spend the night," I said.

His breath smelled of cigarettes and alcohol.

"You got the key—go make a copy and you can stay here whenever you want, even if I'm out of town."

I felt like an adult.

Jeff put a bag on the counter and pulled out a bottle of whiskey. "Want a little?" he asked.

I nodded my head like I went to cocktail parties all the time and he gave me a small glass with ice and a little water and whiskey in it.

It tasted horrible. Like medicine. I liked the wine coolers a lot better.

Jeff poured himself a tall glass, took a swig, and sat on the couch. Within a minute he was snoring so I turned on the TV. A rerun of the *Dick Van Dyke Show* played, so I just hung out watching Alan Brady figure out which wig to put on for his show that night.

"*Hey!*" Jeff yelled.

I jumped. If I were a cat my claws would've been buried deep in the ceiling of his apartment while I swung, looking down at him.

"You all right?" I asked.

He looked at me like he was trying to orient himself to where he was.

My heart beat.

"You want some water?" I asked.

He sat up and nodded his head. I got him a glass of water. He sipped it and stared at the TV.

I waited for the next yell from Jeff, wishing I could go home, but, it was past 10:00 PM, so the buses had stopped running, and it would be like defeat if I called Dad to pick me up.

I'd never seen Jeff that drunk before. He looked at me and I braced myself.

"I'm going to die," he said.

"No," I said, then thought maybe he had AIDS, but only gay people got AIDS. Could he die from something else?

"Jehovah's going to kill me at Armageddon," he said.

"No, he's not."

"You don't know the things I've done. I wish I could. I wish. Your dad. I wish I could be like your dad."

Who would even want to be my dad? He's boring and strict and makes me go out in service all the time, even on Easter and New Year's Day.

"I'm just not a good Jehovah's Witness. You. Gabe. You listen to your dad. You stay a Jehovah's Witness. You . . . ," and he trailed off to sleep.

I was all nerves. He started snoring again.

I would rather have been Jeff than Dad. Girls liked Jeff. He rode a motorcycle. He smoked, I mean, used to smoke.

I went into Jeff's bedroom and set the alarm for 7:30 and fell asleep in my clothes on top of his sheets. When I woke up Jeff was sleeping next to me.

I got my shoes on and took the 43 Sam Trans bus back home.

There were mainly commuters on the bus. Mostly women. Minority women.

I looked out the window and watched Millbrae flash by me. I pretended I was on an airplane heading out of the country, to Europe or South America or Australia. At my stop I got off and went to my room to get ready for service.

Jeff never talked about Jehovah killing him again. I never brought it up.

I couldn't picture living on paradise earth after Armageddon if Jeff wasn't there.

Jeff had a way about him. It kept us all on edge. He'd be in town for a while at his apartment upstairs from Grandpa's shop, going to meetings at the Kingdom Hall, practicing his bass, helping Dad and Grandpa Barry if the car repair jobs were piling up, then he'd take a vacation without telling anyone. Six months could go by and we'd find out he was playing bass for Neil Diamond on tour in Europe. Dad liked Neil Diamond. I could see the pride in his eyes. The excitement in knowing there was one degree of separation between him and the Solitary Man himself.

I was in no mood for my cousin Karen. I didn't feel like taking any shit. I was sure everyone knew about my fantasy lust for Jennifer Jason Leigh. I had found my safe haven in school, and even though it was riddled with disappointment and embarrassing moments, it was better than Karen making fun of me for something.

I hadn't seen Karen or Aunt Laura since they moved to Utah. All I remembered about her was getting made fun of and having to endure her monologues. And Dad telling me not to play stop-time because it might be demonic.

Dad was excited to see Aunt Laura after so long. He gave me a lecture the night before to be nice to Karen and show her a good time and remember to be an example for Jehovah because more people come into the truth by our example than by our preaching.

"You should take that down," Dad pointed to the Einsturzende Neubauten poster as he surveyed my room for anything that could take away from the name of Jehovah.

I didn't know how to pronounce the name of the band, but Stephen, an exchange student from Germany, had passed out the posters in our social studies class and said they were his favorite band. There was a drawing of a stick figure in the middle of a circle with the word "Einsturzende" above the circle and "Neubauten" below. My parents didn't know it was a band. They thought it was the city in Germany where the boy was from and I didn't correct them because having band posters or T-shirts was wrong as a Jehovah's Witness. It was considered idol worship in the congregation. I couldn't put sports heroes or musicians on my walls for fear they would take the place of Jehovah.

Stephen played their record in class. It sounded like a car accident happening over and over while a cat screamed.

"Why do I have to take it down?" I asked.

"It's just weird looking. Karen might get the wrong idea. Laura's been having a hard time with her husband so she may be looking for answers, and we don't want to be a cause for stumbling."

It didn't matter. I took down the poster just so Karen wouldn't make fun of it. And I hid anything that she could tease me over. I put my Bibles and Bible study books under my bed. She'd never be a Witness and would always be in my life, so why add any fuel to her sinister fire?

Mom came in. "Where are your Bible study books?" she asked.

"I decided to put them under my bed."

Mom smirked and left.

Dad came into my room with a Bible.

"We're supposed to shine as illuminators for the Word of God, Jesus told us in the Gospels."

Then my books were retrieved from under my bed and put back on my bookshelf.

The doorbell rang. I looked from behind my barrier to the living room and in walked Laura and that dumb bit— . . . Karen?

Karen had grown her hair long. Karen smiled and didn't have braces anymore. Karen had, she, I tried not to look, but I couldn't help it—Karen had boobs.

Laura and Dad embraced. Then Karen gave my parents hugs while I hugged Laura.

"There's Maybe Gabey," Aunt Laura said.

I felt warm comfort and protected all at the same time when she said those words.

Karen gave me a hug. I think it's the first time I had ever hugged her. I felt her breasts against my chest.

"Good to see you, cuz," she said and pulled away.

She winked at me after the hug. I know this because I was straining to keep my eyes focused on her eyes and not on her chest.

"Can we go out to get coffee?" Laura asked Mom and Dad. They got the message that there were some private things they needed to discuss and agreed that Karen and I could stay home and watch TV.

We turned on the TV.

"You don't have cable?" Karen complained.

Same old nagging Karen. With breasts.

"No."

"That's gay," she said. I ignored her as we watched *$10,000 Pyramid*.

"Mom's pregnant, but she's thinking of aborting the baby because it might be retarded," she said after a few minutes of watching Dick Clark give clues to a contestant on the game show.

I felt bad for Karen. There was nothing I could say. It sounded awful. I looked at Karen to show her some sympathy, but her boobs were distracting any sympathy my face could muster. I thought it was better to stay quiet and watch the TV with her in silence, like I was really thinking about how horrible it was that Aunt Laura was going to abort a retarded baby.

"I'm getting a drink," Karen said and went into the kitchen.

"Cool," I mumbled, then glanced at her butt for a second as she moved away. Her butt curved and moved like a woman's when she walked.

A couple of minutes later she came out with two glasses and handed me one.

"What's this?" I asked.

"Just try it."

It tasted sweet and sugary. I took a big gulp and my nose felt like it exploded.

"You're going to get me in trouble—you went into my parents' alcohol cupboard?"

Jesus turned water into wine, but only for adults, since the Bible also said to follow the laws of government as long as they don't interfere with Jehovah's laws. It was only okay to drink if I was twenty-one.

"Don't worry," she said. "I only took a little bit out of all the bottles and added some vanilla extract and soda. Then I filled the bottles with a little water. Your parents will never know."

"Yeah, they will."

"No, Gabe, I'm an expert at this. My mom draws lines on where the level is on her vodka bottles whenever she can remember. I just pour a little water in to bring it back up to the level. I did the same with your parents' hooch, so don't worry about it."

Hooch?

"But you don't know my dad. He'll—"

"*Drink!*" she yelled.

I drank and finally started not to care about Dad or my books or Karen's breasts. She pulled out a cigarette.

"They'll smell that," I said, grinning from the buzz.

"Let's go on the balcony."

I walked behind her as she led me to our concrete slab of a balcony, looking at her butt, and we sat on the balcony as she smoked clove cigarettes.

"How did you get those?"

"Want one?"

I shook my head no, feeling a little woozy from the scientific experiment she made from my parents' kitchen.

She sucked in and blew out a sweet smell that I'd never smelled before from cigarettes.

"That smells good," I said.

She sucked and blew a plume of smoke right at my face.

The traffic from El Camino sped in the distance, momentarily safe from teenage terrorists with flying wet Nerf footballs. A man yelled in Chinese at another man downstairs across the alley by the Chinese restaurant. I lay back and looked up at the sky.

"What's Utah like?"

"Sucks."

"Are you glad to be back?"

"We're not staying in California; we're just visiting. In a few months I should hitchhike out here and find a place to crash."

She said it so matter-of-factly that I was impressed. She sounded like an adult with resolve.

"Wanna see them?" she asked.

I didn't know what she was talking about. My face must've been a big question mark and she answered it.

"My tits. You've been staring at them for, like, five minutes."

In my drunken haze, I'd miscalculated time. I thought I had just glanced at them.

Just hearing her say "tits" sparked a reaction in my pants. The rest of my body was catatonic.

She sucked in another drag from her clove cigarette, put it down, and pulled her shirt off. She unsnapped her bra from the back and it dropped to her lap and her tits, her breasts, were in front of me. She blew out the sweet smell of smoke. I inhaled. She wasn't my cousin. She wasn't the bitch of boring monologues who made me feel bad for being younger than she was. I stared at her breasts. Her nipples were pink. Her breasts were white, whiter than her body.

She cupped her hands around the bottom of them and pressed her breasts together.

"Dad likes it when I do this," she said.

Dad? She's been? How long has? I didn't think about the horrific consequences of the sexual abuse she was receiving. All I saw were breasts.

I nodded slowly, not taking my eyes off of them for fear of never seeing breasts again, embracing every moment they hung in the night air.

"Touch them."

The hypnosis hadn't ceased. I couldn't move. Breasts. In front of me. Alcohol in my veins. She picked up my hand and pulled it to her right breast.

I grabbed.

"Ow, not that hard. Softer."

I pulled back. She took my hand, "Give it another try."

She took my forefinger and thumb and grazed them across her nipple.

My penis throbbed in my pants.

"Do you have a boner?" she asked.

It snapped me out of my trance. I, I, I, was touching breasts. My cousin's breasts. Her, soft, tender, put, put, "put your shirt back on," I said and pulled away.

"I know you haven't seen or touched tits before." Smug Karen was back. It was all a set-up, but what a sweet, sweet—no, it didn't matter. My penis throbbed and her breasts would be forever imprinted on my mind.

"Thanks," I said.

Thanks for forever changing my life. Thanks for making it awkward ever to see you again at family gatherings. Thanks for the mental fuel I need to masturbate to your lovely breasts. Thanks for making our relationship a car wreck. Thanks for the beautiful, soft, bouncy, and silent monologue.

She pulled out another clove and smoked it. Looking at nothing, but contemplating everything.

I felt bad for my boner that wouldn't go down.

"Why did you show me your—" I couldn't say breasts or boobs or tits or ya-yas or. . .

She puffed away.

"You Jehovahs are no fun."

"You said your dad—?" I offered, remembering what she'd said. What a dichotomy, the beauty of a topless teenager and the ugliness of molestation.

"Don't tell anyone," she demanded.

My palms were instantly clammy. I was glad I didn't have to shake someone's hand anytime soon.

"Are you okay?" I asked.

"Why wouldn't I be?"

"I mean. Your— . Does he— ?"

"What's your sick mind thinking?"

That your dad puts his finger in your vagina, that your vagina looks like Jennifer Jason Leigh's because you have the same hair color as she has. About how he could get arrested. About how sorry I feel for you and how protective of your sexuality I became the instant it hit me that your dad plays with your breasts and maybe even does more than that.

"Do you want to talk about it?"

"What's to talk about? You got your feel."

They felt *great*.

"Why did you let me squeeze your— ?" Again I couldn't finish the sentence.

She inhaled another drag from her clove and blew it out as she talked.

"He only did it once."

The buzz wore off.

"We could do a stop-time," I said.

"I'd rather smoke."

My hands on her breasts had felt like an odd version of our stop-time game. I wanted to cleanse myself by playing it for real.

Mom, Dad, and Laura came home.

"C'mon, Karen, let's go," Laura said.

"You're welcome here," Dad said.

"No, we'll stay at Mom's. She has more room and is really excited we're in town."

Karen gave me a hug goodbye. I felt her breasts against my chest as she hugged me. It wasn't erotic. It was a secret. It was anthropologized. I wanted to cry but held back the tears. Crying would tell the secret Karen wanted me to keep.

Wait. Did I just sin?

Sisters weren't allowed to give Bible lectures in the congregation but they could demonstrate their faith in a similar way by giving demonstrations of Bible studies on the platform.

To the side of the lectern where brothers usually gave Bible talks was a table with two chairs and microphones. One meeting a week, on Thursday nights, sisters used the table to give their pretend Bible studies in five minutes for everyone to hear. Sometimes they'd mix it up a bit and pretend they were out in service or on a return visit or helping an inactive person come back into the truth so that person could reap the rewards of living forever that they came so precariously close to relinquishing by not being active in the preaching work or coming to meetings.

This Thursday, my family sat in the second row. Sister Rodgers, facing our direction, was playing the part of the inactive person who needed help. I glanced at her breasts. They looked bigger than Karen's, but Sister Rodgers was in her forties and fat. They looked like they could be pointier than Karen's round breasts.

"Sometimes a future paradise earth doesn't seem real," Sister Rodgers said to Sister Gomez.

"That's why we need the constant reminders that we get by attending the congregation meetings. Close your eyes and think of your favorite animal. What is it?"

"A lion."

"Have you ever pet a lion?"

"No, a lion would bite me."

"In paradise Jehovah will make all the animals peaceful with humans. We can pet lions and tigers and even have them as pets."

"How will we have electricity after Jehovah destroys the wicked people at Armageddon?"

"We won't need electricity; we can even live in tents if we have to. The Israelites did this in the Bible. Jehovah even gave them instructions on how to keep the camps clean. Turn with me to Deuteronomy 23:13. It says, 'A peg should be at your service along with your implements, and it must occur that when you squat outside, you must also dig a hole with it and turn and cover your excrement.'"

I started to fade out. None of the information was new to me; it was continued reminders so we would stay on Jehovah's side and wouldn't be destroyed at Armageddon.

I glanced back a couple of rows and Camille sat with her crooked teeth. Her breasts had sprouted to about the same size as Karen's.

I'm at Jehovah's place of worship. I'm on holy ground and I'm thinking about what's underneath the sisters' blouses.

I walked to the bathroom past the rows of brothers and sisters. Past Arlene. Her nipples must've been brown because she was Filipino. I knew they looked great because she was eighteen and they were big. She was engaged to Darren. They sat and held hands, displaying their affection to the rest of us aching teens.

Ally. Oh, Ally. Ally's breasts were huge. She was slightly overweight, but it would've been killer to see her breasts. Definitely pink nipples. I wanted to smash my face into those breasts. The forbidden fruit. Forbidden. I needed to get my thinking straight.

In the bathroom at the urinal it was hard for me to start peeing since I had a soft-on. I felt bad for obsessing in the Kingdom Hall. I wondered if I was losing Jehovah's blessing.

Karen had gotten me drunk. And I hadn't touched them on my own. She'd made me touch them. So that couldn't mean I'd committed a sin. There was no reason to confess to the elders because it wasn't technically a sin, I figured.

It was all her fault. She'd breast-raped me. I'd be okay. Jehovah would let me through Armageddon. I'd been a victim.

And Karen didn't need more trouble from her mom. She had enough problems. No. It had been like accidentally seeing her undress or in the shower. She was my cousin. Family. Family sometimes saw each other naked.

It was hard to remember. I'd been drunk. That's a sin too, but I hadn't asked her to make the drink. I hadn't even known what it was until she'd forced it on me. I was a victim. I hadn't sinned. I'd been sinned to.

I washed my hands and walked back to our second-row seats. I closed my eyes to concentrate on what it would be like to pet a lion in the new system.

I got a job at Remington's. It was a restaurant at the El Rancho Hotel about half a block from our apartment building. I was hired as a busboy. It was exciting to come home with hard currency after a shift—$30. Sometimes $40 if it was a really busy night. I worked on Wednesday, Friday, and Saturday nights—non-congregation meeting nights. I set up my first bank account. It felt like freedom.

On my first day off we went swimming at Darren and Arlene's house. They lived a few apartment buildings away from me, in the second biggest Jehovah's Witness complex in Millbrae, maybe one-quarter filled with Jehovah's Witnesses. The swimming pool at their place was in the center of the apartment complex. Balconies on all four sides overlooked the swimming pool. An old man on the third floor smoked his pipe and watched as we swam and jumped off the diving board.

Jin wore his T-shirt when we went swimming because we'd stare at the man-boobs he was developing and wonder if it was erotic or gross, not knowing what to say about them.

Peter stood on the roof of the complex, four stories above the swimming pool. He'd gone up to the fire escape and found the roof access door open.

Jin and I clapped as did a bunch of college-age guys who shared one of the apartments in the complex.

"Go!" they yelled.

I held my breath as Peter disappeared from view. The next thing I saw was him leaping through the air, past the old man smoking, past the fat lady's apartment on the second floor. It felt like watching a slow-motion replay of a dive in the Olympics. I couldn't take my eyes off of him. I couldn't gauge if he was going to hit the water or splat on the pavement. Everyone was alert as his life hung in the balance, gravity dictating whether Peter was going to have a future or not.

Splash!

He hit the water hard. I finally breathed and waited for Peter to come out of the pool. I counted, nine-one thousand, ten-one thousand, eleven-one thousand, twelve—

"Hunh!" Peter sucked in the air as he came out of the water.

The college guys cheered. He went over to them and they all exchanged high-fives.

I was jealous. That was the first time any of those guys acknowledged us. I thought they would kick our asses at some point. Peter had new friends.

When his stepdad found out about his acrobatics, Peter was

grounded and sent to the solitary lockdown of his parents' room with only Bible drama tapes and *Watchtower* publications.

We couldn't go to school dances. Jehovah's Witnesses couldn't do any extracurricular activities after school. No sports. No math club. Especially no school dances. Drugs, sex, and alcohol happened at school dances.

I hated hearing how great the band or DJ was the Monday after a school dance. It felt like we were missing out on life. And entering our senior year, when everyone pretty much started to realize they'd never see Peter, Jin, the sisters, or me at a school dance, our classmates finally stopped asking why.

We did have Witness parties. That's what everyone called them. It was like a school dance except with stricter chaperones and careful music selection.

Millbrae Congregation frowned on Witness parties, so we never hosted one.

"It's too easy for teens to get into trouble. If someone gets in trouble on your property, it's part of your responsibility as well," Brother Miller advised Dad when I asked if I could throw a Witness party at the shop under Jeff's apartment.

Brother Gonzalez from the San Bruno Spanish Congregation invited us to a Witness party in San Francisco. Jin's and Peter's parents were cool with it. All of our parents called the father of the brother throwing the party, Brother Peterson. He reassured them that there would be chaperones and no alcohol and that the music had been carefully screened. It went over well, like telling a Jewish woman that her daughter is marrying a successful Jewish doctor.

I bought Converse high-tops. Chuck Taylors. Pegged my pants with safety pins from the inside. I wore a black button-down shirt. I figured the pegged pants and high-tops reflected my personality well.

Jin wore a jean jacket and white pants. He couldn't button the jacket around his stomach, so he just left it open. He slicked down his coarse black hair.

Peter wore his checkered Vans and yellow pants. He actually pegged them with his mom's thread and needle. He taught himself how to sew one time when he was grounded and stuck listening to Bible drama tapes. At first he used the needles he found in his mother's drawer to prick the skin on his arm until it bled. Then he got the notion to figure out how to peg pants. He had the time. The next time he was grounded, I made sure to give him a pair of my pants to sew.

I was scared about dancing at the party. I watched Depeche Mode's "People Are People" video over and over again. I copied the lead singer's moves in front of a mirror. How he kept his head almost still but moved his arms and shoulders from side to side with the beat.

I invited Jasmine and her forever sidekick sister Camille to come with us. Camille called me ten minutes before they were supposed to be dropped off at my apartment so we could all ride over together.

"We can't go," she said.

"Why? Your mom already said yes."

"Sorry," she said.

There would be no showing off my dance moves to Jasmine that night.

Damn.

On the bright side, this opened up the possibility of meeting sisters from other congregations. I had never asked a sister to dance in my life, so I was a bit nervous. I thought bringing our own dance partners would've taken care of that. Now I was stranded.

Brother Gonzalez, Francesco, had a car that his dad had let him borrow, and he picked us up for the party. He played the Quake, a new wave radio station, in the car on the way to the party.

"How long have you known Carl?" I asked. He was Brother Peterson's son, the one throwing the Witness party.

"About five years," Francesco said and turned up the radio because the Quake was playing the latest release from Scritti Politti.

We all bobbed our heads in Francesco's Buick. Groovin' to Scritti Politti's "Perfect Way" as we drove past Candlestick Park on 101 North.

The Giants were playing a night game and the stadium spotlights lit up the sky. The party was in the Glen Park neighborhood of San

Francisco at the top of a hill in a confusing mess of streets that I never could've navigated without prolonged study of a city map.

We had to park the car about four blocks away. I wasn't used to that since I lived in the suburbs, where you parked in front of your house or in your carport. Parking four blocks away was normal in San Francisco.

As we walked closer to the party we heard the music booming. We walked into the house, up a flight of stairs, and into a front room converted to a dance floor for the night. "Billie Jean" by Michael Jackson played on the stereo. Carl Peterson had made mix tapes before the party.

The windows were fogged up and it was hot in the room.

Brother Peterson pointed to us to come into the kitchen with him.

"Are these the brothers from Millbrae Congregation?" Carl's dad asked Francesco, and we were all introduced.

He asked about Brother Borg and we replied that he was recovering well from the surgery. It felt like a trick question to make sure Francesco wasn't bringing worldly people into his house—human contraband.

Brother Peterson offered us soda and chips and told us to have a good time.

Two black sisters came into the kitchen, patting their foreheads with napkins to wipe off the sweat. I was instantly intimidated because it was obvious they had been dancing for a while, which meant they really knew how to dance.

The taller girl, Daphne, walked over and introduced herself and her friend Shelley. Shelley had braces and was the cutest sweaty black sister I had ever seen. She had full lips, and her skin was chocolate brown. Her hair was slicked into a pony tail. She wore white shorts and a white tank top. She was barefoot.

"Millbrae, huh?" she said.

"Yeah, what about you?" I asked.

"Twin Peaks Congregation. I live in Bernal Heights."

She sucked down a full glass of Coke and poured another.

"Pioneer or anything?" she asked.

"When I get out of school. I auxiliary pioneered a few months ago."

"Yeah, I'm going to pioneer when I get out of school, too." I watched her lips as she told me her spiritual goals. I looked at her legs. I glanced at her toes as she wiped her face. She had cute toenails. No polish and cut just right. Her second toe was the same height as her big toe. I thought about doing return visits with her, smashed against her thighs in the back seat of a car.

"Dig if you will the picture of you and I engaged in a kiss," Prince called from the stereo in the other room.

"Oh, this is the jam!" Daphne said and grabbed Shelley's arm. Shelley grabbed my hand and I wanted to scream for help from Jin and Peter, who were giving me the thumbs-up.

It felt good holding Shelley's hand and I made sure to stay attached to her until we hit the dance floor.

Shelley danced up and down and really kept with the beat.

In my head I counted, "1. 2. 3. And 1. 2. 3. And 1. 2. 3." And I did my imitation of Depeche Mode, trying not to look at Shelley for too long, looking at the wall, concentrating on the beat of the song, trying to look like it was nothin' but a thang.

The next song was "Tenderness" by General Public and everybody in the room cheered and kept dancing.

I felt warm hands over my eyes. I tried to turn around.

"No, you have to guess who," the girl's voice said.

"Courtney?" I said and tried to turn around. Courtney was a girl I had met at an assembly, and I knew she went to one of the San Francisco congregations.

She let go of my eyes and let me turn around.

"I'm sorry. I thought you were someone else. I'm sorry," she said when she realized I wasn't whoever.

Nothing to be sorry about. I'm here pathetically doing my Depeche Mode dance while two black sisters dance circles around me. Thanks for the save.

"No problem. I'm Gabe," I said over the music.

"I'm Julia," she said.

"Can I buy you a drink?" I said. Cheesy. I wanted to smack myself.

I wanted those words to come back into my mouth. She gave me a blank look. That song by the Specials, "Blank Expression," came into my mind, but General Public segued into George Benson's "Gimme the Night." George Benson was a Jehovah's Witness and a necessary staple to every Witness party playlist.

Julia was pretty. She had white-blond hair that went straight down, almost to her butt. She wore a vest, and her arms showed that she was very slightly overweight. Then she smiled. Her smile showed her teeth. Her straight white teeth. Lickable teeth.

Uncle Jeff popped up on my left shoulder. "Girls want it, too. Just touch them like they're cotton. Touch the back of their thighs. Remember the elbows. Then pull back."

Then Jeff said, "Pussy farts" in my head and I instantly turned red.

In the kitchen she told me she was from North Beach Congregation.

"Are there a lot of Italians in that Kingdom Hall?" I asked.

"More Chinese than Italians."

We drank and I fumbled for more conversation.

"Are you a pioneer?" I asked.

"Are you a cop?"

I felt like the biggest Jehovah's Witness dork in the world. At a Jehovah's Witness party.

"I'm just studying. My grandma is a Jehovah's Witness," she said. "Are you a pioneer or something?"

"Not yet."

"So, you're going to be?" she asked.

"I guess."

"You're not sure?"

"I just turned seventeen. I feel like I should be thinking about seventeen-year-old things, not about adult things"—that came out of my mouth before I could take it back. That came out of my mouth and it was the most truth I had ever spoken to a girl. That came out of my mouth and I waited for the music to stop, all the lights to brighten in my direction, and a night of back-pedaling from what I had just voiced to begin.

"I know what you mean," she replied.

She knew what I meant? She?

"Let's go outside," she said and turned toward the stairs that led to the front door. I scouted the placement of the chaperones. Brother Miller popped up on my right shoulder and said, "Teens get into trouble at Witness parties." I thought, if I do anything with this girl and she never becomes a Jehovah's Witness, that would mean I had stumbled her, and Jesus said it was better that a boulder be tied around your neck and for you to be dumped into the ocean than to stumble someone.

Back of thighs. Elbows.

Downstairs I followed.

I didn't want to offend her.

Jin and Peter danced with the black sisters in the crowd of fifty or so Witnesses.

Man, Peter couldn't dance. But Jin, for a fat Korean guy, he really could groove. I was completely intimidated.

"What are we—?" Julia put her finger to her mouth and shushed me, waving for me to follow her.

San Francisco was deep into Indian summer. A perfect night for a Giants game. A perfect night for a walk with Julia.

I felt like I might have Tourette's syndrome and uncontrollably say "pussy farts" for no reason. Thanks, Uncle Jeff.

A block away there was a bench in front of a house and we sat on it.

"That's the first time a Jehovah's Witness has ever said anything like that to me," she said. "I never expected to hear it. Everyone says they're going to pioneer. Like robots."

We sat. I didn't reply.

"Do you believe they're telling the truth?"

No elbow rubbings would be happening after that question.

"It's the truth," I said. I felt it. I knew it. What else is there?

She sat silent. She pulled out a cigarette and I tried to look cool but scanned the area in case we were being watched.

She lit it. It was a clove. The smell put Karen's breasts into my brain. I instantly wondered about Julia's nipples.

She blew the smoke out.

"Are we friends?" she asked.

"Sure."

"I mean, are you a teller or do you keep secrets?"

"I can keep a secret."

"It's not like I want to keep having sex or anything. I've only done it twice and both times it was uncomfortable and just hurt."

All I could think of was that she knew what a penis looked like. She could imagine what was between my legs. I felt exposed.

"I like smoking, but I can quit anytime," she said.

Un-huh. Hrmm. What was my position? Am I a Jehovah's Witness who's supposed to be encouraging her? Will I smell like smoke? I can't go back into the party if I smell like smoke.

"I think I'll miss Halloween the most," she said.

Halloween? More than sex? More than cloves? More than school dances and not having to preach to your friends on Saturday mornings?

"Why aren't you saying anything?" she asked.

I didn't know what to say. I started to pray to Jehovah, *Please help me to say the right things so she's not . . .* , and it trailed off into a memory of Jennifer Jason Leigh's bushy triangle.

She slapped my arm. I looked down to a spot of blood.

"Mosquito," she said.

Clove smoke went through my brain . . . in my head someone was holding up breast flashcards one by one. I turned and looked at the half-worldly girl.

Jeff jumped on my right shoulder and beat the shit out of Brother Miller and told me, "She wants you."

I put my hand on her breast over her shirt.

Slap.

That was to my face.

"You're pathetic," she said.

Busted. She'll tell her grandma, and the elders would tie a rope around my neck and attach it to a boulder and dump me into the ocean.

"You have to kiss a girl first," she said and took a drag from her clove cigarette.

She put her mouth to mine and blew the smoke in. She pulled away and I exhaled second-hand clove smoke. I went back in for more and glided my tongue along her teeth like Jared had advised Peter. I planted my tongue between her bottom teeth and gums.

She pulled out and pushed me back.

"Are you trying to give me a dental exam?" she asked. "I'm going back." She got up.

I knew I couldn't go back into the party smelling like tobacco.

"Julia," I said, "are you going to tell anyone?"

She saw the panic in my face. She saw the shower of anguish that overtook me.

She sat back down. Close to me. She put her hand on my shoulder and took my hand to put it around her shoulder.

We sat.

I smelled her perfume. Her tobacco smell. My body relaxed and she buried her head deeper into my chest.

"Can I get your phone number so we—"

"Shut up," she said.

Everyone started clearing out of the party and walked to their bus stops and cars.

She got up and ran to the sisters who'd brought her to the party. They gave me a hard stare.

No goodbye. No phone number. No last name.

"Where ya been, Dags?" Jin said as they walked toward me. The car was a few more blocks away. Jin was as drenched in sweat as the black sisters had been.

"Chillin'," I said.

Francesco gave me an odd look and we walked to his car.

It was 10:30 PM. An appropriate time for a Witness party to end.

On the way home I rubbed my chest where Julia had buried her head. I wanted to keep that feeling as long as I could.

We walked into the Kingdom Hall. The Dagslands. Good Jehovah's Witness family. Poor Sister Dagsland with her chronic fatigue syndrome. She'll be healed in paradise. What a good boy Gabe is becoming!

Jeff hadn't made it to a meeting in a few weeks. Brother Connelly said Jeff had called him and said that he had to go on tour to pay off some bills.

I looked through the crowd of Witnesses. Along the wall at the back of the Kingdom Hall a line formed for Witnesses who needed to get the latest issues of the *Watchtower* and *Awake!* or other literature. I walked into the auditorium area and saw Jasmine talking to Sister Sorisho.

"What happened last night? Why didn't you come to the party?" I asked Jasmine.

Jasmine's eyes lit up. I turned around and Dan Abrahamson walked up to us and gave Jasmine a hug.

In front of me. In front of everyone in the Kingdom Hall.

He didn't say hi to me, just whisked Jasmine away and they found a couple of seats and sat down together.

Together?

I asked Sister Sorisho what had just happened. She had a smile on her face.

"Jasmine and Dan got engaged over the weekend."

I had masturbated after the Witness party to a lustful fantasy involving Julia. Her smell. Her touch. I melded Julia's head with Jennifer Jason Leigh's naked body. Julia had that puff of hair between her legs. Jennifer Jason Leigh's puff of hair. I pumped and killed all those sperm and flushed them down the toilet and into the San Francisco Bay.

Jasmine and Dan were going to get married. God was punishing me.

"When?" I asked Sister Sorisho.

There was no marriage date. They were going to take things slow.

Blue balls for Dan. Blue balls for all of us.

They held hands.

He had an uptightness to his stature. I couldn't picture them doing any other sex but missionary position. I had seen the *Kama Sutra* when Jared brought a copy to school. They'd never do doggy or other positions. And Jasmine would start pooping out Jehovah's Witness kids as soon as they got married.

She was on her way to proper Christian wife normalcy.

I wanted to stop time. To click freeze on the remote and stop the human race from moving inevitably forward through the universe in the space-time continuum. Forward from when we were sitting together in the back seat of Sister Sandoval's car, or when Jasmine sat on my lap on the way to Burger King in Arlene's car, and her dark legs meshed with mine, both of us sweaty from the summer day. We'd hit a bump in the road, and it was my lap dance.

Freeze.

But life moves forward, and Dan and Jasmine held hands. It was the Dan and Jasmine Show.

Then Ally came up to me and showed me her engagement ring. What was in the air?

"Jim asked me to marry him," she glowed.

I knew they'd been dating, but wow, that was fast.

She'd met Jim Stevens, a brother from New Jersey, at the district assembly. He'd recently moved to Daly City and ran a car-washing business. A proprietor. A businessman. An entrepreneur of sorts.

He was an average-looking guy. Twenty-three. And he had his own apartment. An easy marriage transition, not like for some of the eighteen-year-olds who got married and had to live in their parents' garages for a while until their jobs paid enough for them to move into cement slabs of apartments near their friends and start having kids.

Twenty-three. Ready to go.

Ally loved him, even his nose that was pointed slightly toward the ground.

He was a nice guy with a high voice.

They needed no time. Jim would see those huge breasts and pink nipples within three months of their meeting.

Jim was in step behind her. He shook my hand and I congratulated him. Then he and Ally sat with Dan and Jasmine. All holding hands, displaying affection.

And just like that, Jasmine was forever gone. My heart was an empty pit. Not even masturbating could take my mind off of her and how she hadn't waited for me to turn eighteen and get a janitor job or work at Grandpa's car repair shop to support us.

Ally and Jim were to get married first, and Ally chose Jasmine as one of her bridesmaids. I was an usher and assigned to help people to their seats.

I took the weekend off from Remington's to go to the rehearsal dinner and to the wedding.

Ally glowed.

I liked Jim.

Ally's cousins and brothers and sisters came from all around the United States; she had a big family, mostly older than she was. Both families had some worldly relatives, but the majority were decent Witnesses. Ally had a cousin named Krissy. She wasn't too bad looking. She had dirty-blond hair and a strong, almost Nordic-looking face. But she was ready to balloon. Those hips were for baby makin' and those calves were for jiggling. I knew she was just trying to maintain until a man entered into the contract of marriage with her, the vow of the covenant, then, *bam!* Late-night drive-throughs would fill in any emotional gaps she suppressed. Trouble with Mom, trouble with Dad—it wouldn't need to be as extreme as Peter's sadistic stepfather or his passive mom, but something off, just enough, and hunger would set in, insatiable hunger for something else out of life, something that would never be revealed . . . maybe the urge to be a dancer, a burlesque dancer, or a member in a band.

A purpose.

A purpose crushed down.

A purpose smashed down because she was a Jehovah's Witness.

A purpose substituted by a Double Ultimate Cheeseburger from Jack in the Box.

It was a *Phil Donahue* show in the making.

There weren't any potentials among the sisters at the rehearsal dinner. Nothing to take my mind off Jasmine.

Jasmine and Dan, Ally and Jim, corresponding families . . . I could've used an alcoholic recipe the likes of the one Karen had made for me before showing her breasts.

Dinner was excruciating. Krissy was nice, though. I even flirted a bit with her, but there was no way, nothing further. She returned my flirting, and then Dan left early from the dinner.

There was an empty seat next to Jasmine. A void. A vacuum.

Jasmine looked awkward, like I had never seen her before. Ally's parents made speeches. Jim's parents made toasts. Jasmine sat alone. Krissy ached for attention. And me? All I wanted was a beer or something with vodka in it.

Jin and Peter didn't come, even though they were assigned to be ushers, too. They didn't ask their parents. They went skateboarding, and I should've gone with them. How did they know the rehearsal dinner was going to be lame? It was the first time I'd been really close to a wedding, so I wanted to taste the joys.

Eh?

After dinner, a few of us ended up at Arlene and Darren's house. Darren had to go to his night job at UPS, which paid union wages and gave him good benefits. He loaded trucks all night.

There was champagne and beer. I took one without asking. Jim was the oldest person in the room and he didn't care if I drank or not. We hung out and listened to records and drank.

The beer tasted like the land of milk and honey.

That was the after party. The real shindig. And Ally sat on Jim's lap, reminding me of all the bumps in the road from Mills High School to Burger King and back. Jasmine and Camille and Krissy went into the bedroom with champagne and closed the door. I enjoyed my Löwenbräu, and my second. An hour later I had a pleasant beer buzz. New Order's "Blue Monday" was on the record player, and Jasmine, Krissy, and Camille came out of the bedroom. Krissy drank out of a bottle of champagne and passed it to Jasmine, who quenched her thirst. Wow. Nice chug. She was on her way to becoming a secret sinning alcoholic wife . . . easier to get away with that than other things. So many Jehovah's Witnesses hit the drinking hard because it was the only acceptable vice (in moderation, and moderation can be interpreted differently for everyone).

Jesus turned water into wine and an organization of Jehovah's Witnesses into borderline alcoholics.

I drank another beer, and Jasmine was in her dress. It was light red, almost pink, and her white stockings contrasted well with her black buckled shoes. Her hair was a bit tousled and I glanced at her dark eyes, and she looked at me.

"WHAT ARE YOU LOOKING AT?" Jasmine yelled.

Everyone in the room stopped and I had no idea if that was a confrontation or a general question I needed to answer. I wanted to make my face blank. Without emotion. I wanted to appear transparent. I wanted to have a slight, "Hrmm, what's this you're inquiring of, young lady" look on my face.

I tried to look like that, but the beers in my system made my face sag a bit.

"STOP LOOKING AT ME."

Silence.

I looked away.

No one intervened. They all thought this was some type of real conflict between Jasmine and me. Something that needed a resolution. I had no idea what to do or why she was attacking me. Her words took up the whole room. I had never seen her take up the whole anything before.

I walked over and changed the record to Depeche Mode and everyone started talking again. A bit louder because I turned up the volume, in case Jasmine wanted to continue her one-way conversation with me.

"I HATE YOU." It was a deep growl from the abdomen, of a possessed woman about to undergo stigmata. I was impressed, considering Jasmine's slight build, which I had made a point of brushing up against most of my post-pubescent life.

I turned around and she pointed at me.

"I HATE YOU. STOP LOOKING AT ME."

Everyone looked at me.

"I wasn't looking at you," I said, sounding more like a sheep trapped in a barbed wire fence than a man who could cope with the energy building in the room.

Maybe she'd read an erotic thought from my mind. They were coming more often. Maybe she'd seen that I wished I had X-ray vision and would've loved to see if her nipples were pink or brown.

"STOP . . ." and then she started mumbling stuff that was incoherent.

"She's going to puke," Arlene said as Jasmine jumped up and stumbled to the bathroom, spewing whatever the demon inside her decided to spray on the bathroom walls and floor and toilets. It smelled. I was tempted to see if there was a pattern to her vomit, if any phrases were sprayed on the walls.

Mene, Mene, Tekel, and Parsin.

Everything returned to normal. As normal as it could be with a puking Jasmine in the bathroom and Krissy letting out huge alcoholic burps, then giggling afterward. I laughed and was a bit turned on that she was so free with her bodily functions, though I was still shaken from Jasmine's outburst.

Jim helped me take my mind off it.

"Do you like ELO?" he asked and put on *Out of the Blue*. He really grooved to it.

"What was that about?" he whispered.

"I have no idea."

"That was strange. Do you like ELO?"

"Sure, they're cool," I lied, even though his enthusiasm was infectious.

The party ended with a whimper. Jasmine passed out mostly cleaned up on Arlene's bed. I had to sneak a peek at her. The *she* who hated me. The *she* who saw through me. The *she* who would never be a *my*. Her mouth hung open. She was on her side. A bucket was next to the bed. She snored. I looked at her petite body all curled up. I looked at her lips.

My only hope was that she'd cheat on Dan with me because she knew I was her true love.

It didn't even seem like a sin in my mind. It only seemed inevitable. We'd cheat. I'd ruin their marriage. When I was over eighteen and had a steady job and could afford an apartment.

The next day at the wedding Jasmine didn't say hi or look at me. In her hokey purple bridesmaid's dress she still managed to look like an Italian goddess.

Glancing at her made my brain hurt and reminded me that if she caught my eye she might scream that she hated me again to everyone in the room, at the Kingdom Hall, or at the Millbrae Recreation Center, where the reception was held.

She danced the wedding party dance with Dan. They looked great. He was a handsome guy. I wished I was in his situation.

The reception was in full swing. Everyone had eaten their dinner and the dance floor started to pick up. I danced with Krissy. I asked her about the Jasmine thing from the rehearsal-dinner after party, and she said she vaguely remembered but had been too drunk really to comprehend the situation. She liked her liquor. I asked if they'd talked about me when they went into the bedroom, and Krissy smiled.

What?

"What?" I asked.

"Well, Jasmine talked about you a little bit."

"What did she say?" I asked.

"She said you were a nice guy."

Nice guy?

"What else?"

"She said . . . " Then Krissy looked into my eyes—those begging eyes stared into my soul. It made me scared, that she saw a bit too deep into me. I wasn't eager to see that deep into myself.

"She said that if you asked me out I should say yes."

Then she put her head on my shoulder for the rest of the extended wedding-party dance, and I saw a movie of my future filled with a fast-food-craving wife and living with her parents in their garage in Vacaville while I slaved fifty hours a week as a floor cleaner or at some other job so we could have benefits.

"Ouch," she said after I accidentally stepped on her foot. When the dance was over we pulled apart and she looked into my eyes and I looked toward the floor, wondering if that was it, if I should just muster up the courage to ask her to be my girlfriend.

I said I needed to go to the bathroom. Like it was an emergency. Like there was a chance I'd made a little squirt from my butt and now would not be the most prudent time to continue this conversation. She let me go.

I would've gnawed my leg off to get out of that bear trap.

Dan was in the bathroom.

"Good wedding, huh?" he said.

I looked in the mirror, at my tuxedo and big crooked bow tie. A deep sadness registered on my face. I couldn't make it go away. After Dan left, I tried various smiles. I couldn't smile without looking like a pedophile slowly driving a van with blacked-out windows by an elementary school during recess. I felt pressure on my chest. Could I die of a heart attack at age seventeen?

Peter gave me his trademark smirk when I came out of the bathroom.

"What?"

"Debbie."

"Who?"

"Four o'clock," and there was Debbie.

"I'm going to ask her to dance."

"She's hot. What Kingdom Hall does she go to?" I wondered out loud.

"I don't know."

The chicken wasn't settling too well in my stomach. I should've checked the steak box on my RSVP.

Since the whole Kingdom Hall was there as well as other visiting Witnesses and I was in the wedding party, it was okay for me to have a glass of wine to celebrate. Underage drinking was okay under adult supervision and during special occasions. I made sure to sneak a couple of refills as well.

"This is the last piece of cake—we should leave," Jin said with his mouth full. He knew exactly where the food was, but he wasn't a good gauge when it came to scoping out the sisters, since he had a hard time getting any sisterly Witness play. He'd learned to say, "Two servings please" in English before he'd learned to say, "Will you dance with me?"

"Peter found someone," I said, and we looked over at him and Debbie. They moved to the dance floor. For a slow song, thank God, since Peter couldn't dance.

A tug to my arm and I was in Krissy's grip again, slow dancing to "Always and Forever." She burped. I loved it when she burped. She was obviously getting a bit tipsy.

The reception was about two blocks from the shop and Jeff's apartment. Jeff was back in town but couldn't make the wedding. I had my permanent key. I wanted to walk to his place and watch HBO and just go to bed.

Peter came up to me after the dance, after I led Krissy back to a chair and put her down. His face was white.

"She said she wants to go hang out in her car."

"Really, what congregation is she in?"

"She's not a Witness," Peter said. He was half excited at the offer and half terrified that something would happen that could get him disfellowshipped.

"Her husband lives back East and she told me she's horny, and she stuck her tongue in my ear while we danced."

Opportunity knocked.

"Fuck," Peter whispered to me.

It meant he wanted to take it there. A worldly girl was offering herself to him, and he was seriously considering it.

But it was a Witness wedding. And who knew who she was connected to in the organization of Jehovah's Witnesses? A chat with her cousin about her snogging a cute, freckled seventeen-year-old at Ally's wedding could get back to the elders through the network of Witnesses eager to find out about the sins of others and inform the elders, to do their duty to the congregation and to Jehovah.

Opportunity knocked but it was time to turn the lights out and pretend no one was home.

"Jin," I tapped him on the shoulder, "let's go to Jeff's."

Jin smiled and I could almost see the thought bubble above his head, containing cupboards full of junk food at Jeff's.

Dad gave me the okay and said I could sleep at Jeff's if I wanted to.

Jasmine ogled Dan. Ally ogled Jim. Jim was mere hours from seeing Ally's huge breasts on their honeymoon night. Unless they had sinned and she'd already given him the chance for some touching and caressing.

Dan's balls were turning bluer by the minute. The DJ played Kool and the Gang's "Celebration." I watched the crowded dance floor. Even Brother Miller was dancing, with his pathetic side-to-side shuffle. He looked like a speed skater with epilepsy. His eyes were closed to concentrate on the music. He wasn't squinting and looking into anyone's soul.

I couldn't even pretend to have fun. To see Jasmine with Dan.

Debbie walked in our direction, oozing sexuality. As she got closer it was obvious she had to be thirty. Experienced. Ready for Peter to stick his penis into her vagina. A real vagina. A warm woman to hold instead of having to tug with his right hand.

"Get me out of here—this isn't good," Peter said.

We hit the exit and Peter fled, like he was Joseph fleeing Potifer's wife. His emotion turned into laughter and we all laughed and wrestled and kicked small rocks to each other on the sidewalk like they were soccer balls.

At Jeff's we hooked up the Intellivision and played video games.

"You could've gotten laid," I said.

"Don't rub it in," Peter replied.

"Can I eat these Ho Hos?" Jin said.

I heard a bump on the stairs that led up to Jeff's. Assuming it was Jeff coming back, I looked down but it was Krissy. She sat on one of the stairs resting before moving on. She must've followed us.

"Krissy?" I said.

She puked on the stairs. Yup, she was drunk.

"Ew," Peter and Jin plugged their noses. It was rank.

I walked to Krissy and helped her up the stairs, avoiding her puke breath whenever she talked to me.

"You're a great guy."

Hold breath—reply—"Thanks."

"You have nice eyes."

Hold breath—reply—"Thanks."

As I walked her to Jeff's bed she started to heave again. I got her to the bathroom, but not in enough time to avoid splatter on the rug and video game console. The Intellivision died. Peter and Jin looked at me.

Then Jin started heaving. Sympathy dry heaves from hearing and smelling Krissy.

"C'mon, Jin," Peter said and helped him downstairs. His face was fading to white.

I heard him spitting on the shop floor.

"Throw me a towel," Peter said. I tossed one down the stairs for him to clean up Jin's wedding-cake vomit puddle and ran back to attend to Krissy.

"We're leaving. He's going to keep throwing up if he smells that," Peter yelled from downstairs, helping Jin outside.

For a guy whose number one pursuit in life was consuming junk food, I wouldn't have guessed him to be a sympathy vomiter.

Krissy lay by the toilet and I scrubbed the stains on the rug with some cleaner. The Intellivision was ruined.

"Bluuuugh," Krissy started up again from the bathroom. It was obvious she'd checked "chicken" on her RSVP and had had a bunch of chocolate almonds that were set out on the tables at the reception.

Her hair was in the toilet. I flushed and pulled her hair back.

In Jeff's fridge there were some wine coolers. I cracked one open and went back into the bathroom and stayed with Krissy while she moaned, heaved, and wept between her puking. When her stomach calmed down enough, I led her to Jeff's bed and put a bucket next to it, like I saw had been done for Jasmine.

Krissy moaned.

"It's okay. Relax and sleep."

I knew Jeff wouldn't mind sleeping on the couch—I'd take the floor—so Krissy could feel better. He'd told me many times about his days of partying too hard.

"Dress," she said.

"What?"

"Off."

She wanted me to help take her bridesmaid's dress off. If I were sick and wearing that purple egg suit, I'd want it off, too.

I took it off while trying not to look at her white bra and panties and her milky-white belly, slightly protruded, and her muscular thighs that I'd never seen or realized she ran or did whatever she did and her square shoulders and those bra straps hanging onto her shoulders.

"Mmmm," she said and looked at me.

I looked away and tried to put her out of my mind. I tried to put the thought of taking off her bra and panties out of my mind. Definitely pink nipples. And I tried not to think about snuggling up next to her and embracing her half-naked body, feeling her soft skin against mine.

I turned her on her side. Her skin was clammy and wet from the alcohol coursing through her veins.

I watched *RoboCop* on HBO while Krissy slept it off. I called Jasmine and Camille's house but there was no answer. I didn't know where she was staying. I called Ally's mom's house. No answer.

She'd be too hard to move anyway.

I fell asleep thinking, *I'd buy that for a dollar.*

I woke up and heard bacon crackling on the stove. I still wore my tux shirt and pants and glossy leather shoes.

It took me a minute to figure out I had slept at Jeff's.

Fraggle Rock played on HBO.

I was glad Jeff had made it home. I felt like I really needed to talk to him again about the torment I'd been going through with Jasmine. From the early lustful days to her engagement to her drunken outburst. Emotions pushed on my heart and vital organs. They needed release. And I could trust Jeff. He wouldn't tell anyone. He wouldn't tell Mom and Dad.

My eyes finally opened all the way and I did a big stretch.

"Finally," Krissy said.

It felt like a nail had been hammered into my eyeball.

I turned around as Krissy poured orange juice into a couple of glasses. In her bra and panties.

She came over and handed me a glass.

"Rise and shine," she said.

Some mornings I awoke with a boner and some mornings I didn't. That morning I was boner-less until I saw Krissy bopping around Jeff's place in her bra and panties. I tried to stare at her eyes but involuntarily kept surveying her other goods.

I drank the juice and she took the bacon and eggs off of the stove.

"Jeff?" I called out.

"No one else is here. Do you share this place with someone?"

I explained the situation. It was Sunday. 10:15. I had a couple of hours before I needed to get back home to go to the Kingdom Hall with my parents for the Watchtower study.

Krissy handed me breakfast and sat down.

I ate breakfast with a girl in her underwear.

The emotional charge from Jasmine was nowhere near the surface of my brain.

Power.

Her body, her skin, and her being in her underwear had power over me. I finally got the courage to speak.

"How are you feeling?"

"I woke up at 7 and drank tons of water. Then found some aspirin and vitamins and took a bunch. Thanks for helping me last night."

She was a pro when it came to hangovers.

"You remember?"

"Most of it. Did you take advantage of me?"

"No, you told me to take your dress off," I pled innocent.

"I'm kidding. I know."

We ate.

"Does this bother you?" she asked.

"What?"

"That I'm in my underwear?"

God. No. I've been waiting for a moment like this, I've been waiting to see a girl in her underwear, I've been waiting, no bother, no way, let's make out. Let's.

"Oh, no," I said like it happened all the time.

She took my empty plate away and washed the dishes. She sat back down and we watched the 49er game since *Fraggle Rock* was lame.

She kissed me on the cheek.

"Thanks. You're a nice guy," she said and put her arm around the back of my neck.

I put my hand on her hand. I played with her fingers and she leaned in a little closer.

I kissed her cheek.

She kissed my cheek again.

I kissed the side of her mouth.

She kissed me and opened her mouth, automatically opening my mouth.

IT instantly throbbed since Krissy was in her underwear. I didn't go for gliding my tongue between her teeth and gums because I'd learned from my mistake with Julia at the Witness party. Instead I rolled my tongue around hers. I lightly touched the back of her neck. She moaned.

Thanks, Jeff.

I rubbed her elbows and she pulled them back.

"What are you doing?"

"Rubbing your elbows."

"Don't," and she came back in and we rolled our tongues together.

After we kissed a little more she got up and said she had to get over to Jim and Ally's apartment. They wouldn't be home since they'd left for their honeymoon, but Ally's mom was going to pick her up to take her to the train station at noon. She put her brides-maid's dress back on. In the bathroom, she rubbed out the remain-ing puke stains.

I found a Pink Floyd T-shirt and a pair of Jeff's jeans. Both were huge and baggy on me. I cuffed up the jeans but his belt wouldn't come in enough to hold them up on my waist. I found one of his ties in his closet and wrapped it tight into a knot around the jeans.

Krissy came out of the bathroom in her purple egg dress. I didn't need X-ray vision to know exactly what her bra and pant ies looked like.

I tucked in the Pink Floyd T-shirt so it didn't look like a skirt on me. I felt like a kid playing adult in those clothes.

We walked to the bus stop. She held my hand.

"Not here," I said, fearing that the wrong person might drive by and see us. We were on my turf. No one from Vacaville Congregation was going to see her.

On the bus I surveyed the passengers. No one looked familiar. And I got a really good look at everyone because they all stared at us like we were circus performers. Her in her bridesmaid's dress with her makeup mostly washed off and her hair tousled, and me in my uncle's oversized clothes, looking like I'd picked them up from a dumpster that unfortunately didn't have my size.

We sat down and I held her hand. The bus passed my apartment and we went the two more stops to Ally and Jim's place. We didn't hold hands as we walked.

"I'll give you my phone number at Ally's," she said.

Ally's used to mean Ally's at Ally's mom's house. Now it meant Ally's at Ally's place. Life as I knew it was changing.

We got in the door and she went into the bedroom and came out with her phone number on a piece of paper.

"I'll try to visit soon," she said.

I put her phone number in my back pocket.

She kissed me on the lips. Neither of us opened our mouths.

Just a long, tender kiss as I put my hands around the back of her bridesmaid's dress.

"Go—they'll be here any minute."

I walked home to get ready for the meeting and *Watchtower* study. No one was the wiser. No one knew what had just happened. I felt a little guilty, but the taste memory of Krissy's tongue in my mouth overrode the other feelings creeping up.

"You should've brought a change of clothes," Dad said as I came in the door.

"I know."

"Did Peter and Jin get home okay?"

"Yeah." Did they?

"Good. At least no one will miss the meeting then. Hurry up—we leave in ten minutes."

As I dressed I rolled my tongue around in my mouth. I licked my teeth. I puckered up. I put Krissy's address in my underwear drawer.

Monday at my locker, Peter and Jin came up to me.

"What happened with Krissy?" Peter asked.

I turned around and couldn't hold back my evil grin.

"She got better?"

"What did Jeff do when he came home?"

"He never came home."

They looked confused.

"She made me breakfast."

Peter's jaw dropped.

"We kissed. She," I added, trying not to get a boner while telling the story, "she was in her bra and underwear and we kissed."

Peter smiled.

"You better be careful, dude," Jin said as sugar powder from his doughnut blew into the air.

"What are you talking about?"

"Did you go further than kissing?" he asked.

What was he all of a sudden, his commie Korean dad?

"No, we just made out," I said.

Peter winked.

"Are you going out or something now?" Jin asked.

"Yeah, I think she's my girlfriend."

"You're too young to date," he said.

The bell rang and Jin left for class. I looked at Peter and he started blinking in a weird way, like it was involuntary.

"Are you okay?" I asked.

"I-I-I-I, fine," he stuttered.

"What's wrong, Peter?"

He looked toward the center courtyard.

"Dad took me to breakfast yesterday."

"Doesn't your dad have a janitorial job on Sunday mornings?"

"My f-f-f-father. Robert. He's out of prison."

He hadn't seen his dad in over ten years and rarely talked about him.

"Is he cool?"

"When he dropped me off at home T-T-Terry y-y-el—screamed at him. He said I can never see him again and they're getting a restraining order. He's going to die at Armageddon Terry s-s-aid, so why see my dad when he h-has a death sentence?"

"I hate Terry. What are you going to do?"

He shrugged his shoulders and walked away.

Peter stuttered when talking about his real father. I never asked Peter about him unless we were alone. I knew to patiently wait for his stutter to end. He wasn't uncomfortable stuttering around me. At least he could control his bowels better than when he was eight years old, when they remembered the horrors of his real father's abuse.

Camille came up to me. "Walk me to class?" she said.

It didn't faze me like before. All of a sudden she didn't irritate me. It was the first month of our senior year of high school. I no longer cared that Jasmine had graduated. She was pioneering.

As I walked Camille to class and she told me about how much fun the rest of Jim and Ally's wedding had been and about Jasmine and Dan's engagement plans and about her having to chaperone them, I didn't feel bad. Krissy really gave me something. Krissy gave me freedom. There was more to life than Millbrae Congregation, Mills High School. I had Krissy's phone number at home to prove it.

"Thanks," Camille said after I had completely ignored her as we walked and just reevaluated how great my life was becoming, was going to be, from that moment forward. I felt fine. I was at peace. It was okay that she had told on me, about my letter to her, years before, and couldn't keep her mouth shut about anything. It didn't matter. Breakfast with Krissy had changed my life. It even made me like Camille a little more as a person.

"Have a great day, Camille," I said as I dropped her off at history class. And I meant it. She looked at me. She knew something had changed. She smiled and showed me those crooked teeth.

"You too," she replied and stayed near the door of her class and watched me walk down the hallway to my biology class.

Thursday night Brother Rodgers asked to talk to me after the meeting. I tried to think of any possible technicalities I could've been involved in. No one knew about Krissy and we hadn't committed "sins," but they'd still probably want to talk to me if they really knew what happened so we wouldn't "go any further."

Ally and Jim were on their honeymoon in Hawaii. Jim was playing with those large breasts, sucking on those pink nipples.

Jasmine and Dan held hands.

I asked Dad if he knew what the elders' meeting was about. He asked if I was worried, if I should confess something. It was the closest I ever came to punching Dad. That wasn't the comforting answer I needed. It was then I realized that between the congregation and his son, Dad chose the congregation. The congregation was his god.

"Thanks for talking with us, Brother Dagsland. We just have a question for you regarding something that happened last week," Brother Rodgers said as two other elders looked on with stern faces, the weight of the holiness and cleanliness of the congregation on their shoulders.

Shit. They knew about Krissy. How did they find out? It was cool. I knew making out wouldn't get me into too much trouble. It might take some explaining, about her being in her bra and panties and us being unchaperoned. Something that they'd urge me to avoid, but nothing to pin a sin on me for. It would take some explaining to Dad. Yep, it was going to be a rough ride home on that one. I'd probably have to give Jeff his apartment key back.

"We want to ask you about Jasmine and what happened after the rehearsal dinner. In your opinion, was she drunk?"

Shitfaced.

"Uh, I'm not sure. I left early," I replied.

"Did you notice her drinking?"

Chugging.

"She had a glass of champagne, I think. There were adults around and it was a special occasion."

"So nothing was out of the ordinary?"

Does a demonic voice of I HATE YOU coming from a petite Italian girl who then ran to the bathroom to throw up satanic green spew on the walls spelling Mene Mene Tekel and Parsin (the hand-writing on the wall) count as out of the ordinary?

"No, it was actually pretty boring. I left early," I replied.

"Thanks, Brother Dagsland. That's all," they said and asked me to leave the back room so they could get on with their investigation.

Jasmine called me the next day after school. After the elders' meeting. After holding Dan's hand. Kissing him in front of Camille, their chaperone, who was supposed to be making sure they didn't take it any further until their wedding day.

Blue balls for us all.

"Did the elders talk to you?" she asked.

I wondered about bringing up her drunken rage toward me or how she didn't want me to look at her anymore or how she didn't even say hi to me at the wedding and why we hadn't talked until then.

"Yeah, what's going on?" I said.

"What did you say to them?"

"They asked me if you were drunk and I said you seemed fine to me."

There was silence. I heard her breathing. I pressed the phone tighter to my ear.

"I think they're going to reprove me."

"Why?" I asked.

"Because they think I got drunk that night."

Oh, that.

"It's better than being disfellowshipped," I said.

She laughed. It was a desperate laugh with a pinch of relief. Laughing, then silence. I heard her breathing again.

"How's Dan?" I asked, though I wanted to yell with the same demonic possession she'd dredged up from her core last Friday at Ally's apartment.

"He's fine. He's scared we won't be able to have our wedding at the Kingdom Hall if I get reproved."

"Do you know when you're going to get married?"

"No, we're holding off until we find out what happens with the elders."

"Oh."

Silence.

All my feelings came back. Krissy couldn't stop them.

"Why didn't you talk to me at the wedding?"

"Why didn't you talk to me?"

"Because you screamed you hated me and didn't want me to look at you."

"I was drunk," she said. I could tell she wished she hadn't confirmed that out loud.

"Do you hate me?"

"No."

"Why did you say it?"

"I don't know. I was drunk."

Silence.

"Do you like Krissy?" she asked.

Leave Krissy out of this.

"Do you like Dan?"

"Yeah, that's a stupid question."

Silence.

"I don't like him," I said. There. Finally. It was out in the open.

"I need to go. Goodbye," and she hung up the phone.

"See ya Sunday," I said to a dial tone.

I should've told the elders you smoked a pack of cigarettes and took all your clothes off and asked me to have sex with you and probably couldn't remember that part because you were so drunk.

See you Sunday.

Brother Miller came up to me before the next Thursday-night meeting.

"Gabe, could you join us in the back room after the meeting?"

Of course I couldn't say no. There was no need to be nervous since it was probably just a follow-up meeting regarding Jasmine.

She was talking to me at the meetings again. I wasn't sure if she was just being nice so I'd stick to my story that she wasn't drunk. She sat there hand in hand with Dan. Yuck.

"We're ready," Brother Miller said, and I walked into the back room followed by Dad and Brother Rodgers.

"Gabe, we need to ask you a few questions."

Someone had left a black comb at the Kingdom Hall and hadn't claimed it from the lost-and-found. It lay alone on one of the two empty shelves in the back room under piles of *Watchtower* publications.

Brothers Miller, Rodgers, and McMurphy were silent as they looked at their notes. Dad held his Bible and waited. I sat in the middle, my chair facing all of the elders and Dad. My brain wandered in the silence. A flash of Karen came into my mind. Maybe I wasn't clean. Maybe Jehovah had turned events to make the elders find out about Karen.

I started feeling guilty.

All right, I did it. I felt my cousin's breasts. They were *grrrreat.* Breasts are soft. Nipples are perky. I would touch every breast of every girl I ever met if I could. Karen used the word "tits." *Tits.* Squeeze. Caress. Cup. Feel. Touch. Lightly pinch. I couldn't wait to see Krissy's breasts.

"It's been brought to our attention that you stayed the night with a girl," Brother Miller started.

Huh?

I looked at Dad for help but God must've given him a divine slap on the back when he went into stern-elder-look mode, because he still had the weight of God furrowing his brow.

"I'm not sure, um, what?" I fumbled.

Brother Miller squinted his eyes and tried to read my soul. I had seen him do it during Bible studies and when he was giving a talk to the congregation, but never directly at me. Then he pulled out his reading glasses and went over his notes.

"Krissy?" he said.

Krissy?

Dad?

"Dad?"

"From Vacaville Congregation," Brother Miller clarified, then gave me the squint.

We did nothing technically wrong. I'd just give Jeff the key to his place until I could prove myself responsible to my parents again.

"You spent the night with her."

"No, she slept on the bed and I slept on the couch." The Holy Spirit of God ungripped my tongue. "We only kissed."

Dad's face registered confusion. Kissed?

"Brother Dagsland, according to the witness who brought this to our attention, Jeff wasn't home and you stayed alone with Krissy."

"Oh, that, yeah. I didn't tell Dad about that because I didn't want him to worry about Jeff or how Peter and Jin got home. Is everything okay?"

"You lied to your father?" Brother Miller caught that and squinted.

I tried to look away from Brother Miller to Brother Rodgers, who sucked in a breath through his teeth with his mouth open while keeping eye contact with me. I never noticed how straight his teeth were. I wondered if they were dentures. He closed his mouth before I could conduct further analysis.

"No, well, I didn't tell him."

"What we're concerned about is Krissy."

Okay?

"And you spent the night with her," Brother Miller continued to lead the elders' end of the conversation.

"Yeah. No. Well, not spend the night, like slept together. She slept in Jeff's room and I slept on the couch. She was sick. Something she must've eaten at the wedding. She threw up so I let her use the bathroom until she was done being sick. Then she went to bed."

In her bra and panties. Mmm.

"Was anyone else in the house when you stayed together?"

"Jin and Peter left. Jin got sick from the smell of the vomit. I was trying to be a gentleman and let her get over the food poisoning or whatever she had after the wedding."

I was ready to get up and go since we were all straightened out.

"Gabe, it is in fact a sin when a man and woman spend the night together in a house alone if they aren't married."

"No, I slept on the couch. She was sick. We only kissed for a minute." What were they not getting?

"It doesn't matter if sexual activity occurred or not; it's a sin."

Huh?

"Huh?"

While Brother Miller squinted to see my soul, Brother Rodgers said, "Spending the night with a woman alone whether or not sexual activity happened is a sin, and no one would ever know if anything sexual really did happen." Brother Rodgers took another breath through his teeth. This time it made a small whistling sound.

"I don't—"

"It's explained right here in the 1983 *Watchtower* that spending the night together is loose conduct, and from what we understand, you and Krissy spent the night together. Do you deny this?"

"No, she slept on Jeff's bed and I slept on the couch. I didn't—"

"Let me explain, Gabe. If your mom stayed the night at my house alone, your father could divorce her because it would seem obvious that she cheated on him. Do you understand the gravity of the situation?"

Yeah, but Mom would be asleep the whole time and all you would do is squint while you concentrated on masturbating in the bathroom.

I didn't reply. I was hoodwinked. Sucker punched. Confused.

"Okay," Brother Miller continued, "we're going to have to

arrange a judicial committee regarding this sin. Gabe, are you available on Wednesday night at 7:00 PM?"

I looked to Dad for help.

"Seven PM is fine," Dad replied for me.

"Gabe, can you excuse us for a few minutes? Your dad will be out shortly," Brother Miller said.

They were going to have a committee meeting about me and they didn't even know about Karen and how could just sleeping in the same apartment as Krissy be considered a sin?

Dad drove us home.

"I don't get it," I said.

Dad hadn't realized how serious my actions were either, but since it was considered loose conduct, I needed to have a judicial committee.

"Don't worry, Gabe. You're a good brother. They'll take that into consideration," he said.

That didn't feel like consolation. That felt like something you say to someone before you stick a horse needle into the bottom of their foot and say, "This will only hurt a little bit."

I got home and dialed Krissy's number. She answered the phone.

"Hi, Krissy. How are you?"

"Who is this?"

"It's Gabe."

Silence.

"I'm not supposed to talk to you," and she hung up the phone.

My heart raced.

Not supposed to talk to me? What the . . . ?

I called Ally. She and Jim hadn't been back to the Kingdom Hall yet, but they'd been back from their honeymoon for a few days.

Jim answered. "Hey, buddy," he said. He sounded different. Like he was sucking Ally's breasts every night. Like all he'd done since the wedding reception was rehydrate, make protein shakes, and jump back into bed.

"Yeah, Hawaii was great. We had a blast," he said and continued telling me about the ocean and the brunch they'd had with fresh fish at the top of a hotel on Waikiki where they could see Diamond Head and how they drove by Tom Selleck's house and it all went in one ear and out the other because I needed to speak to Ally.

"Ally," he yelled, and then asked, "How you been, man?"

"Eh," I said, and Ally grabbed the phone. She was probably naked.

"Hey, Gabe."

"Hey, Ally. I heard you had fun." I didn't want to hit her right away with the third degree.

"What happened with you and Krissy?" she asked.

Where was the billboard announcing that something had happened with Krissy and me?

"That's why I called. The elders talked to me last night about Krissy and I called her but she wouldn't talk to me."

"She doesn't want to get disfellowshipped."

"I didn't even know we could get disfellowshipped for just staying in the same house together. Did she tell you?"

"No," Ally said with a mumble.

"Who told?" I asked. "C'mon, Ally."

"You didn't hear it from me."

"Okay, okay."

"Camille."

That crooked-toothed cunt. How did she find out?

"It should be fine. All we did was kiss," I said.

"You didn't know she's engaged?" Ally asked.

"Uh, no?"

It turned out Camille and Jasmine didn't know either until Krissy called them, being new friends and everything, and spilled all the beans about how much she liked me but how her fiancé would break up with her if he found out and what should she do, blah, blah, blah. Krissy didn't know that anything she told Camille and Jasmine about me went straight to their mom, then to my mom, and this time to Dad and the elders.

I tried to picture who Krissy could be engaged to. Hopefully not a violent man.

"Why would Camille tell?"

"Her mom was out in evening service with Brother Miller and she just mentioned it. Then he called Camille and asked her everything she knew, so she told him."

If only to staple shut that mouth.

"Thanks, Ally."

"Are you going to be okay?" she asked. Her concern comforted me.

"Hang in there, bro," Jim called from the background.

What would Jesus do?

At the committee meeting Brothers Miller, Rogers, and McMurphy sat across from me, and Dad sat with me, facing the elders.

Since I was under eighteen and Dad was an active Jehovah's Witness, it was the organizational policy that he be present for the judicial committee.

"Krissy says you took her dress off. She admitted she was drunk, but"—Brother Rodgers flipped through his notes and made a small whistling sound while breathing through his clenched teeth—"according to your statement you said she had food poisoning. Did you know she was drunk?"

Shitfaced.

"Yeah," I said in a whisper.

"Why did you lie to us?"

It wasn't starting on the right foot.

"I, I didn't want her to get into trouble."

"Did you know she's engaged?" Brother McMurphy asked.

Twenty-eight-year-old Brother McMurphy. He was eager to get questions in that were relevant, probably so he could advance to more interesting cases of adultery and intentional sodomy and molestation. He looked like a young Phil Donahue and I almost expected him to put a microphone in my face after he asked the question.

"No, I didn't know she was engaged."

"Why did you take her dress off?"

I looked for his talk-show-host microphone.

"She asked me to. She had puke on it. I helped her while she was in the bathroom and she wanted to go to bed and get out of the big bridesmaid's dress."

"She asked you?" Brother Miller asked, then squinted for my answer.

"Yes."

The brothers looked down, all flipped through their notes.

It was like they used to be a synchronized swim team and now were elders in a judicial committee.

"Well, according to her, she doesn't remember asking you or what happened after her dress was off. Did you get into bed with her?"

"No."

"Hmm," Brother Miller squinted.

"Did you take your clothes off before getting into bed with her?"

"No, and I told you I didn't get into bed with her." Brother McMurphy was trying to trick me. He really wanted to get to some heavier cases and wanted to show the other elders that even though he was young, he was ready for cross-examination, for being a pathetic Sonny Crockett of the elders. I was getting pissed. My cooperation dissipated.

"She said you kissed," Brother Rodgers said.

"Yes, I told you that."

Dad made an uncomfortable shift in his folding chair.

"Did you insert your tongue in her mouth?"

Silence.

"Yes."

Dad breathed heavily.

"Did you touch her breasts?"

"No."

"She was in her underwear, though."

"Yes."

Ve have vays of making you talk.

I tried to figure Krissy's angle in this. Of course she was trying to keep her engagement together. Of course she'd slanted this to look like it was my fault.

Brother Rodgers sucked in his breath and said, "Were any of her breast or vaginal areas exposed when you kissed?"

It started to feel like an invasive doctor's exam.

"No."

"After you took her dress off when she was drunk, did you look under her clothes to see her vagina or breasts?" Brother McMurphy said. His wife was from Japan. She didn't speak too much English. If she did she probably would never have married him. She just bowed her head and said hi a lot.

I wondered if she kept saying hi when she and Brother McMurphy had sex.

"No, I didn't see her vagina and breasts." Were they getting off on this?

"Did any arousal occur when you kissed Krissy with your tongue?" Brother Miller took over.

Hell yes.

"No."

They all looked at each other. There was no way to prove that one, and I didn't feel like talking about erections in front of Dad.

So it went. They read me scriptures and continued to explain how serious it was that we spent the night together, how it was loose conduct, and a disfellowshipping offense.

They asked if I had anything to add. The Holy Spirit moved me to stand up for myself.

"I don't get it. I helped her. She was drunk and puking. I cleaned up her puke. Jin had to leave because it smelled so bad. I didn't ask her to follow us from the wedding reception. I pulled her hair out of the toilet. It was the right thing to do. It's what Jesus would've done."

By their faces, I knew that was the wrong thing to say. Brother Miller let out a gasp like I had just sinned against the Holy Spirit.

"She's the first girl I ever kissed. I'm seventeen. I know a lot of other Jehovah's Witnesses who have kissed more girls than me."

Talk to Francesco; he's kissed half the Witness girls in San Francisco, from what I understood.

"I know I shouldn't have kissed her. But it didn't go any further. We didn't commit a sin. She was sick and I let her sleep there. I fell asleep in the other room, watching TV. I, I think anyone, any

Jehovah's Witness, would've done what I did in that situation. I was trying to be a good guy."

I wanted for them to agree with me and to be exonerated.

"Brother Dagsland, Gabe, could you excuse us?" Brother Miller said without squinting, without looking further into my soul.

Dad and I waited in the Kingdom Hall auditorium. The door to the back room closed.

Dad asked for Jeff's shop key. I gave it to him. He said that he couldn't trust me and would put me on restriction until I could gain his trust again. I understood.

"Krissy was the first girl you ever kissed?" Dad asked.

"Yes," I confessed. I felt like crying. Julia and her secondhand clove-smoke kiss didn't feel like it counted as a first kiss since it went so horrid.

"Is that what we've taught you all of these years?" He couldn't meet my eyes. I had disgraced the family.

The elders called us back into the room for their decision. I secretly hoped they'd take away the privilege of giving talks at the theocratic ministry school because I hated giving those six-minute Bible talks on the Kingdom Hall stage.

When Brothers Miller, Rogers, and McMurphy disfellowshipped me, it didn't register.

The body of elders, acting under the direction of Jehovah's organization, had decided to disfellowship me.

Brother Miller, the chairman of the judicial committee, said a bunch of stuff after that. Write a letter after one year when you feel you're capable of being reinstated, and other rules for the disfellowshipped.

I just stared at Brother Rodgers' hair. I had never realized it was a comb-over. I tried to figure out how far back his hairline went.

". . . you can't talk to anyone who's a Jehovah's Witness, you can't . . ."

Brother Miller. How many times had we preached together? How many stupid jokes had he told me? Now I couldn't talk to him or Peter or Sister Feeney, even though I didn't care about that gossiping, meddling old fart with runs in her nylons.

". . . and we urge you to study the . . ."

I looked over to the comb that I'd seen earlier in the lost-and-found and decided I needed a comb. I acted surprised when I saw it, like I was thinking, *Ah, finally, I've been looking all over for you* . . . And instead of putting the comb in my pocket I grasped it fondly and ran my fingernail against its teeth.

". . . do you understand what we've told you?"

I felt like saying *No*. I wish Krissy and I had sex twenty times and she felt my balls and I played with her breasts and this is the comb I've been looking for because I combed her blond pubic hairs before I stuck my penis in her and she's pregnant but I advised her to get an abortion.

That! That felt like sin. Not what actually happened, which was a whole lot of nothing. One big monster of a technicality. But since I didn't think it was a big deal, even after they read me some scriptures from the Bible and interpreted what I did as sin, I still didn't get it. How could I be repentant when I didn't sin? If Uncle Jeff had showed up that night like he was supposed to, this wouldn't have even been happening. But he didn't, and she slumbered, and I slept, and my cousin Karen's breasts were never even brought up, which I decided was best kept a secret at that point.

Everything was confidential. The three elders couldn't discuss with anyone, even the other elders, what happened behind those closed doors. The rest of the elders and the congregation would only find out the decision, that I was disfellowshipped.

As Dad and I left the room, I wondered if I should've lied and explained how wrong I was and how it all came clear to me in a dream about the disgrace I'd brought upon my family and the congregation.

Announcements of disfellowshippings were scheduled for Thursday-night meetings at the Kingdom Hall. Every week right after we sang the second Kingdom Melody there was a talk called "Announcements" in which a ministerial servant, a junior elder, would read letters from the governing body at the Watchtower Bible and Tract Society, remind the congregation to fill out their time slips to keep track of how many hours they'd gone out preaching, to pick up their latest *Watchtowers*, and stuff like that. If someone was disfellowshipped, the brother doing the "Announcements" part would call the head of the judicial committee to come to the stage and announce who was disfellowshipped.

"Brother Miller has an announcement to make."

That's all the junior elder said after the Kingdom Melody song. The audience went stone quiet. They knew whenever an elder was brought up to the stage before the "Announcements" that it was usually to tell the congregation about a disfellowshipping.

Brother Miller walked up and kept a sullen straight face, something he must've learned to do at the elders' school they had to attend twice a year. They probably had to perfect the look in the mirror.

"The Millbrae Congregation elders, under the direction of God and his Holy Spirit, have decided that Gabriel Dagsland is disfellowshipped. If anyone has questions on how to treat a disfellowshipped person, you can approach me after the meeting."

The shortened version would have been "You know Gabe? He is now a piece of shit that you don't want to step on or go near."

When he made the announcement everyone kept their head very still and I pressed a tooth of that comb in my pocket between my thumbnail and thumb until it bled a little, diverting my hurt so I wouldn't cry.

I'd have no choice but to go to every single meeting, Tuesday, Thursday, Sunday, while nobody acknowledged or talked to me. I didn't want to die at Armageddon. I wanted back. I wanted to talk to my only family and friends I had ever known.

Jasmine walked by and kept her head down so we wouldn't make eye contact. Ally sat in her seat and talked with Arlene. She caught me with her eyes and then looked away.

I should've fondled every woman's breasts in the Kingdom Hall before I got disfellowshipped.

I was about to get up from my seat after the meeting and leave when Peter and his family passed me on the way out. Peter's arm was freshly broken from another skateboarding accident. He had accidents all the time. He was fearless. And his stepfather, Terry, had replaced Bubbles the spoon with severe groundings, taking everything out of his room and leaving only a tape recorder and cassettes of Bible dramas, which he had to listen to over and over again. He'd recite them to us whenever we were skating ramps.

"Hotep, tell Moses I will not let the Israelites go and ask them who is this Jehovah that I should free the Jews?"

Peter sounded exactly like the Jehovah's Witness actors at the Watchtower Society who were commissioned to play those parts on tape, and we'd laugh so hard, not only because Peter could imitate every actor from every Bible drama cassette released by the Jehovah's Witnesses, but at the absurdity of his lengthy and frequent punishments.

He'd drink a whole bottle of cold medicine or vanilla extract or anything with alcohol or codeine in it to numb himself before going back into the room of Bible drama tapes. And when he skated he'd do handplants and 360s on the ramp; he'd grind on the copping and fall flat on his back and would limp home in agony to find out he'd fractured his ankle or that his knee had fluid in it that needed to be extracted immediately.

He was my hero in that regard. I was scared of everything. Whenever I'd skate a ramp, I would gyrate a little back and forth, then let someone else take a turn. I couldn't drop in, I couldn't get to the vertical, I couldn't even do a 180. Peter did it all and he paid the price, but he learned and got to the next level. He was more of a man than I could ever be.

And I couldn't talk to him anymore.

I couldn't even listen to him stutter when he talked about his real dad. I thought about the times he pooped his pants when we were kids. I wouldn't have cared if he still pooped them if only I could've talked to him. If he tried to talk to me and was caught, he could get disfellowshipped.

From then on, I stared straight ahead at the meetings, listening to the hollow sound in my head reminding me that I was being punished by God himself. Maybe God was actually getting back at me for being drunk with Karen and feeling her breasts. God knew all. He was just. Maybe that was his justice for me?

Dad tried to get me to appeal the decision but I couldn't go through four more hours of drilling and interrogation and trick questions to make sure nothing had happened between Krissy and me. That we'd only slept in the same place was in itself supposedly a sin. That alone could be reason enough for Jehovah to kill me at Armageddon with the rest of the wicked world.

School was even harder than the meetings. Camille saw me in the hall after I was announced disfellowshipped and turned her face to the wall. I looked to the ground. What I would've given even just to take her to class.

Jin saw me at my locker and hung back until I got my books out. Then when I walked toward my English class he continued walking forward.

At lunch Jin, Peter, Jared, and Tom played Hacky Sack.

"Hey, Dags," Jared called and kicked the Hacky Sack in my direction. I let it drop and threw it back to Jared. Peter and Jin kept their eyes on the ground.

"Not today," I said, feeling like I was about to cry.

"What's his problem?" Tom said.

Even my few worldly friends were being cut off because Peter and Jin also hung out with them.

I hadn't realized how often I passed the Witnesses who'd set up the literature booth at school. I saw them all the time in the hallways. We'd always said hi, but no more. Lunchtime was now alone time. Isolation. Just like the meetings.

Alone.

We had an open campus so I could've walked to the Burlingame Plaza for lunch, but walking alone would've been even more embarrassing. Disfellowshipped and pathetic.

I walked into the school library voluntarily for the first time in my life. To hide. But I had to go past the Bible literature table to get to the library. Jennifer, Kim, John, and David all stopped what they were doing and stared into the distance like they were statues, so there wouldn't be any eye contact with me.

In the library, Stan, the half-blind guy in a wheelchair, drooled in the corner. Eddie the midget had a pocket calculator out and solved difficult trigonometry equations. During fifth and sixth period he went to Stanford to get an early start on his education to become a doctor. The librarian, the wrinkled failed poet, the queen of the *shhh,* stamped books that were written by others, not her.

In the library I was lost. I went to the 809.02–812.04 aisle and pretended to look at the books. I pulled out a book by Pablo Neruda. A poet. I walked to a table and copied a love poem out of the book. After the lunch bell rang I was tardy to my next class because I was slipping the anonymous poem into Camille's locker.

I was sure that would give her a thrill.

Mom slept and I watched TV. I heard Peter and Jin skateboarding in the cemented courtyard of our building. I could hear Jin breathing heavily. He was continuing to gain weight. His food addiction was a curse to his intestines.

Dad came home from work at 5:30. Mom got up and put three frozen dinners into the oven. The house had a silence to it. An emptiness that wasn't there before I was disfellowshipped.

I had to wait in the front room while Dad and Mom prayed over the food. I could enter the kitchen to sit down with them when I heard Dad saying, "In Jesus' name, amen." Being disfellowshipped meant I couldn't pray with my family. The only reason I was still able to live at home was because I was under eighteen.

Every bite of food felt loud. Loud against the silence. The silence that was a good friend to my loneliness.

"I'm going to listen to Kingdom Melodies when I go to sleep from now on," I said to break the awful silence.

"That's a start," Dad said.

Mom kept eating.

As my immediate family, they could talk to me, not about spiritual stuff, but we lived together. If I'd been over eighteen and Dad didn't kick me out of the house, he would lose his privilege of being an elder and maybe get in some trouble himself.

"And I'm going to make sure to study harder for every meeting," I continued.

"I hope so," Dad said.

"That's good to hear, sweetie," Mom said.

We continued to eat.

"Alan, we got a postcard from Jeff today. He's in Paris. He says it's beautiful and he'll be back in a few months."

"Did he say what he was doing in Paris?" I asked.

"Here's the postcard." She handed me a photo of the Eiffel Tower and smiled. "In the new system, after Armageddon, we can go to Paris."

I pictured Jeff driving a motorcycle on the freeways of Paris.

"It's probably good Jeff is out of the country. Sometimes he's not the best association," Dad said, looking at me.

I realized I missed Jeff a lot. And he wasn't an active Jehovah's Witness, so he could've talked to me.

I went back to the 811 aisle in the library the next day at lunch break and opened a few more poetry books.

One poet wrote about trees and nature. Boring. If I hated a book I'd put it in backward, white paper facing out instead of the spine. I figured it was the least I could do for the high school librarian, giving her a break from stamping due dates on books.

Then I found Kerouac. I read his poem "Mexican Loneliness" and all of a sudden in my head, I started thinking like a poet.

I checked the Kerouac book out of the library and received the passive-aggressive due-date stamp from the failed wrinkled ex-poet.

Instead of going to the library the next day during lunch, I sat in the courtyard among the well-adjusted, socializing teens with my notepad and book. I'd read one of Kerouac's poems and then observe. Kerouac was all about the observation, the taking in of life, grooving on it, then writing about it. I watched girls in short skirts. I watched jocks. I wrote poetry. Then I slipped the poems into the lockers of people I didn't know. My poetry of observations of people while watching them during lunch break. They could read them at their leisure. Sometimes they were sexual; sometimes they explained the mastery of the proper caressing of a breast. Other poems were hostile. "You Make Me Sick"–type titles would flow out of me. I left one of those in Peter's locker just to mess with his head.

I found out Kerouac had written a book called *Big Sur*, about him and his friends starting the Beat generation. I asked the wrinkly librarian about the Beats and her face lit up.

"You have to read *On the Road*," she said.

It took me a week to read *On the Road*. I walked differently in school. I held my head higher. At the mall I bought a Charlie Parker cassette. Dad was surprised I was choosing such clean music—jazz, better than rock, which was influenced by Satan. If you played some of those records backward, Satan would leave messages, subliminal messages, but jazz and classical were pure music, Dad said.

I be-bopped around school. Charlie Parker's music played in my head. I started to wear my wingtips to school. I found some photos of Kerouac with the help of the librarian, who told me her first name was Flo, short for Florence, and I begged my parents to buy me flannel shirts and khaki pants. I'd tuck the flannels into my pants and strut with my wingtips.

People began to notice.

"What are you reading? Ker-ook?" they'd ask.

"It's pronounced Care-Oh-Whack."

"Cool."

Then I found out about banned books. I didn't know some schools had even banned *Huckleberry Finn*. I wished our school did; that book bored me. The list also had books they didn't have in our high school library, either.

I asked Flo about *Ulysses*, *Canterbury Tales*, and *Lady Chatterley's Lover*. She said the school didn't have those books, but the public library had them.

I asked if she liked any of the ones I had underlined. She looked into my eyes and I saw what she'd looked like thirty years ago in college. She was a bombshell. She was a hot young poet. Her blue eyes must've knocked the guys on their asses.

She looked at the paper and underlined *Tropic of Cancer* and gave it back to me and turned around to her regular librarian duties.

At the Millbrae Public Library I brought Henry Miller's book from the stacks to the librarian so she could stamp a due date on it. She looked me up and down as she examined my library card. It was like the contents of the book were so graphic she wasn't sure if she should ask to see an ID.

Walking down the street with a book in my hand that wasn't a Bible felt electric. I could hold my head up in my regular street clothes, with literature that had nothing to do with the Watchtower Society. Feeling great even though I was sentenced to social solitary confinement by the elders.

Then I saw her. Julia. The clove-smoking relative of a Jehovah's Witness. Who'd shared a tender moment with me and whose tobacco breath would forever be imprinted in my head like a nicotine stain.

I crossed the street, *Tropic of Cancer* in my hand, focusing on her tasty lips.

"Julia," I said.

"Yes?"

"How have you been?"

Her friends looked at her, then at me.

"Good . . . you seem familiar. What's your name?"

"Gabe?" My voice cracked a bit. Her eyes made the connection.

"The Jehovah's Witness party," she said like she had just won a game-show quiz.

I nodded, relieved.

"I stopped that nonsense," she said. "Thank God I never became a Jehovah's Witness."

I stepped closer.

"It's great to see you," I said. Phone number? Secret date? Cloves?

"Cool. See you," she said as she walked away. Her friends were giggling.

I read about twenty pages of the book, which was all I needed to read to know that this would be my favorite book in the world. Among other things, it gave me much appreciation for the beauty of the cunt. Cunt: c-u-n-t. The word flirted in my sightlines.

All those years of reading every *Watchtower* and *Awake!* and the other publications from the Watchtower Bible and Tract Society had made me hate reading because it was so boring, but it had also prepared me to read real books, which were a lot more enjoyable to read than articles on the fall of Jerusalem in 586 B.C.E. and why 1914 had been the beginning of the last days leading to Armageddon.

I asked for more hours at my busboy job at Remington's. Remington's was part of the El Rancho hotel, so sometimes the waiters let me take care of room-service orders and keep the whole tip. Another great thing about having your social life ripped out from you like a jugular vein is all the money you can save by not going out with friends. Six more months and I figured I would have enough money to get a decent car.

"Six Heinekens and a ham and cheese sandwich cut in half," the lady from room 224 ordered.

It was 11:00 PM. Room service went until 2:00 AM. I had the place to myself and was doing my first real shift as a room-service waiter. Easy money. I sat around reading, and when the phone rang, whatever the order, 18 percent of the bill would automatically go into my bank account.

I also had the key to the bar, since the bar usually closed with the restaurant at 10:00 PM. I ordered two more Heinekens for room 228, even though room 228 hadn't ordered beer. The bar kept strict inventory and I didn't want to get fired like Guillermo did when they found out he'd stolen a bottle of champagne on his shift. Working at Remington's was the only place I didn't feel like a misfit or disfellowshipped, and I was excited to talk to any foreigner who stopped over in San Francisco from Australia or Europe and wanted to stay a few days and see the sights of the Bay Area.

I drank part of one of the beers while getting the tray ready for room 224. Salt, pepper, utensils. I had learned while working on a few room-service orders on other shifts that forgetting to include a packet of mustard meant a mad sprint back to the restaurant to retrieve it.

The lady opened the door. She was in her bra. Guillermo, who used to be the full-time room-service waiter, had told me there were times when men or women would answer the door naked and you just had to pretend it was normal and that it happened all the time.

A lot different from door-to-door preaching.

I pretended it was normal and she asked me to put the tray on the table in front of the television. I caught a glimpse of another girl in the bathroom. She was naked and put on a robe while she came out and gave me a knowing smirk. I smiled back.

Back at the restaurant as I put the cash into the register all I could think about was the curve of the girl's hips to her butt as she put the robe on and greeted me. IT was hard in my pants. I thought about masturbating in the bathroom with the fresh thought of the lady in the bra and the nude girl in my mind. They were either sisters or friends. The lady in the bra looked a bit older, and her hair was feathered. She was clinging to the Farah Fawcett look while the robe girl had her hair in a bob, streaked with blond highlights.

The room-service phone rang and startled me from my erotic thoughts.

"Is this the room-service waiter?" the lady asked.

"Yes, what can I get for you?"

"You just came to our room with the beer and sandwich and we were wondering"—I heard a giggle from the background—"if you'd like to come back and help us finish our beers."

My penis throbbed, but I knew God was looking down on me. It was a test. I knew I could die at Armageddon for sure because they were worldly girls and would want to have sex. My mind raced and vigilance won out.

"Thanks, but I have a lot of homework to do," and I slammed the phone down and ran to the men's urinal.

It took less than a minute from the first tug.

I had been disfellowshipped for nine months. I went to every meeting with my parents and had three months before I could apply for reinstatement.

Time went by fast, since my job at Remington's and literary fascination took over the gaping hole of socializing.

There was an article in the school paper about the poems I was leaving in lockers. The paper published one I'd left for Lorie, which explained the delicate fabric of a cotton tank top and how only a perfectly framed woman could do it justice. The school paper asked that the anonymous poet make himself known. I was tempted. But I'd left poems in all of the Jehovah's Witnesses lockers, and that would've meant I was trying to associate with them, which would prolong my disfellowshipping. None of those were personal or divulged anything that would point to me.

Like the poem I wrote about a crooked-toothed traitor. I put that in Anne-Marie's locker, not Camille's. Anne-Marie had straight teeth so I knew she'd see it for its artistic value and not take offense to it.

I had a hard time going to the bathroom at school. The toilets were always filthy. I was scared who would come into the bathroom—if I would involuntarily fart and walk out to a group of kids laughing. Since I was the only high school kid wearing wingtips to school, they'd look under the stall and know it was me.

The misfit.

The man without friends.

Disfellowshipped. Weird. Farting freak.

But the diarrhea was going to push its way out no matter what, so I walked into the bathroom. No one was there. I entered a stall and let it out. My bowels burst forth and I flushed the toilet to try to cover over the noise my butt was making.

The bathroom door opened and I tried to hold it in for a minute. I tensed. I tried not to moan from the cramps, waiting to hear someone peeing in a urinal. Nothing. Maybe someone had opened the door and decided not to come in. I counted to ten. At seven I gave up and let the rest out.

"You really stink, Dags," I heard from behind the door. I sucked back in and flushed. It was Peter.

"Hi?"

"What did you eat?"

I let the rest out but it was mostly farts, then came out of the stall.

"Why are you talking to me?" I asked.

"Wash your hands," he said, and I washed.

He gave me a hug.

"I can't take it anymore. I miss you," he said.

"How's Jin?"

"Getting fatter."

"I noticed."

"How are you?" Peter asked. He meant it. No one had asked me that for a while. Not a lot of people talked to me in general.

"Shitty," I said.

"Me too."

"Yeah, but you're not the one who's disfellowshipped," I snapped.

He looked at me.

"I'm sorry," I said.

"It's weird not talking to you."

"I know."

Charles, a sophomore, came into the bathroom. He looked at the stalls, then looked at us and walked out.

"What happened to Krissy?" I asked.

"She got publicly reproved and is married."

Bitch.

"Did you see who she married?"

"Yeah, this older guy. She's fat now. I saw pictures of them."

Of course she's fat.

"How's Jasmine and Dan?"

"You still like Jasmine?" Peter asked.

"What are you talking about?" I had only told Jeff.

"C'mon, friends know."

"Yeah," I shrugged.

"After she got publicly reproved for getting drunk, her and Dan decided to wait at least one year before they get married."

"That's why he hasn't been to our Kingdom Hall for a while?"

"Yep."

Opportunity? Jasmine, how do you feel about disfellowshipped brothers a year younger than you?

"Do your Bible drama thing for me?"

"Why?" he asked.

"I didn't realize how much I missed hearing you do your imitations."

He spouted off just like Moses, like the Jehovah's Witness actor from the Watchtower Society did on the Bible drama tape, when Moses made water come out of a rock after the Israelites were complaining in the wilderness. I cracked up.

"Can you come back soon?" he asked.

"Next month I'm sending in the letter," I said.

"I don't ever want to not be able to talk to you again," he said. "Let's promise if either of us ever gets d-d-d-disfellowshipped in the future, we'll s-s-still meet secretly."

That was the first time I had ever heard him stutter without mentioning his sperm dad.

"I could meet you at the garbage cans with a Nerf football tonight," I offered.

"I'm grounded. Next Thursday after school. I'll go skateboarding and we could meet there."

"Cool."

"I'll try to make us hamburgers so we can just hang out and talk."

"Sounds good."

He left and I waited two minutes and left after him so no Jehovah's Witnesses could suspect we talked in the bathroom and get him in trouble.

"What's up, dork?" Karen said when I answered the phone.

"Karen?"

"Yeah, who did you think?"

"I don't . . . How are you? Where are you?"

"Eh, I'm the same, and you?"

"Same."

"I heard you got disfellowed or something."

"How did you know that?"

"Did they find out you felt my tits?"

"No!"

"Good, because Mom would freak out."

Uh, yeah.

"Wait, did you feel another girl's tits?"

"No, it was something stupid. Can we stop talking about . . ." and then I whispered, "tits?"

"I'm coming back to California," she said.

"Your mom keeps calling Dad. She's really upset. Why did you run away?"

"It's not running away when you're over eighteen," she replied. "There's a guy I'm meeting out there. He's going to take care of me for a while until I get my feet on the ground."

"Your boyfriend?"

"He thinks so, yeah. I guess. How's your love life?"

"Shitty."

"You're a Jehovah; why did I even ask?"

Fucking Karen.

"When are you coming out?"

"You can't tell anyone, okay?"

"Yeah."

"I'm already here."

"What? You don't want to call your mom and at least tell her you're okay?"

"Fuck her and Ernie," she said. It was the first time I heard her refer to her dad by his first name.

"Did something happen?"

"Can we not talk about it?"

"Do you want to meet?" I craved association. Companionship. From anyone. Even my psycho cousin with the only real breasts I had seen and touched.

"You have to come up to San Francisco. If I go to Millbrae your parents and their Jehovah narcs might see me."

I arranged to meet her on Saturday. Mom and Dad had started trusting me again, and I was going to be eighteen really soon anyway. I reassured them that I knew the bus routes and explained that I wanted to go book shopping. Since I had been studying for all my meetings they were fine if I read "secular" material as long as it wasn't riddled with sex or violence. They didn't read anything not published by the Watchtower Bible and Tract Society, so they never checked up on the stuff I brought home. I wanted to buy *Notes of a Dirty Old Man* by Bukowski, so I wasn't lying.

I met Karen at City Lights, the bookstore on Kerouac Alley in North Beach. She was taller. Skinnier. Her breasts almost seemed smaller than I remembered them. Her hair was dreadlocked and she had a nose ring.

"I would've never recognized you."

"You grew up, too." She looked at my wingtips, then messed up my hair with both of her hands.

She was staying in North Beach, in a room above the Condor. The afternoon prostitutes hustled on Broadway. Karen said hi to one as we walked down the street.

We played video games at the arcade. We didn't talk, just got used to our new selves. Her new look. I felt kind of proud to be with her. She looked tough.

"You should figure out a way to stay the night. We could go see some bands," she said.

She told me about Mabuhay Gardens and the Rock on Broadway.

About Black Flag and how Henry Rollins, the lead singer, had signed her *Slip It In* record.

She had been in town for a month before contacting me. I felt a little betrayed.

We ate at a deli. She took her hoodie off and I saw bruises on her arms.

"Is that from your boyfriend?" Automatically thinking about Laura and Ernie and how her father felt her up. All of a sudden I wanted to kill Ernie.

"No, it's from slam pits," she said like I was an idiot.

"When I felt your, you know, uh . . ." I started.

"My tits." She was bold.

"Yeah, you said your dad . . . did he . . ."

"No, Dad never touched me. I just wanted you to feel me up that night. It was really important to me so I lied to you. I don't know why."

"That's pretty fucked up."

"Wanting you to touch my tits that night was pretty fucked up anyway."

She was slam dancing at punk shows. She was dangerous. She was different, yet the same. She was someone to hang out with.

We decided to meet again the next Saturday, since I had to get to work by 7:00 PM.

We walked to Stockton Street in Chinatown. "The 30 bus will take you right to the train station," Karen said.

It was getting dark.

"I'm glad you're here."

"Go home," she said with a slug to my arm. I watched her walk with attitude back toward North Beach.

She was excited that Agent Orange was in town and playing the On Broadway that night.

I sat quietly at the Kingdom Hall on Sunday, waiting for the Bible discourse to begin. Not allowed to talk to or acknowledge anyone. I was a plague. No one came near me as I sat in my seat.

A whiff of strawberries entered my nose. Jasmine still used the same shampoo she had used since she was eleven. I turned around, cautiously, slightly. She was two rows behind me, laughing with Sister Sorisho.

I closed my eyes and traveled to a time when we were in the back seat of a car, when her nylons rubbed up against my slacks. Return visits with Jasmine ruled. Now she was almost nineteen and in her prime of life. On her way to becoming a Mrs. I read literature, and she didn't. She couldn't know that I was reading Henry Miller and Charles Bukowski. She wouldn't understand that I was coming to terms with the animal inside me, with the man I was becoming. The man who craved.

The man who had no clue how to satisfy his cravings without secretly sinning. Masturbating. I was feeling less guilty every time I did it. God gave it to me. He put my penis within reaching range of my hand.

It was spiritual for me, though I'd probably stop when I was reinstated. My social needs were being met by stroking my penis. I'd be approved again soon to make it through Armageddon and live forever.

Would Jack Kerouac and Henry Miller be brought back to life in the new system? The men who understood what I was going through. The men who let their animals out and ravaged what they needed.

The End was around the corner. Armageddon was close because the Watchtower Society said that all the time. I needed to get back "into the flock," the congregation. I needed God and the elders' approval.

Peter brought the hamburgers as promised. They were lukewarm by the time he got to the area by the garbage cans outside of the apartment complex. The spot of our earlier Nerf football terrorism.

"I want to kill Terry," Peter said.

I guess he'd stopped calling his stepfather "dad."

"I've always wanted to kill Terry," I said.

That Vietnam War veteran bastard. He clung to being a Jehovah's Witness like it was the military. Like he was sergeant. He lorded it over Peter. Probably since Peter was really almost a man, there was more tension, testosterone-fueled tension in that house.

I ate the hamburger. There was mayo on it. I felt like scraping it off but I didn't want to show any ingratitude to Peter for hanging out with me, for breaking bread with me, the disfellowshipped one.

"And my mom just keeps taking his c-c-c-crap. She never stands up for me. She never stands up for herself," Peter continued.

He paused and ate. I was finished with my hamburger and drank the Fresca he brought.

Peter told me how he was grounded and left alone in the room with only Bible study books and no tape-recorded Bible dramas. Terry heard him imitating the tapes and thought he was mocking the organization. He performed an aikido move he learned in the army on Peter, bending his thumb backward until all Peter could do was kneel to the floor and cry. His mom did nothing but continued drinking her vodka.

"Has he ever done anything like that to you before?" I asked.

"No, usually he hits me with a belt or something. If I don't cry he uses the metal end. A few months ago, the metal end didn't even make me cry. I laughed. I looked at him and laughed. Then he kneed me in the balls."

"Fuck."

"Yeah, f-f-fuck," Peter replied. "I've been grounded a lot lately, as you can tell."

"I'm sorry, man."

"I'm not. One of these days I'm going to kill him. Mom will stop drinking and won't be as depressed. She'd probably be happier with him gone." She was going through vodka like it was water. Jesus turned water into wine and Peter's mom into a catatonic drunk.

"Peter, what about the consequences?"

The look in his eyes scared me, like he was really planning on murdering Terry.

"I don't care if I get disfellowshipped for it. It'll be worth it."

"But, dude, you'll get thrown in jail."

We sat in silence. We'd grown up with the discipline that happened inside the congregation and tried so hard to avoid it so we could keep talking to our family and friends; it was easy to forget that there could be consequences outside of the congregation and in society.

"He just cracked your thumb and you couldn't move?"

"He said it was aikido or something. He learned it in the army."

"I want to know how to do that."

"I don't ever want to feel that pain again," Peter said.

It had been so long since we could actually talk to each other, we made sure to cut any small talk and go straight for the heavy stuff.

I spilled my guts to him about Jasmine. Stuff he already knew, so I was just confirming it. And I told him about Karen, about the night I felt her breasts. He was totally grossed out, but then he asked if he could meet her.

I never thought of setting Peter up with my cousin because she's worldly.

"I'll tell you before I kill him," Peter said.

"You're not going to kill Terry."

"If I can figure out a way to get away with it I will," he said as he picked up his skateboard. "Gotta go. Wanna meet tomorrow?"

"Sure."

I sat at the garbage cans, smelling the refuse and thinking about the heavy stuff of life and death while other eighteen-year-olds were thinking of college and getting laid and drinking at keg parties.

Jeff gave up even trying to be a Jehovah's Witness. He lived in Paris for most of the year playing bass for a cabaret act. It was good money and when he came home he looked like a changed man. No more rock T-shirts and sneakers. He dressed in boots, his hair was long and slicked back, and he didn't shave as much.

"Paris rules," he told me.

He was pissed to hear I had been disfellowshipped and was sorry he couldn't have been in the United States to hang out with me when all my other friends abandoned me. I told him about everything I was reading. Kerouac, Bukowski, and stuff. He was impressed and he liked my wingtips.

"You're halfway to Paris already, Gabe," he said.

"What were the girls like?" I asked.

"I'll tell you in a few years."

The phone rang in his apartment and he answered.

"Hello? *Ah, salut; ça va? Oui. Ah, oui, je comprends. Oui, ce soir. Ciao.*"

Wow.

"Who was that?"

"One of the dancers in the show I worked for; her sister is an au pair living in San Mateo. I promised to meet her and bring gifts from her family."

"French sounds cool. How much do you know?"

"I had to learn fast. Nobody really spoke English, especially in the part of Paris I stayed at. It was either Arabic or French. It started to click. My friend Pascal helped me."

Pascal. I wanted a friend in France named Pascal.

"Can I stay here tonight?" I asked.

"Sure, double-check with Alan. I don't want him up my ass."

I never thought of Dad being up Jeff's ass.

"Dad said it was cool. I'm not really going to stay here though. I'm staying with Karen in San Francisco."

"Laura's kid?"

"Yeah."

"She's here?"

I forgot I wasn't supposed to tell anyone, but Jeff didn't feel like anyone and he promised to keep it a secret. He even gave me some money and told me to show Karen a good time. I think he felt guilty that I was still disfellowshipped and he hadn't been around for me when I needed him most.

Karen and I stood in line at Wolfgang's to see Verbal Abuse, Fang, and English Dogs. I tried to keep from shaking with anticipation. The energy was thick in the line. Karen knew a few of the punk rockers.

After we got our hands stamped we left the club with Jimmy Thorn. I'm pretty sure that wasn't his real last name. He was twenty-one and bought us a pint of vodka. Karen and I went around the corner in front of a church and poured out half of our Cokes to make room for the vodka.

The ocean wind blew down Columbus. I had my wingtips on, and the cold nighttime San Francisco wind blew through my jacket to my bones. The vodka went down with a bit of pain, then felt smooth. Karen always figured out how to get alcohol.

"Let's go to your place," I said, starting to shiver in the cold.

"Can't. We're staying at Beth's place tonight."

"What happened?"

"That guy who set me up in a place to live, the fucker who thought he was my boyfriend, turned out he was trying to be a pimp, but he's such a fucking amateur. I found out he's targeting the punk girls and boys. A few people work for him but get strung out on shit really fast. He takes his boys and girls to Polk Street. Beth said I could crash with her for a few weeks."

"Did you . . . ?"

"God, no. I'm not a fucking whore."

Just a girl who showed her tits to her cousin when she was younger.

Walking down Columbus, we passed restaurants and cafés.

If she wasn't my cousin and she was a Jehovah's Witness she'd be a catch. For a moment I thought of walking hand in hand with her around the Ring at the district assembly, showing her off to aching sixteen- and seventeen-year-olds.

We walked by a café called the Steps of Rome on our way back to the show. The vodka buzz was pleasant and settling in.

Then I saw her. My heart, struck with an arrow, broke open. Dizzy, slight blackout. Regained consciousness and Karen thought I stumbled and started to fall because of the alcohol.

I'd seen and had been ignored by Jasmine at the meetings at the Kingdom Hall for almost a year. She was with Dan and Jim and Ally and Camille. There were two other guys with them, obviously Jehovah's Witnesses, who looked like they were vying for Camille's attention.

I wanted to duck. To run. To take an alternate route to the club.

"What's wrong?" Karen noticed.

"I—"

Then I looked at Karen with her dreads and her nose ring.

"Let me put my arm around you and get coffee. There's someone I want to make jealous."

Karen jumped in the air and took a couple of skips.

"An adventure, I love it. I feel like we're in *Ferris Bueller's Day Off.*"

We went into the Steps of Rome and ordered. Out of the corner of my eye I saw Dan notice me first. Then they all took turns looking at us, me with Karen, our arms around each other.

"Which one?" Karen asked.

"The table back there. Black hair. She's the darkest one with the uptight-looking white guy."

"Does she go to your school?"

"She graduated. She's a Witness."

"Why don't you say some—... oh yeah. The disfellowed thing." She grabbed my butt for extra credit, trying to help me make Jasmine jealous.

"Uh, cousin?" I said.

"Just fucking with them," and she brought her hand up again over my shoulder.

As I ordered coffee, I finished the vodka and Coke. I felt great. Punk rock show great. And there was also an urge to go over to that table and spill my guts to everyone there: Jasmine, I think I love you. Dan, can I take Jasmine away from you for a minute? Oh, the urge was there.

We got coffee and sat. The Witnesses. My former friends and my love interest kept their eyes averted, just like when Krissy made me breakfast in her bra and panties and I tried my best to keep eye contact with her eyes, not her milky-white exposed skin.

"Fuck this," Karen said and walked over to the table.

No, do not tell Jasmine. Oh God, no. Karen. Fuck. You're going to ruin everything. Karen didn't know I was on my way back into the congregation.

She spoke loud enough so I could hear her. "You Jehovahs call yourselves Christian? And you can't even talk to Gabe? Your friend. Is that something Jesus would do?" and she walked away.

My heart pounded. None of them turned around to look at me.

"Fuck them. Let's go." Karen grabbed my hand and led me to the club.

Yeah. Fuck them. I had a buzz. I was meeting people called Jimmy Thorn and Kaos Kelly and Lucian. I wanted to change my name. I introduced myself to her friends at the club as Dags. Karen didn't know my friends sometimes called me that.

At the show the first band played and punkers slam danced. They were scary. I jumped up and down on the side of the stage away from the slam pit.

Karen talked with Beth, whom we met up with at the club and who turned out to be really sweet. She was from Greece, and she and her girlfriend had just moved to San Francisco. She showed me her tattoo of the Black Flag logo on her shoulder. Her girlfriend was rich and didn't like punk rock, but they loved each other and had been going out for three years. I think Beth was the first real lesbian I'd ever met. Then I wondered if Karen could be a lesbian.

Talking to Beth and Karen and the other punks, just talking to people without worrying if they were Jehovah's Witnesses or not, or if they were observing my actions in case they needed to tell the elders of any possible sins, was liberating.

After the show, Beth hailed a cab. We went through the Broadway tunnel and stopped at Divisidero and Broadway. There was a doorman at their old apartment building. He said hi to Beth and us. Beth said, "Hey, Gilbert," and we went up to Angela and Beth's place. It was on the third floor. My clothes were wet from jumping around and getting beer spilled on me. We all smelled like smoke.

I looked out the window. I saw the Golden Gate Bridge lit up in the night, partially engulfed in fog. I saw Alcatraz. I heard fog horns from ships in the distance.

Angela didn't look like a punk or even a lesbian. She looked like a kindergarten teacher with an understanding quality about her. An openness you need to be a good school teacher. Approachable.

And she had a Greek nose just like Beth.

I was with Greeks. The Apostle Paul preached to the Greeks. Lesbians. Lesbos. Isn't that Greek?

Angela gave me a blanket and pillow and I made a bed for myself on the couch. There were no curtains on the windows. Beth and Angela slept together. Karen went to bed in the guest room. I fell asleep to the panoramic view of San Francisco.

The next morning we ate breakfast at a small table in the kitchen, looking at the stunning view of Sausalito. Beth and Angela had thick robes on. Karen was in her T-shirt and sweats. I was in my change of clothes. Last night's clothing was in a sweat-and-beer-soaked pile plopped next to the sofa in the living room.

It felt like a family. Karen was family. Beth and Angela, a few years older than us, could've been our adoptive parents.

Karen spilled the beans about me being a Jehovah's Witness and disfellowshipped. Thanks, Karen. I went through the explanation of what everything meant, like how I couldn't celebrate holidays and I was still a virgin.

"You don't believe in homosexuality, then?" Angela asked. Not in a threatening way, more like she was researching a paper for her anthropology class.

"I don't know; you're the first homosexuals I've met and you seem great to me."

"He's adorable," said Beth.

It was the most accepted I had felt in a while. And I was adorable.

That Sunday, the Bible talk was on the joys of being Jehovah's chosen people. I watched Jin. Over the previous months I'd noticed that he participated in commenting on questions during the *Watchtower* study and that during the public talk he took copious notes. I didn't know what had changed to make him so involved in researching further into the Bible, when going to three meetings a week and preaching on top of that felt like enough Bible for me.

Jin walked down the aisle and toward the bathroom during the Watchtower study and dropped a note on my lap as he passed me. It was folded.

He went back to his seat after using the restroom like nothing had happened. I brought my *Watchtower* with me to the men's room in the back of the Kingdom Hall. No one was in there, so I read the note.

"If you can meet me tomorrow at 12:30 PM at Millbrae Park, wipe your forehead as I walk by you to leave the Kingdom Hall. If you can't meet me scratch your chest."

I felt like the note would self-destruct in ten seconds. I flushed it down the toilet and went back to my seat. I wiped my forehead when he walked by.

Grandma Sara was diagnosed with colon cancer. The doctor gave her six weeks to three months to live. They didn't catch the cancer cells in time to perform chemotherapy.

I called 411 and got her phone number and called her after not being allowed to speak to her since I was three years old.

"Grandma?" I answered when she said hello.

There was silence.

"Gabe, not-a-good you call here," she said in her Italian accent.

"I don't want you to die," I said, then wished I hadn't said that.

"God, he wants a-me in heaven," she said. I forgot she was Catholic.

"Should . . . " I paused. "Should I come to visit you?"

I didn't even know what she looked like anymore.

"Not good you call," she said and hung up.

I met Jin at Millbrae Park. "Dags," he said and gave me a pudgy bear hug.

"I missed you, man," I said.

No more small talk for me. I wanted to get to the love, the months of lost time and affection from my friends and spiritual family of hundreds.

"I'm going to disassociate myself," he said.

Disassociation

To disassociate yourself, you write a letter to the elders stating that you no longer want to be a Jehovah's Witness. When the disassociation takes place, you are treated like a disfellowshipped person. It used to be that if you disassociated yourself from the religion, you could still associate with other Witnesses (at their discretion), but that changed in 1980.

"You can't do that," I pleaded with Jin. Why would he jeopardize ever being able to talk to anyone he grew up with?

"My dad found this," he said, pulling out the book *Crisis of Conscience* by Raymond Franz. It was apostate literature. Even having a copy of that book could lead you to get disfellowshipped. It scared me when he showed me the book, like a demon would possess me if I even touched it. The evil spirits would throw me to the ground and Jin would have to call the elders so they could pray and get them off of me.

"After Dad found it I started asking him questions. Like, if the book of Revelation says there will be a great crowd who will make it through Armageddon, that no man will be able to number, and the Watchtower Society tells us exactly how many Jehovah's Witnesses there are every year, doesn't that mean you shouldn't have to be a Jehovah's Witness to make it into paradise?"

"I never thought of that," I said, picturing Jin's commie Korean Jehovah's Witness dad yelling at him in the gibberish I'd heard them communicate in before.

"It says no man will be able to number, and those who make it into paradise will be like the sands of the sea."

"So, you're saying a lot more will make it than all the Jehovah's Witnesses on the earth? What did your dad say after you told him that?"

"He said the Watchtower Society gave us the information and they are God's channel to his people. So the scripture probably means there will be fewer Witnesses making it into the new system because of people with secret sins. So I asked, what about the people behind the Iron Curtain? Most of them don't even know what a Jehovah's Witness is, so they're going to all die just because they don't know. He answered and said if Jehovah reads it in their hearts, he'll get the information to them they need so they can become baptized Jehovah's Witnesses."

The questions Jin was asking were reasonable. Stuff I'd never really thought about.

"He said I shouldn't question the governing body and the Watchtower Society and that I sounded like an apostate. I told him he was ignorant for calling me that because I'm not yelling insults to Jehovah's Witnesses at assemblies while they walk by, I'm asking important questions. He says I'm going against the Society and if I'm doing that I'm going against Jehovah. I replied the Apostle Paul said to search out the scriptures for yourselves to make sure. All I wanted to do was make sure."

We looked at each other. It was great just to look Jin in the eye for the first time in ten months.

"I can't go out and preach to people about things that aren't based on the Bible," he said. "I'm not drinking or kissing girls or doing anything wrong, I'm just trying to figure it out, and my dad wants to tell the elders and get me disfellowshipped. I'm not wasting my time. I'm writing the letter."

Jin was going to get kicked out of his house for sure.

"Where are you going to live?"

He looked away at a mom pushing her child on the swing set. She was barefoot in the sand on the playground. She glanced over at us, then looked away.

"I'm moving back to Korea. My cousin works at a nightclub in Seoul; he's going to teach me how to be a bartender."

That sounded exotic. I didn't even know they had nightclubs in Korea. I had never thought about it.

"Do you think my cousin Karen and Uncle Jeff are going to die at Armageddon?"

"Like the sands of the sea, Gabe. A God of love wouldn't kill her."

"She does a lot of bad things," I said.

"Bad by whose standards?"

It did seem really strange to dwell on the fact, the idea, that if God is love, he'd kill my cousin, my family, Aunt Laura. Why would God hurt us like that?

• • •

In the back room after the Thursday night meeting, I sat surrounded by Brother Miller, Brother McMurphy, and Brother Rodgers. Dad wasn't with us, since I had turned eighteen. There was one week of school left before I graduated. Looking at the elders sitting across from me, all I could think of was what a horrible dancer Brother Miller had been at Ally's wedding.

They looked at their notes and I sat silent. I looked over to the lost-and-found shelf and saw a leather-bound notebook. I felt like taking it.

Ah, there it is.

If they didn't reinstate me, I'd take it. If I was reinstated, whoever left that notebook at the Kingdom Hall would probably be happy I was reapproved for association and wouldn't mind if I took it.

"Do you have a worldly girlfriend?" Brother Miller asked and squinted.

"No," I said.

He cleared his throat and Brother Rodgers sucked in air through his teeth.

"Gabe, lying to us isn't going to get you reinstated."

"I'm not lying."

They looked through their notes.

"You were seen in San Francisco a month ago with your arm around a woman with dreadlocks and a nose ring," Brother Miller stated.

I laughed.

"We don't find that funny," Brother McMurphy replied.

"That's my cousin."

They looked confused. Since Karen had finally called her mom and calmed her down, Dad knew, so telling the elders Karen was in town was no big deal.

"You put your arm around your cousin while walking around town?" Brother McMurphy came at me with the trick question.

Bad cop.

"We're close," I said.

Crooked-toothed Camille probably couldn't wait to tell on me after she saw me and Karen at the Steps of Rome.

"Your cousin has dreadlocks, huh?" Brother Rodgers asked. More curious than accusing.

"Yeah, she thinks she's a Rastafarian."

He smiled.

"Gabe, we were concerned about that and wouldn't be able to reinstate you if you were dating a worldly girl. In fact, we're relieved. You've shown yourself humble, making all the meetings and not speaking to any other Jehovah's Witnesses. We have to ask, have you spent the night alone with anyone of the opposite sex or committed any sins since our last meeting?"

"No."

The word m-a-s-t-u-r-b-a-t-i-o-n spelled out in my cum-clouded vision.

"Gabe, welcome back to the Christian congregation."

The elders told me I couldn't comment at meetings or pioneer or have any responsibilities for a while and that they'd meet with me in six months to discuss giving me my privileges back.

They all hugged me. My ill feelings dissipated. I was accepted by God again. I didn't want to screw that up for nothing

I watched TV, completely engrossed in an episode of *Three's Company*.

The misfit chain attached to my ankle was releasing. Armageddon hadn't come when I was disfellowshipped. I still had a chance.

It had been twelve hours since I was reinstated, and I hadn't masturbated once. Though Suzanne Somers did look hot in her tight shirt and shorts.

Dad came home from work.

"Why did you call Mom?" Dad asked.

"I didn't call her. I knew she was sleeping."

"My mom, your grandma?"

I didn't think it was a big deal.

"She's dying," I said.

It must've been the right answer because he had nothing to say in reply. He sat on the couch and watched *Three's Company* with me. Suzanne Somers jumped up and down in her tight shirt and her boobs bounced and bounced.

"Grandma died last night," Dad said, then just left the room.

Good. I got to talk to her before she died. I cared more about getting Dad pissed off about it than actually having closure with an old woman I didn't even know.

I went into the bathroom. I figured a celebratory masturbation session was appropriate because I was reinstated. And then I would stop playing with myself forever.

At school the next day, Jared, Tom, Jin, and Peter were playing Hacky Sack. Jin ate a Slim Jim.

"Peter, Jin, what's up? Hey, guys."

"Are you done being a snob?" Tom asked.

I ignored him.

"You're back?" Peter said.

"Back, baby, back!"

"What are you guys talking about?" Jared asked.

"We'll see you later," Peter said as he, Jin, and I walked away.

"Peter, how's life?" I asked, hoping he was in a less homicidal mood than during our stealth conversations at the garbage cans.

He just said fine and didn't acknowledge any murderous plot against Terry. Ignorance is bliss.

The last day of school was the next Wednesday. Today was Friday. Only three school days left of normalcy, of being able to hang out with my friends during senior year. I was ready to soak up every second I could, make those three days feel like nine months, no matter what had changed.

"Jin's been driving me nuts with his apostate lecturing," Peter said.

"Shut up. It's the truth," Jin replied.

I felt out of place. These weren't the same Hacky Sackers from before I was disfellowshipped. And Jin was going to Korea. I was jealous.

• • •

"Hello?" I answered the phone.

"Hi."

"Who's this?"

There was a pause.

"It's Jasmine."

Jasmine, calling to tell me she loved me and was going to dump Dan.

"It's nice to hear your voice," I said.

"Me too, I mean, it's nice too. Uh, how have you been?"

"Better, and I can talk to you, so I'm great."

"Who's that girl you're dating?"

"That's my cousin."

"You're dating your cousin?"

"God. No. She was just messing with you, you guys, because I saw you in the corner of the café that night."

"Your cousin's a bitch."

"Uh, huh," I said but immediately felt defensive and bad for not sticking up for her.

"How's Dan?" I asked.

"He's taking too long to set a wedding date. He keeps pushing it forward."

"That's lame."

"Yeah, I don't know. I probably shouldn't even be telling you that."

"Since I've been disfellowshipped, it's been pretty important for me not to talk too much small talk. Just to get to the point. Since I've had the privilege taken away, I crave talking to people, and getting to the point fast."

"Oh?"

She was scared a bit with my frankness.

"I need to go," she said.

"Okay, goodbye," I said.

The goodbye felt final.

Dad came home from work and I was watching TV. I waited for him to tell me to turn off the TV and read my *Watchtower*, but he ignored me and went straight into the bedroom.

Elder business.

I felt like jumping up to the kitchen to listen on the phone. I had seen the other side of the door to that back room at the Kingdom Hall.

It all starts with a phone call. A call from elder to elder to elder, and then the time is set. The execution day awaits. The three Judges sit before the accused, the potential threat to the cleanliness of the congregation.

I wondered what Dad felt like, choosing the future of all those people, making those confidential phone calls, extracting intimate details from "sinners" about where they'd put their penises and how swollen they'd been and reading them scriptures from the Bible showing that Satan was directly related to every action, every ounce of pleasure they'd taken from that horrific moment when they'd touched the wrong person in the wrong place or slept on the couch while an engaged, manipulative bridesmaid snored through the crusty vomit in her nose.

I promised myself that when I became an elder, I'd be nice and not try to ask stupid trick questions like Brother McMurphy.

I turned down the volume on the TV to see if I could hear Dad making confidential judicial plans. I didn't hear anything.

Saturday I went to my first service meeting in a year. I looked forward to it and dreaded it at the same time. Mom asked if we could preach together. It told her I'd rather work with someone else, someone I hadn't been able to talk to for a while. Anyone I hadn't been able to talk to for a while. She understood. Dad stayed in bed. Sometimes his elder meetings went really late.

The service group was me, Jasmine, Brother Miller, Sister Feeney, Ally and Jim, Darren and Arlene, Brother Albertson, and Mom. Brother Miller said the prayer at the service meeting and I kept my head down and eyes open to stare at Jasmine's sweet toes. He said "Amen" and we were all given our assignments. Mom was partnered up with Sister Feeney. Sister Feeney was excited because she and Mom hadn't preached together for some time. Brother Miller paired himself up with Brother Albertson. The other husbands and wives worked together, so Jasmine and I were the only people without prearranged partners. Dan was supposed to show up for service, but he didn't, so Brother Miller paired us together.

Jasmine, out in service with me again. I secretly hoped to brush up against her, to be smashed together in the back seat of a car. I couldn't believe my luck.

She wore a man's black button-up shirt with a black skirt. Nylons and grayish-blue shoes. She looked sleek. Her hair contrasted well with her outfit. It was like she was dressed up enough to be a news anchor reporting on a funeral.

It was the usual door-to-door preaching. Not interesteds. Not at homes.

We did house over house with Brother Albertson and Brother Miller. We didn't talk about much more than what we were going to say at the next door and what scriptures we were using for our presentation. That was fine. I'd take any talking I could get from her. But I still felt like grabbing Jasmine by her arms and shaking her until the buttons flew off her shirt, exposing her lace black bra. Let's talk for real. Break up with Dan. I'm back. I can't pioneer anyway so I'll work at Remington's full-time and support us. I have enough money saved up to rent a small apartment, a love nest of sorts.

"You guys go ahead and finish this block," Brother Miller said. He took Brother Albertson on a Bible study and Jasmine and I continued alone.

A college-age girl took the *Watchtower* and *Awake!* from Jasmine. Jasmine wrote down the address to set it up for a return visit in a couple of weeks. When she was done writing she still didn't move forward.

I was lusting over a Vespa parked across the street and turned around to see if Jasmine was ready to move on to the next door. She was looking down. Hair covering her face. She wiped a couple of tears from her eyes and walked in front of me.

"Are you crying, Jasmine?"

"No, let's just finish this block."

"Do you want to talk?"

She sniffled and said, "No."

At the end of the block we waited for the rest of the service group.

And waited.

After about ten minutes of strained silence and the throbbing urge to throw her down on the sidewalk and make out, I suggested we drive her mom's station wagon around the territory to see if we'd missed the rest of the service group or if they needed help working the rest of their territory. She accepted the suggestion and we walked the block to her house and got the car.

The afternoon fog started coming over the mountain in Millbrae.

We couldn't find them.

I suggested a coffee break since there was a good chance we would run into the service group there anyway. That was another fun thing about service, always knowing a maple bar or hot chocolate waited for you after you finished preaching in the territory. So we drove to Rolling Pin Donuts on El Camino.

We ate our bear claw and chocolate old-fashioned in silence as the radio in the doughnut shop played that old light rock song "Killing Me Softly."

No one showed up at the doughnut shop.

"Do you want to go bowling?" She almost spewed hot chocolate out of her nose when I said that.

"Are you kidding?" she said.

"Why not?" I said.

She didn't have an answer for me.

As we drove to the bowling alley I looked out the window. Along El Camino we passed concrete apartments, Chinese restaurants, video stores, strip malls, dive bars.

My window was open—and a door that the universe had left unlocked, so I could crawl through and resolve something that had been a part of my life for years.

"Jasmine." She continued to concentrate on her driving and looked exactly like she did when she showed off on the monkey bars when we were kids. "Do you remember when we would go out in service when we were younger?"

"Of course," she replied.

"I'm not really talking about service. I'm talking about return visits."

"Okay?"

"When we'd sit together in the back seat of the car and be crushed up against each other."

Jasmine didn't say anything.

I tried to read her mind:

– You pathetic pubescent horny little toad

or

– Of course I remember. I used to sleep with your high school photo next to me in bed and kiss it good night.

Silence hung in the air, and apartments and small strip malls continued to fly by as she drove us forty miles an hour down El Camino to King's Bowling Alley.

"I remember," she finally said.

"I always tried to make sure I sat next to you when we'd do return visits or go to Burger King at school for lunch."

She smiled.

"Did you know that?"

She didn't answer. I was laying my heart open. We were talking again. I needed to know and I didn't care what she thought of me so I went for it.

"I wasn't sure if you sat next to me on purpose," she said.

I decided to swing at the fastball. I would either hit it out of the park or get called on strike three.

"Those moments," I said, then looked at her concentrating on the road, driving forward, moving us forward, "those times meant a lot to me."

I said it. It was out. "Those times" could've been translated as "you." *You* meant a lot to me.

"You meant a lot to me," I said.

It hung there in the air. My feelings.

I couldn't gauge the look on her face. It was serious. She navigated the car forward. My balls shrunk by the second.

That was it. That was the last. Jasmine would never go out in service with me again. I was a gushing post-pubescent dork. A boy who held on to his crushes for years. A crush on a woman who was engaged and ready to walk down the aisle into Dan's arms. At least she was stuck bowling with me. I wished it were a date. I'm sure she was trying to figure out a way to get out of it and just drop me off at home.

The clerk gave us lane 11. A professional bowler was on lane 16. Every time he put a ball down toward the pins it would spin like it was just about to roll into the gutter, then would come back and make a strike. Creedence Clearwater Revival played on the sound system.

Jasmine laced up her size 6 bowling shoes, which contrasted horribly with her dress and nylons. The counter guy gave her a pair of socks to put over her nylons.

I entered Knut as my name in the electronic scoring system. She put EO.

"Why EO?" I asked.

"I don't know, I guess I was thinking of that Michael Jackson movie in Disneyland. Why Knut?"

"Knut Hamsun. He's my favorite writer at the moment."

At least the Creedence and noise of the bowling alley masked our awkwardness around each other.

"You were reading a lot when you were disfellowshipped."

"Still do. I'm kind of happy in a strange way that I was disfellowshipped. I would've never found out about my favorite writers, or it would've taken longer for me to find them." I was saying too much. I should've just said, "Yes, I did." I sounded pompous.

She bowled. I bowled. She had this cute awkward sway and hesitated right before putting the bowl down the alley. We continued to play and didn't talk.

Knut had 73 by the seventh frame and EO had 52 by the eighth frame. Jasmine looked at me.

"I'm engaged," she said.

No shit!

"I know."

She bowled her next frame.

"Do you think it's appropriate to say stuff like that to a woman who is about to get married?" She was mad.

It was a lecture from my dad all of a sudden.

I shook my head no. I couldn't look her in the eyes. I couldn't even look at her legs and those ugly bowling shoes. She sat down and huffed. I got the courage to look in her direction. She was watching the pro on lane 16 bowl. She had the same gaze she had when all of us splashed around in the pool when we were younger, and she stared into another place, or the future. Her legs were crossed and her left foot was moving up and down, like she was tapping it on the floor, waiting, just waiting for the game to be over with.

The pro on lane 16 nailed another strike. He had gloves on and everything.

"Bette Davis Eyes" by Kim Carnes played over the sound system. Jasmine took a sip of her Coke. I HATE YOU echoed through my brain.

"Why do you hate me?"

"Urgh, I don't hate you."

"At the party at Ally and Jim's you said you hated me."

If this was going to be our last alone time together I wanted answers.

"Oh, that."

The electronic scoreboard blinked for Knut to bowl.

"Why?" I asked.

"I've seen the crazy way you look at me. Sometimes it's like you disapprove of me."

"For what?"

"I don't know. Like when I talked to other brothers. You looked weird. I can't explain it. Like you're happy for me and relieved or something."

"That's why you hate me?"

"Yeah, that's pretty much it," she said fast. I bet she figured if she spoke faster our game would end quicker and she could get rid of me.

"You scared me that night."

"I barely remember. Arlene told me what I said to you."

"Why didn't you talk to me about it?"

"I don't know."

"Picture being me leaving the party early thinking you hated me and didn't want me to ever look at you."

I bowled for Knut and came back.

We finished bowling without saying too much and left.

In the car in the parking lot underneath the bowling alley it was dark. She started the car, put it into gear, then slammed it back into park and pushed the emergency break down with her left foot.

"You can't do that."

"I— didn't— what?" I asked.

"Why?" she whispered and switched the ignition off.

"You're pathetic, you know that?" she said. "You're— fuck!" and she slammed her hand against the steering wheel.

She hadn't said fuck in all the years I knew her. I remembered when she even told on me and got me in trouble once when we were kids for saying the word. I was ready to get out and walk home.

"I hated you because," she paused, "because I liked you and all you cared about was meeting other sisters and," she started to cry, "so I wasn't going to wait [sniffle]. You wanted Camille [sniffle]. I couldn't [sniffle] . . ."

I moved over and wiped her tears with my shirt as best as I could. She looked at me with the weird smile you can sometimes get when you're sobbing.

"I need to blow my nose," she sobbed with a laugh and pointed at the glove box. I found a tissue and put it against her nose and she blew into my hand. I wiped her nose and tossed the tissue into the back seat.

I kissed her on the nose.

"Don't," she said.

I kissed her lips and pulled back waiting for the second "Don't." It never came.

Our tongues rolled around. Her tongue tasted like an ice-cold Coke.

In that dark, dank parking lot underneath King's Bowling Alley we kissed. In her mom's brown station wagon. In the front seat, mashed up against each other, the same way I used to coordinate it in the back seat on return visits chaperoned by Sister Sandoval. My

fantasy coming true. The steering wheel was in the way so we natu-
rally fell onto the bench seat. She angled on top of me. Our kissing
continued. Our tongues didn't stop. I held her close. I embraced her
like I had never embraced anyone before.

Close.

Intimate.

Except those words didn't exist during that lapse of morals; no
words existed in that gap of time when our two bodies exchanged
saliva, trusting our mouths, our tongues, together.

Then I pushed her away. She looked at me a bit confused. I was a
man possessed. I ripped her shirt open. The buttons flew all across
the car. Her bra was blue. I doubt she'd thought her bra needed to
match anything she was wearing that day. Her bra was blue under
her black shirt.

Then I saw the look on her face. Frightened. I'd gone too far. I'd
just opened the door to something else.

She fell on top of me and as we kissed further, she pressed her
bra into my shirt. I pulled my shirt up to feel her bra against my
chest. I put my hand on her bra. I lightly lifted the underwire and
felt the bottom of one of her breasts. Kissing. I pulled her bra up
over her breasts.

Dark nipples. Her nipples were dark.

I didn't rub her elbows. I didn't think of Jeff's advice. There was
no dental exam kissing. She liked it. Pulling back, moving forward,
tongues back in each other's mouth.

She squirmed for a couple of seconds in my grasp before she
said, before she whispered, "Too fast, slow down. Don't." She sat
up and pulled her shirt around her bra. I rolled my tongue in my
mouth to prolong the taste of the inside of her mouth.

My shirt was around my neck. I scrounged around the car for
her buttons. For the evidence of our passion.

She held her shirt together as we drove to Burlingame Plaza.

"Size two," she said as I left the car and walked into the women's
clothing store.

"Can I help you?" the clerk said to me like I was a pervert or a
transvestite.

"I need a dark button-up shirt, size two," I said with as much authority as I could muster.

She showed me a couple of shirts. The closest was more of a blouse. I bought it with my busboy/room service money. Twenty-three dollars. My first gift to Jasmine was to replace a shirt I'd ripped off of her, like Charles Bukowski would've, like Jack Kerouac would've, like Jeff probably did to girls in France.

Jasmine changed into the blouse in the car. Just watching her dress was intimate. I felt like I was being embraced by an angel using her naked body and wings to cover me completely and protect me from anything that was unsafe in the world.

Jasmine combed her tangled hair and reapplied her lipstick. She gave me a mirror. Her lipstick was on my lips and face and neck. I wanted to tattoo those marks to my face forever.

We drove away and passed strip malls, Lyon's restaurant, Chinese food joints, our bowling alley and its parking lot that would always be a UNESCO landmark in my heart.

She parked a few streets from my apartment. She knew the rules. Being alone together for too long could raise suspicion and land us in the back room with the elders asking about our every move. Drilling us. Giving us trick questions. Playing good cop, bad cop to make sure we hadn't crossed any sinful boundaries, disrupting the cleanliness of the congregation.

Did you touch?

Did you fondle?

Did you pet?

Did you penetrate?

Are Jasmine's nipples pink or brown?

She turned the car off.

"I'll tell them I just walked home from the territory," I said.

"I'll tell them I drove around and couldn't find anyone. Then I lost you so I just went home."

Then we sat a little longer in silence. We didn't move.

"I've," she said, "I've thought about you. I've thought about this. I've . . ." and she let it drop.

"Yeah, I thought about it too. For years," I said.

I wanted to kiss her again, but the spotlight of the sun was upon us and you just never knew who could be driving by at the wrong time.

"Goodbye?" I said.

"See ya," she said.

I jumped out of that den of sin and eroticism. One of her buttons was still in my pocket. I gripped it tight. That was the best day of preaching I had in my entire life.

I called Karen.

"Remember Jasmine?"

"No."

"The dark girl at the Steps of Rome."

"Oh, yeah."

"I just made out with her."

"That's what you called to tell me?"

"I thought you'd be proud or something."

"You're pathetic," she said.

"Why did you say that?"

"Are you still coming to San Francisco tomorrow night for the Butthole Surfers show?"

"Definitely. See you then," and I hung up the phone.

At the meeting on Sunday Dan wasn't there. Jasmine sat with Camille. They both came up and talked to me after the meeting. When Camille talked I just watched her crooked teeth click together. Blah, blah, blah, blah, blah.

Monday at school I played Hacky Sack with Jared, Tom, Peter, and Jin. Just like old times. Just like it should've been for the last year instead of me being disfellowshipped for being a gentleman to drunk Krissy.

Jin whispered he wanted to cut class. Fifth period. I had never cut a class before. It was just P.E. for me. I had no final exam so I agreed. Jin impressed me because he was never dangerous.

I went to the library first and interrupted Flo as she stamped and sorted books. She smiled when she saw me. I told her all about Jasmine and what was going on. I told her why I'd been in the library so much for the past year. Her cousin's husband was a Jehovah's Witness. She knew a lot about it.

I told her about Dan. Her head tilted slightly to the left and her eyes concentrated on mine. I confessed about Karen. About her breasts and how she was back in town and how I worried about her.

She put her hand over her mouth when I mentioned Karen's breasts.

I spilled it all, then asked her what I should do.

"You're a great storyteller," she said.

"This isn't a story; this is my life."

"Do you love Jasmine?"

"Yeah, I mean, I've always loved her I think."

"And she loves you back."

"I guess so."

"Go with your heart," she said.

Into my mind popped the scripture read over and over again at the Kingdom Hall: *The heart is treacherous and deceitful above all things.*

"What if," I looked at Flo, "what if I can't figure out what my heart is telling me to do?"

"You'll know. It will tell you exactly what to do. The feeling will be strong. Don't push the feeling down with what your brain is thinking. Let the feeling grab you and do what you need to do."

"What if what I need to do ends up hurting people?"

"Gabe, you don't get to go through life without some battle wounds," she said. "Even the right decisions hurt sometimes."

I left Flo and I was more confused than when I had gone in to get help. She gave me a goodbye hug. I assured her I'd come back to visit next year and she smiled.

"I'll give you another one if you do," she said.

"It's all there." Jin handed me the book he'd showed me when we'd met last time, at the park. *Crisis of Conscience*. There were a lot of underlines and bookmarks because he had really studied it since our last meeting. It was written by a member of the Governing Body who'd left the Society—an exposé of the inner workings of the Jehovah's Witness organization. It was apostate literature. We had been told over and over that anything written about the Jehovah's Witnesses that wasn't published by the Watchtower Bible and Tract Society was apostasy.

The author, Raymond Franz, had been shunned by other members of the Governing Body because he researched and asked questions that went against the beliefs of Jehovah's Witnesses. They finally disfellowshipped him on a technicality. Because he was disfellowshipped, no one could talk to him, ask him why he was disfellowshipped, or question the decision of the elders who did it. Anyone who wanted to stay a Jehovah's Witness and still talk to their family couldn't read or even possess a copy of the book.

"This is apostate literature," I said and gave it back to him. It felt heavy in my hands and on my heart even to touch it.

"No, stop it. There's a reason why the Society calls everything that's written about them apostate. It's because they don't want you to know some important stuff."

"Did you read the rest of it?"

"Yes. It's bad. It's worse than I thought. He says the exact same thing I figured out about the great crowd including more than just Jehovah's Witnesses. And there's a chapter on Jehovah's Witnesses in Malawi that made me cry."

Jin was really affected by it. It seemed he was more passionate about it than junk food.

"My elders' meeting is next week. I didn't write my disassociation letter yet."

"Lie to them," I pleaded. "Pretend you got the book by accident and you plan on burning it. Don't get disfellowshipped."

"You'll still stay in touch with me no matter what happens, right?" he asked.

"Of course," I replied, but I wasn't sure. If I talked to him I could get disfellowshipped too. And with what had just happened with Jasmine, I wanted to make absolutely sure I didn't mess that up.

I told him about Jasmine and he congratulated me, but he was worried that Dan would kick my ass.

"Peter and I will have your back," he said.

"He's grounded," Terry said, hanging up the phone without further conversation.

I was ready to kill that military fuck for Peter myself.

I hadn't seen Peter for a few days. I missed him so much, I walked to his apartment and tapped on his window, which was over my head. It was a small window for their dank apartment, barely enough to let the fresh air in. It slid open. All I saw was a hand and I prayed it wasn't Peter's mom or Terry.

"Hello?" Peter said.

"Hey, man, are you okay?"

"No," Peter said without hesitating. "I turn eighteen in three months and Terry grounds me for a month this time. Can you sneak me your transistor radio? I'm losing my mind here."

"Yeah, want some R-rated movies too?" I joked.

"I wish. Terry watches our only TV all day in the front room. He is taking vacation days from work so he's home all day. This sucks."

There was a thump that came from the front room. Peter and I stayed silent. The phone rang and I could hear Terry's muffled voice through the thin wall.

"Did Jin show you that book?" Peter whispered.

"Yeah," I said.

"Pretty fucked up, huh?"

I wasn't sure if he was referring to Jin having the book or to the contents and how messed up the Watchtower Bible and Tract Society was.

"It's all wrong. I can't believe Mom and Terry made me be a Jehovah's Witness," he finally said.

"You didn't tell your parents that you read the book, did you?"

"No," he said. He sounded like he was about to cry. I put my back against the cold stucco wall underneath the window. It felt like I was visiting Peter in prison. I pictured him killing Terry and prison visits becoming a reality.

"Peter," I said, "let's get an apartment together. I'm making enough money and I could get you a job at Remington's."

He was really silent. Then I heard a sniffle.

"Just think—this'll be the last time you're ever grounded."

I turned around and put my face to the wall, wishing I could wipe Peter's tears away.

"Okay," he said.

"So you better enjoy the last of that room while you can."

He laughed.

"What are you laughing at?" Terry came into the bedroom.

"I wasn't laughing. I was crying," Peter said as I tiptoed away from the window.

I bought a copy of the *Millbrae Sun* and circled studio apartments that were $450 a month and under. I knew he wouldn't be able to pay rent for a couple of months and I wanted to make sure I had enough money left over from the deposit to buy a motor scooter.

"Beth and Angela want to fuck me," Karen said as we waited in line at the Stone, across the street from the Rock on Broadway, to see the Dead Kennedys.

"And?" I asked.

"And, I ain't no lesbo," she said.

Beth wasn't at the show. Karen talked to a few friends before the band went on. I hung out with Jimmy Thorn in the back by the bar. He pulled out his flask and dumped a bunch of whiskey into my Coke. He told me about a band, Mudhoney, that he'd just seen, a band from Seattle, and about a record label called Sub Pop.

"They're like the MC5, but more punk rock," he said.

I didn't know who the MC5 were. I nodded my head; it helped the alcohol soak in.

After the show we got in Karen's van. She'd bought it earlier that week. She told me her grandma on her dad's side had left her a trust fund that matured when she turned nineteen. I didn't ask how much money she had. I asked why she bought a van and not a car.

"In case I ever need to leave town, I could pack all my shit and go."

"You're not in any trouble, are you?" I asked.

She slugged me on the arm as we entered the Broadway Tunnel.

We drove back to Beth and Angela's place.

"You have to sleep in my room," Karen said.

I put a blanket on the floor.

"No, in my bed."

"Uh, cousin?"

"I told Beth that you weren't a blood cousin but a third cousin through marriage and that we'd been fucking for a while."

"Okay?"

"Seriously, help me and get in bed."

I lay next to Karen. On my back. Staring at the ceiling, waiting for sleep to come, hoping I wouldn't fart in the middle of the night.

Karen fell asleep quickly. She turned over and one of her dreadlocks tickled my ear.

I felt bad. I felt completely wrong for having an erection just because I was in the same bed as my cousin. I remembered our night on the balcony as I fell asleep.

• • •

The blinds were open and the dawn light crept into the room. I was entangled with Karen under the blanket.

I had a boner. It was pressed against Karen's bare thigh.

I tried to pull back. I could barely see that her eyes were open in the dim light.

"Don't," she whispered. She was awake and moved closer. "Don't move." Her mouth was right in my ear.

"I . . ." I said.

"I know, I feel it. It's okay. Stay."

I stayed. I pressed my boner harder into her thigh. She reached down and smashed her hand against it and tugged.

It was dark. It was my cousin.

"We shouldn't," I said.

"Shhh," she said.

She pulled her underwear off and flipped my penis out through the leg of my underwear. I entered her vagina. It was warm. Really warm. And tighter than I ever thought a vagina would be. My penis felt like it would get stuck in there and fall off.

Stop-time. In my mind there weren't any consequences. No thoughts of diseases, mongoloid inbred babies, committee meetings with the elders. All I felt was enveloped by the warmth that engulfed me. It was so much different than masturbating.

I moved and she winced, "Ow."

"Sorry," I said.

"It hurts a little—just don't move for a minute."

I fell into a deep sleep until noon. When I woke up, Karen sat on the couch in her underwear and tank top, calmly flipping the channels on Beth and Angela's TV set. They had cable. I didn't know what to say. I had a boner that wouldn't go down no matter how hard I tried to think about baseball or sitting in a committee meeting with the elders or anything. My pants were on but it still felt noticeable. I was nauseated.

Karen looked up.

"You okay?" she asked.

"Yeah, I mean, uh, I feel a little weird."

"Gabe," she said, putting the remote down. "Come here."

I looked at her, in her tank top and underwear with a book on her lap and her dreadlocks and nose ring. It was the sexiest thing I had ever seen.

It was wrong. My mind told me to get out of that apartment and run like Joseph did when Potifer's wife tried to seduce him in the Bible.

My heart told me otherwise. It said, *stay*.

The heart is treacherous. My heart said, *yes!*

Yes, without thinking of elders' meetings. How would they find out, anyway?

Yes, my heart said.

The conviction suddenly hit me that every time I held her hand, or even when I'd put my arm around her to get Jasmine jealous, it felt even better than when I finally made out with Jasmine, better than when I finally found out the color of Jasmine's nipples. These feelings crashed down on me all at once. Jasmine might be on my mind, I thought. But the mind was what was treacherous. Karen was in my heart. It had taken a long time to realize that Karen had already been in my heart. For years.

She noticed my penis through my pants. She smiled and unzipped my fly.

"What are you doing?" Mom asked.

"Watching TV," I said.

"No, what are you doing now that you're reinstated?"

"Why is Dad home from work?"

"He's not feeling well, I asked you a question."

I've been fucking my cousin, your niece—what does it look like I've been doing?

"I'm trying to figure things out. Since when does Dad not feel well?"

Dad wouldn't miss a day of work if he was vomiting blood. His whole goal in life was to devote himself to his work with the devotion appropriate to a Jehovah's Witness, and not just be a regular mechanic—which meant he put 120 percent into a job, to show his stepfather that Jehovah's Witnesses were good workers, excellent contributors to society, and that if everyone was a Jehovah's Witness, the world would function smoothly until God finally started Armageddon to kill anyone who wasn't a Jehovah's Witness. Dad tried to leave all his work the way Jehovah's people left the Cow Palace after every district assembly: cleaner and better than before he came to it.

"Dad isn't feeling himself. He wants to do more for Jehovah and he's trying to figure out how. You should be doing the same," she said. "If it wasn't—"

"If it wasn't . . . ?" I asked.

Mom ignored me and went into the kitchen. I followed her.

"If it wasn't what?"

"Forget it, Gabe. Just make sure you make wise choices, wiser choices, so you don't, you know, end up in a situation where you might not be able to pioneer or something."

I think I understood what she was trying to say, or deep down inside I knew what she was trying to say because it felt a little like I needed to throw up.

He bought a roll of stamps. One hundred of them. He mailed the note to everyone in the congregation and included all of the details. How his stepfather, Terry, was a hypocrite and abusive. How the society was wrong about the great crowd. Jin's book from Raymond Franz had convinced Peter that everything we believed was wrong. Peter needed to make a statement. It was even better than killing his stepdad.

In the letter, Peter told the story of the thousands of Jehovah's Witnesses in Malawi in the 1970s who were forbidden by the Governing Body to buy a political card required by the Malawian government and were slaughtered as a result. In response, the Jehovah's Witnesses in Mexico got in touch with the Watchtower Society and begged for clarification because the Mexican Jehovah's Witnesses were bribing officials to give them military cards that showed they'd done their time in the military—and bribing, which hadn't been forbidden in this context by the Governing Body, seemed a lot less Christian than buying a political card, which had been forbidden, and the Jehovah's Witnesses in Malawi were being killed as a result.

The Governing Body wouldn't budge in the Malawi decision. Their reasoning was if they were wrong about it, at least the Jehovah's Witnesses in Malawi were dying for what they thought was righteousness and sacrifice for God.

A death sentence because the Governing Body was too scared to correct the mistake they had made. Too many had died already: to reverse the decision regarding the political card would risk the trust that the world of Jehovah's Witnesses had in the Organization. They saw a few thousand Witnesses sacrificed in the name of Jehovah as necessary for the greater good of the Watchtower Society.

Jesus said he'd run to save one lamb that ran astray from his sheep, Peter wrote. Christ wouldn't have even thought of sacrificing one of his disciples. Following Jesus is the definition of a true Christian.

Peter had read all that in Jin's copy of *Crisis of Conscience* by Raymond Franz.

The book continued that the Mexican Witnesses wrote again. They wanted to know if their carrying military cards and bribing officials was wrong. They were willing to go to prison and more if it was wrong. And they followed the Malawi situation closely. The Society kept reassuring them there were no problems.

When Peter, Jin, and I were seven years old we wrote letters as instructed by the Watchtower Society to the King of Malawi to beg him to stop the killing of our brothers and sisters. Jin wrote his letters in Korean.

The Watchtower Society also pretended to the government of Mexico that they weren't a religion but a cultural organization, so they could own the property of the Kingdom Halls and not lease them from the government the way that all other religions had to. That meant that Mexican Jehovah's Witnesses couldn't pray at meetings or sing Kingdom songs like we did at our Kingdom Halls. Not allowing Jehovah's Witnesses to pray and express their faith was sanctioned by the Watchtower Society. That sounded really shady to me, since we were taught not to let the government get in the way of our worship. It was all done so Jehovah's Witnesses could own real estate in Mexico.

Peter's letter upset me. He photocopied the letters from the Mexican Jehovah's Witnesses and the replies received from the Watchtower Society. It was all from that book. I remembered being told every week when I was a kid that our brothers were dying in the name of Jehovah. It shook me at my core to think that there was the possibility it could've been just an internal struggle for power within the Governing Body. I didn't know how to react or what to think.

But there was more in Peter's letter. He gave the address for how to order a copy of *Crisis of Conscience* by Raymond Franz.

His letter went to everybody.

They found Peter hanging from a tree on the property of Mills High. A eucalyptus tree. There were cigarette burns on his arms. He tied the noose with precision, talent, and care.

The end of his letter said he didn't want to hurt anyone.

If being a Jehovah's Witness was wrong, he couldn't bear to fathom what was right. If brothers were needlessly slaughtered in Malawi, he felt his sacrifice to get the correct information to the members of the congregation was the least he could do. He was braver than Che Guevara.

My feelings were mixed and I was angry at him. Angry and sad and confused.

I found out a week later that they had been planning to disfellowship him. He was caught with the book and the elders asked him to repent. Instead, he asked them to explain the accusations from the book. Their only explanation was it was written by an apostate, and that they were not required to respond to the questions of a godless person. He wouldn't have been able to communicate the truth to anyone if he was living and disfellowshipped. Better to be dead and still a Jehovah's Witness.

He promised to see everyone in the resurrection and asked for the congregation to pay special attention to his mom.

In the note I received, which had all the above information, he added a handwritten message that he loved me and prayed I wouldn't be too mad at him for killing himself and that he hoped it all worked out between Jasmine and me. He said the garbage cans at the apartment building down the block, where we met when I was disfellowshipped, where we terrorized unsuspecting motorists, would always be our spot. If I needed to talk to him, I should go there and maybe he'd hear me somehow.

When I received my copy of the letter I put it in my pocket. My

left leg felt heavier with the weight of it in there. I heard a yelp from
a small dog, like it got stepped on, then realized it came from me.

I held my hand to my mouth but it was too late. The vomit was
already spewing through my fingers.

Peter was announced disfellowshipped at the next meeting.
There was no mention of him killing himself. After his announcement, Brother Rodgers gave a local needs talk about the importance
of avoiding apostate literature. He never said it outright, that Peter
killed himself because Jehovah took away his Holy Spirit. Because
Peter was an apostate. Brother Rodgers just said that even having
apostate literature in your possession could make you lose God's
protection and when we lose that, we're leaving the door open for
Satan to step in. Then he read the scripture about Jesus expelling
the demon from a man into a herd of swine. The herd instantly
killed themselves by jumping off a cliff.

I didn't cry. It didn't feel real. Mom was sleeping more and more.
When she got the letter that Peter addressed to her and everyone in
the congregation, and to the *Millbrae Sun* newspaper, which printed
it two weeks later, Mom slept.

She functioned. She came to the meetings, she showered, and
she used the bathroom, but everything was with a heavy foot and
distant eyes.

I asked Dad what we should do. He put his finger to his mouth.
"*Shhh*."

I didn't know if he wanted *it* quiet or wanted *me* quiet.

Or if he wanted everything quiet.

I wondered if wherever Peter was, it was quiet.

I closed my eyes and listened to the silence. There was never
ultimate silence. A TV was on in the apartment next to ours. There
was the sound of water splashing onto a truck being washed with
a hose in a carport below. There was traffic on El Camino. Idling
cars, cars picking up speed, some louder than others.

I tried to tune out the cars, the water, the TV. I tuned out the
sound of pans clacking in the Chinese restaurant in the alley. I tuned
it all out. That's when I heard it.

Doon, dun. Doon, dun. Doon, dun.

My heartbeat.

I couldn't turn the sound down on that. There would never be complete silence. There would always be something. That didn't comfort me.

The next day Mom slept and Dad went to work, the latest copy of the *Watchtower* folded in his back pocket. When Dad had received the letter, the only thing he said about it to me was, "You're okay about Peter, right?"

"Right."

"Good. You'll see him in the resurrection and that'll be soon since Armageddon is so close."

He took in a breath that wasn't enough so he compensated with a stuttered second breath.

After they announced Peter was disfellowshipped and gave the local needs talk at the Kingdom Hall, the brothers asked me to come into the back room. They bad cop/good copped me regarding Peter.

Did he try to give me apostate literature?

Did I believe what he said in the note?

Did I know he was going to kill himself and send the letter to everyone?

I lied and told them what they wanted to hear. The meeting was fast and they acknowledged sorrow for the loss of my friend.

When I left the meeting, Jin was waiting outside. He wasn't the Jin I had known all my life. He looked me right in the eyes and time stopped. I didn't see the pudgy Korean; I saw deeper. I gave him a firm handshake and he went in for his interrogation.

On the phone I told Karen about Peter.

She came to Millbrae to have coffee with me. We didn't talk about tits or vaginas or sex or anything like that. We sat at Lyon's restaurant putting too much sugar in our continued refills of coffee and staring out the window.

Karen knew when to be quiet. To be silent. That's what connected me to her. She could just *be*. I never felt like I could *be*, only when I was with Karen.

We didn't hold hands. The last thing on my mind was anything that could give me a boner—which was quite rare.

I didn't think about Jasmine. I watched the traffic roll by on El Camino and the caffeine attacked my nervous system. I wanted so much coffee, so much caffeine that my nerve endings would finally collapse and give in and express the sorrow in my heart for Peter.

We hugged at the train station and she went back to her life in San Francisco. I wanted Karen's life. It felt simple, happy, and sad at the right times.

Dad's car was in the driveway; he was home from work early.

In our apartment I saw holes in the wall above the couch.

The first hole was for Dad's mother who ignored him at work and disowned him for being a Jehovah's Witness.

The second hole was for the pressure at work and how everyone made fun of him for being a Jehovah's Witness and how Grandpa Barry treated Dad as an employee and not a person. Grandpa felt protective of Grandma's feelings and hoped that Grandma would one day feel okay with her son, even if that meant her son would quit being a Jehovah's Witness and flaunting it with those damn *Watchtower*s in his back pocket every day at work.

The third hole was for Mom, for not understanding the pressure he was under and sleeping all the time and not making me keep up with my Bible studying.

The fourth hole was for me. For being disfellowshipped and a problem, a burden, for being the son who constantly reminded him that he came from the world, that the product of his sin was right in front of him every day. Me finally growing facial hair and a decent bush of pubes underneath my pants. For the time he took advantage of Mom, took her virginity in the front seat of his '57 Chevy at the drive-in while watching *Five Easy Pieces*. For engaging in premarital sex and how he wished he had the *truth* before he made such a huge mistake.

I didn't know what the fifth hole was for.

"What happened?" I asked Mom. She lay in bed; her eyes were open.

"Where were you?" she asked.

"Are you okay?" I said, fearing that some of Dad's punches weren't accounted for yet and that he might have more to throw. "Where's Dad?"

I turned to the bathroom and the door was locked.

"Dad," I called.

I pictured Mom hiding her bruises.

"Dad!"

No answer. I busted the door down like I had seen Crockett and Tubbs do every week on *Miami Vice* with their shoulders. They never showed how much it hurt after busting open a locked door.

Dad wasn't in the bathroom. I looked at the damaged door and felt guilty, then heard a moan from the bathtub.

Dad was sprawled in the tub behind the shower curtain. There was blood on his knuckles and I couldn't believe I hadn't smelled the vomit when I first busted in.

Mom!

I went to Mom to check for injuries.

"Did. He. Hit. You?"

She looked at me like I was crazy.

"No," she said.

"Let me see," and without her approval I ripped the covers and sheets off of her. She was in her bra and underwear. I scanned her body for bruises or blood. She was clean.

Five punches connected.

I went back to Dad, who stayed quiet in the bathtub.

"Dad, are you okay?" I asked.

He shook his head no.

"Should I call an ambulance?"

He shook his head no.

I was scared to my core and wanted out, but I didn't want to leave Mom alone with Dad. I walked into the bedroom.

"Mom, can you drive me to Jin's?"

She got out of bed like there were no holes in the living-room wall and like Dad wasn't lying in the bathtub with bloody knuckles and in his own throw-up. She got out of bed to drive her son to

Jin's, just like she used to before I learned the bus schedules. She dressed. We got in the car and she drove.

At Jin's I grabbed the keys out of the ignition so she wouldn't leave.

"I'll be right back," I said. She nodded like it was the most normal day of our lives.

"I was wrong," Jin said. Mom drove, and Jin and I sat in the back seat. The radio was on and she wasn't listening to us.

"I shouldn't have questioned Jehovah's organization. I was wrong."

"What about Malawi? What about all the bad things the Watchtower Society did and let happen that you read about?" I asked.

"Jehovah will take care of it," he said.

That's what was always said—wait on Jehovah, he'll take care of things. It was usually said when an elder or other high-ranking official in the Jehovah's Witnesses was doing extreme harm to a congregation or an individual. It was never used when executing immediate justice on a kid busted on a technicality like helping a drunk bridesmaid.

Peter's suicide had scared Jin straight. The committee meetings had scared him straight. He was going to be privately reproved and looked forward to getting all of his privileges back so he could excel as a Jehovah's Witness.

Back at the apartment, Dad wouldn't get out of the bathtub, but he'd taken his shirt with the vomit off and it was in the corner of the bathroom. I threw it in the clothes hamper.

"Dad, get out of the bathtub," I pleaded.

Jin and Mom stayed in the kitchen. Jin asked her to play a Bible drama and she put in a cassette that was about the Israelites, one that Peter had memorized. When she'd heard Peter recite it, she'd been excited I had chosen such fine association and said there was hope for me yet.

There was nothing. Dad held his left hand over his right. I popped open some hydrogen peroxide and poured it on his hands. He cocked his left arm back like he was going to punch me but his eyes looked elsewhere. I put the bottle next to the tub. He could do that shit on his own.

I got on the phone and called Brother Miller. It was the only thing I could think of. I didn't want to get Dad in trouble, but I didn't want him to hurt us. I moved the Einsturzende Neubauten poster to the front room to cover up Dad's five holes.

Brother Miller came over with Brother Albertson. Both were dressed in suits and held Bibles in their hands.

"Hi, Gabe. Where's your father?" Brother Miller asked. He didn't squint; my soul wasn't in question.

I put my hand to my mouth and tears streamed down my cheeks onto the floor without any warning. I pointed with my other hand to the bathroom and went over to my partitioned-off bedroom area next to the front room. Ten minutes later they came out of the bathroom and I waited for Dad to follow them, looking normal, like nothing had happened, ready to resume life as he had been living it.

"Gabe, do you know if your father has any secret sins?" Brother Miller asked and squinted.

I looked confused.

"You father seems to have lost Jehovah's Holy Spirit and must feel guilty about something to act this way. We prayed with him, but he didn't move, so now we're worried about him and the cleanliness of the congregation."

I looked confused but secretly seethed inside. I wondered what it would look like smashing a brick against Brother Miller's head and seeing the blood gush out from his ears.

"No, Dad doesn't sin," I said.

"There's nothing we can do for him unless he is honest and confesses."

Two bricks, one for each of them, hitting the floor, blood splattered all over. Mom would help me clean it up because it was her nature. Where would I dispose of the bodies? Could I strip them naked and put them in a sexual position in a carport downstairs so it would look like they had sinned and killed themselves over the guilt of their homosexual lust?

"It's important that Brother Dagsland be truthful with us so your house can have Jehovah's Holy Spirit in it again," Brother Albertson said. I felt like offering him a drink to go break his years of sobriety for God.

Jin left after the elders left. He also talked to me like an elder. Like Dad. Like his Korean dad. Jin, the Jin I had grown up with, had left the building. Dad was still in the bathtub—his pants smelled like pee. Jin left and Mom went to bed.

Peter's funeral couldn't be held at the Kingdom Hall. As a Jehovah's Witness, if you couldn't have your wedding or funeral at the Kingdom Hall, it was a huge disgrace. In Peter's case, it was not only because he'd been disfellowshipped when he died but because there was speculation that since he killed himself he might not be resurrected.

I felt tempted to join Peter. To put it all behind me with one last gasp for air. But I had a little hope for the future.

At the funeral there were only about thirty people. Some from the Kingdom Hall. Jin wasn't there. I longed for his presence. Mom was in bed and Dad was in the bathtub.

Jasmine wasn't there. I burned inside because of that.

Uncle Jeff gave me a hug. "Peter was a great kid," he said.

I looked at Jeff. Really looked at him—looked through him. My heart told me something. It said, "Be like Jeff." Jeff felt like an anchor, an anchor that could leave at any moment to play gypsy in Romania or something, but everything else was changing too fast.

He didn't break eye contact with me.

"You're going to be all right, kiddo," he said.

Maybe, I thought. Maybe.

Peter's mom's brother gave the talk. He had been a Protestant priest and assured Mandy and Terry that it would be a nondenominational funeral. Terry made sure that he didn't mention the letter. Mandy requested that he didn't mention Peter was disfellowshipped. The man asked us to bow our heads and reflect on Peter for a minute before he started his talk. A photo of Peter, his senior picture, was at the front of the room.

Jared and Tom showed up and sat behind me. We bowed our heads. I closed my eyes tight. I concentrated on Peter. On us running together, skateboarding together. Then my concentration broke when someone sat beside me on my right. Karen.

She grabbed my hand and held it.

Jared and Tom looked at Karen and me and smiled. They didn't know she was my cousin; they thought she was my hot girlfriend. Wait, she *was* my hot girlfriend. Karen gripped my hand like no one ever had before. She was infusing me with life force.

"Even though Peter had troubles in his life, we still loved him," Mandy's brother started.

My mind floated outside of the Millbrae Recreation Center and into space. Karen gripped my hand tight. Fingers intertwined.

The sermon continued but I was with Peter at Lyon's restaurant. We were putting sugar in the salt container at the table and laughing. Nothing profound, just him and me being teenage terrorists and giggling until tears came out of our eyes.

Karen's van was parked outside. Before we left I hugged Mandy. Terry put out his hand for me to shake it. "At least some of Peter's good-for-nothing friends showed up," he said.

I left his hand hanging and walked away.

"How are you, Dags?" Karen said while we drove away.

"I feel like there's a fire in me. I feel, I feel like I should be sad, but I'm not. I don't know what I feel. Thanks for holding my hand. It felt like stop-time."

She smiled. At the intersection on El Camino I asked her to make a right instead of a left, where my apartment was.

"I need to find something out," I said. She didn't question me.

We drove to Jasmine's house. Camille answered the door. She was shocked to see me there.

"Why didn't you go the funeral?" I asked.

"You should leave."

"No, why didn't you go to the funeral?" I said louder.

"Is that Gabe?" Dan said as he came to the door.

"Me and you need to talk," he said.

"No, we don't," I replied.

Karen stood next to me.

"Where's Jasmine?" I asked.

Dan stood there without responding. I moved to go inside and he put his hand up to my chest to stop me. Karen whipped out a butterfly knife, flipped it to show the blade.

Dan and I looked at her in shock for packing a weapon; then he stepped out of the way. Jasmine was in the kitchen.

"Why didn't you go the funeral?" I asked.

"What are you doing here? You shouldn't be here."

I looked at Jasmine and my heart felt cold, colder than her tongue tasted after she drank the Coke at the bowling alley. I remembered Camille's expression when she answered the door and it cleared up any confusion I had. And if Camille knew, her mother knew, and if her mother knew, the elders knew.

Dan came into the kitchen. Karen was right on his tail, knife by her side.

"Peter, our friend, dies, and you can't go to the funeral," I said to everyone in the room, including Dan.

"You shouldn't have done that," Dan said. "I'm her fiancé, buddy."

I wished Karen would stab him just for calling me buddy. She walked to the refrigerator. Dan was pissed but wasn't going to do anything.

"The elders know everything," Dan said.

"What do they know?" I directed my question to Jasmine.

She put her head down. Her long dark hair covered her face.

"They know that you took advantage of her. She said to stop and you kept going."

"Is that right, Jasmine?" I asked and she didn't look up.

"The only reason you're still standing is because the elders will disfellowship you again and me and Jasmine want to make sure we can have our wedding at the Kingdom Hall."

If Dan was disciplined by the elders for assaulting me, a Kingdom Hall wedding would've been out of the question.

"That's it?" I said.

She didn't look up.

"Jasmine?" I said louder.

"It's time for you to leave," Dan said.

I saw Camille. She gave me the evilest look I had ever seen from her, probably because she wished I had ripped her shirt to shreds in the front seat of her mom's car.

There was no reason to plead my case. There was no explaining Jasmine lying on top of me, moaning, and sticking her cold tongue deep in my mouth.

Karen and I left.

"I'm sorry," Karen said. I think she meant it for everything.

We went back to my apartment. On the way I told Karen about Mom and Dad. I asked her to stay in the car. She looked relieved.

I put some clothes on my bed and my favorite cassettes and books. I bypassed gathering any *Watchtowers* but I added a Bible to the pile, just in case. I couldn't find a suitcase or bag, so I used a couple of paper grocery bags to store everything. Mom was sound asleep. Actually snoring.

I went into the bathroom to check on Dad. The toilet had overflowed and it smelled like shit in there. Dad looked at me.

"Dad," I said.

He didn't reply but stared at me and slightly smiled.

"Dad, Jasmine and I kissed and I felt her breasts."

He still stared at the wall. It was a relief to tell him that. Almost better than the actual experience had been.

"It was a few weeks ago. She hasn't broken up with Dan yet."

Dad stared into space. Maybe he was telepathically talking to his mother. Confessing his guilt to her. Maybe he'd gotten stuck in another dimension and when he was done getting what he needed off of his chest to his mother, he'd come back.

"I felt Jasmine's breasts," I said and Dad stared off. "That"—the next thing was a bit harder to say, even to a dad who was somewhere else in space—"that was the second time I felt someone's breasts. The first time, it was Karen. Karen let me feel her breasts a few years ago."

I looked to see if that snapped Dad back into the third dimension.

"Karen jacked me off."

I sat in silence. He looked at the wall.

"We had sex."

I got up.

"I masturbate too," I said. "A lot. I'm going to ask Karen to run away with me."

I worried about leaving Dad alone, and Mom didn't seem too capable. The situation was beyond my control. I called Brother Miller.

"Thanks for returning my call, Gabe," he said. Confused, I looked at the answering machine and saw the number three blinking on it. "We'd like to hear from you in your own words exactly what you did to Jasmine in the car at the bowling alley."

"My dad won't leave the bathtub and I'm worried about Mom."

"Are you trying to avoid answering the question, Gabe?"

"No, I'm just, it's Dad— he—" and I tried not to cry but some tears had a mind of their own and splashed onto the carpet.

"According to Sister Jasmine Passeri, you 'pinned her down in the front seat of her mother's car.' Gabe, are you there?"

"Brother Miller, I'd like to tell you everything that happened, right now, in person," I said.

"Great. Brother McMurphy and I will be there in about twenty minutes. Thanks for cooperating, Gabe. When this goes to the judicial committee, it'll be taken into consideration."

I hung up the phone and wrote:

Brother Miller,
Dad is in the bathtub. HELP HIM! I think he might need to be
taken to the hospital.
—Gabe

Then I left Dad in the tub with his pee. I tore the Einsturzende Neubauten poster off the wall to expose Dad's holes.

To show the truth.

I went into the bedroom and kissed Mom on the cheek.

I love you, Mom.

I love you, Dad. I didn't feel like kissing him goodbye.

"You okay, Gabe?" Karen asked.

I didn't answer her and got in the passenger side of her van. We drove to San Francisco in silence.

She brought me to Café La Boheme. Karen read the *SF Weekly* and I just looked out the window and watched the people walk by. Hookers, Mexicans, yuppies, homeless, Asians. It was a racial soup on 24th and Mission. A man yelled into a microphone on the corner. In Spanish. He said, "Blah, blah, blah, Hey-Suse, blah, Dee-ose, blah blah." None of them had a clue about growing up as a Jehovah's Witness. Most were not affected by suicide. None of them had a father in a bathtub and elders trying to track them down. I envied them.

When the café closed Karen and I got in her van and drove back to Beth's apartment. I grabbed her hand before getting out of the van. "Thanks for coming to the funeral and for, you know, being there for me."

She shrugged her shoulders like it was the way things were supposed to be.

I wanted to wait and tell her my plan the next day so it would be special and wouldn't be confused when we celebrated our anniversary with the memory of grief that surrounded me earlier that day. The plan was for Karen and me to get out of town together, away from all of this. We could pull our savings out of the bank and go hang in Los Angeles or New York for a while. We could start a band. We could use her trust fund to go to Paris. Like Henry and June. Like we weren't cousins.

I pictured it all as we walked down Broadway to the apartment.

I wanted to go buy a pack of clove cigarettes and get used to smoking so I could smoke all day in Paris at a café, drinking strong coffee, writing poetry.

The elevator carried us up to Beth's floor. Karen had a key.

"What took you so long?" Beth asked.

"I told you—it was Gabe's best friend, and he had to run an errand."

Beth kissed Karen. On the mouth. An affectionate kiss. Like I had seen from couples. From married people. My heart pushed the blood to my face and Beth noticed. Then Karen noticed.

"Oh, Gabe, I forgot to tell you. Beth and I are moving to Seattle and I'm going to play guitar in her friend's band."

Beth and I? Didn't you fuck me a couple of weeks ago in that room right there?

"Oh," I said.

Beth and Karen. Where was I?

"Shit, I forgot to tell you. Beth finally seduced me to her side and Angela is kicking both of us out."

"You say it like our love is sinister," Beth said and put her arm around Karen. Karen my cousin. Karen my fuck buddy. Karen whom I wanted to run away with.

"What about me?" I looked at Karen. Then I noticed the moving boxes.

"I want to go, leave, I want . . ." and I didn't say *you*, I want *you*. I couldn't bring myself to say it.

"No, silly. You'd be a third wheel with Beth and me."

I wanted to punch my bitch of a cousin. I had nothing to say. Wait—I said:

"But we fucked."

I looked at Beth to see her surprise, but none registered. I wanted to break them up. Karen was mine. Karen lit a cigarette.

"Beth knows all about it," she said, blowing out her mouth and nose. "Gabe, you're my cousin. We can't, uh, fuck. It'll be better this way."

I collapsed and sat Indian style and cried.

For Jasmine.

For Peter.

For Karen.

For being on the brink of losing every one of my friends again.

Karen got an envelope out of her backpack and pulled me up from my pathetic position.

"Beth and I gotta get to the airport to make our flight," she continued as I tried to keep sniffles in. I wiped my face with my sleeve. I was sick to death of all the emotion.

"The van is yours." She pressed the keys into my sweaty hand. "The paperwork is in the envelope. You should leave," she went on, grabbing my shoulders and staring into my teary eyes. "When you figure your shit out, call my mom. She'll know how to find me."

It was final. Like I would never see Karen again. A few minutes earlier I had thought my future was a Karen Fuck Parade in Paris.

I was lonelier than ever.

She didn't kiss me goodbye. She practically shoved me out the door. Outside the apartment building I threw her van keys as hard as I could into the Broadway traffic. They hit a parked Plymouth across the street. I walked slowly across the street through the honking horns and tires screeching to a stop to avoid sending me to the grave—and unfortunately I made it across in one piece to retrieve the keys to the van.

I sat in the van. I started the engine and didn't move. A few cars waited for me to pull out of the parking spot. When they realized I wasn't moving they drove past. A couple honked and flipped me the bird.

Armageddon was the only future I ever knew about. Death to the wicked, life to the righteous Jehovah's Witnesses. I couldn't picture life without Armageddon. I felt God look down from heaven and judge me unworthy. There was no going back. No paradise for me.

I couldn't stand going to the Kingdom Hall three times a week and not talking to anyone. When the congregation found out I was disfellowshipped for screwing my cousin and messing around with Jasmine, my reputation would forever be tarnished. I felt wrecked.

I thought about Peter.

I thought about suicide.

Emotions whirled in my brain and I turned off the engine and fell asleep in the driver's seat, heavy in thought.

I woke up at dawn with a boner. I looked down and laughed. There it was. The thing that got me into this whole mess in the first place. Thanks, God, for putting that there when you created me. Thanks for putting an apple in front of a starving teenager and telling him never to take a bite from it or to suffer a death sentence.

If I was going to die at Armageddon, I was going to die.

Or maybe I wasn't. How could I know? If the Jehovah's Witnesses lied about other things, what would keep them lying about Armageddon?

As I drove south on Highway 101 I punched the steering wheel. I punched it again. I punched the dashboard. For Dad. For Mom. For Jasmine. For Jehovah's Witnesses.

I drove and resisted the overwhelming urge to press the pedal to the floor and swerve across all four lanes, causing a major accident and ending it all.

I punched, and it was on the tip of my tongue. I said it before I could pull it back.

I said, "Fuck God."

My heart jolted like lightning had hit it. Tears streamed down my cheeks. Did God just hear that? Did he care? I pulled over because the crying blurred my eyes.

But there was a dim light flickering in my peripheral vision.

I drove to Jeff's.

He had a girl over. I couldn't move into his place because if Dad snapped out of it and went back to work I'd see him every day in the shop. I needed a clean break. I needed an out.

I told Jeff everything. He sat on the couch with his shirt off while the girl lightly snored in the bedroom. Then I told him my master plan and finally got the nerve to ask him.

"I'm sure he'll say yes," Jeff replied when I told him my idea of staying with Pascal in Paris for a while.

"You need your passport before you go. That'll take around six weeks," he said. "Hell, I'm going back to Paris to work at the night-club again in three months—you're welcome to come with me."

Three months. I could do it. Live out of the van, work a double shift at Remington's. I'd have well over $10,000 to get to Paris and figure it out.

Whatever IT was.

ACKNOWLEDGMENTS

To Lia Garcia for your love and emotional support. To my brother for life, Joseph Sandoval, who has ridden this rollercoaster with me for many years. To Mark Haskell Smith, who has been not only a mentor, but an amazing person on so many levels. Kenneth Hughes, you've made me laugh and cry just when I've needed to do both, and your creative drive is infectious.

Mollie Glick, my agent who came through more than I ever anticipated. Anne Horowitz, the editor extraordinaire who made me dig deeper to make this book shine, giving me weeks of nightmares in the process. All the people at Soft Skull and Counterpoint who have put many hours of hard work into getting this book out.

Thanks to those who have also helped move this book forward and made me a better writer: Richard Nash, Jonathan Evison, Delfin Vigil, Paul Corman-Roberts, Walter Kirn, Rachel Resnick, and Kris Saknussemm.

Thanks to my parents Ken and Torunn DuShane for their support and love.

Gratitude and apologies to Jennifer Jason Leigh.

Tony DuShane writes for the *San Francisco Chronicle*, SFGate.com, *Mother Jones*, *Crawdaddy!*, and other publications. He hosts the radio show *Drinks with Tony*, interviewing writers, musicians, and filmmakers. He lives in San Francisco. This is his first novel.